Enjoy

Gerald R. Mill[...]

02/2023

Enjoy!

Gerald R. Hill

05/12/08

SHARE
the
Happiness

GERALD MILLER

LifeRich Publishing is a registered trademark of The Reader's Digest Association, Inc.

LifeRich Publishing books may be ordered through booksellers or by contacting:

LifeRich Publishing
1663 Liberty Drive
Bloomington, IN 47403
www.liferichpublishing.com
844-686-9607

ISBN: 978-1-4897-4350-3 (sc)
ISBN: 978-1-4897-4349-7 (hc)
ISBN: 978-1-4897-4348-0 (e)

Library of Congress Control Number: 2022915300

Print information available on the last page.

LifeRich Publishing rev. date: 08/15/2022

DEDICATION

This book could not have been completed if this person did not take an interest in the characters. She came forth with numerous ideas where they should go. So I want to thank her for supporting me and being my cheerleader when I needed her.

Thank you Janice for all your help, because without it this book could not have been written.

Jerry!

Chapter 1

As he was walking down the street he realized, he was the new kid on the block. This thought amused him because he had just celebrated his eighty-fourth birthday. At about the same time, a little boy raced down the drive, heading for the street with his mother in hot pursuit. He reached down, grabbed him by the collar and said, "Whoa little man. Better watch out. We don't go into the street."

Just then his mother caught up, out if breath and managed to say, "Thank you". She explained that little Bruce was a handful. She introduced herself as Irene Johnson.

He smiled and told her, "My name is Marvin Malloy. Pleased to meet you. I just moved in with my daughter next door."

Irene then explained that little Bruce sometimes was driving her crazy. Marvin smiled and recalled that he too had been a handful at Bruce's age and his mother's solution to the problem was to take Ten minutes a day to play any game he wanted to play.

Irene thought for a minute and then she said she would try it. As he began walking away he said, "Good luck. Nice to meet you." He continued walking toward the mailbox, wondering what might be in it today. It was too soon for his mail to be sent here, but he was always curious if there would be any surprises.

He remembered when his mom would send him to get the mail. If you forgot the combination the teller would just get it for you. Yes, friendlier days. When he opened the box he saw a lot of advertisements, a few bills, and a magazine. He glanced at the magazine and saw a picture of a pretty lady who looked to be in her late sixties or early seventies. He saw her name in bold letters: Amanda Watkins, Prime Minister of England. He studied her look for a few minutes, then started for home, feeling a sudden swagger in his step. He decided he liked this new feeling.

When he came into the house, he laid down the mail and glanced at the magazine. He studied the lady's eyes closely; he couldn't look away. He saw something, but he didn't quite know what. Intrigued, he opened his computer and typed in "Amanda Watkins." The screen went crazy, and hundreds of articles appeared, most were political, but a few were personal. He ignored the political and went straight to the personals. As he was reading, he learned that she had three grown children, two boys, one girl. She had been married to her husband for thirty-five years until he died in a plane crash along with her daughter and Son-in-law.

After reading about it, he felt sad for her loss. He knew what she had been through. Losing your spouse and your child could have devastating results if you let it but there was always sadness. Some days were very bad, and some days happiness sneaked in. You longed for the happy days. He looked back at her picture, and he studied her eyes; he could see the sadness. He studied further and thought, in the corners he could see flashes of happiness. This photograph was amazing. He decided right then he would write her a letter, knowing she might never see it. The strong feelings he was experiencing toward her seemed to be uncontrollable. He brought up Word on his computer and began.

My Dear Ms. Watkins,

My name is Marvin Malloy, I live in Arizona, USA, I am an Eighty-four-year-old widower. I was fascinated by your recent magazine picture. Now I do know that you will never see this letter, for I believe that you have readers to sort out the good from the not- so- good ones, before they are passed on to you. This one will go into the not so good pile, but for my own satisfaction I will write it anyway.

After seeing your picture, I noticed your eyes; I could see the hurt of losing your husband. I looked deeper, and I could also see flashes of happiness moving in. Having had these same experiences, I would very much like to have a conversation with you about our losses and how we dealt with them. No press and no politics- just two people who need someone to talk to and listen to. I will be in London on holiday in thirty days, staying in a Bed and Breakfast whose name escapes me now. If you care to, let's set up at least a thirty-minute appointment to just talk. To the reader who is reading this, have a heart and put this in the interesting pile. Thank you for your time and God Bless. Marvin Malloy 222-555-5015. Time was slipping away, and the day of his leaving was drawing closer. He was becoming anxious to start his trip.

Chapter 2

MARVIN PICKED UP THE BROCHURE and re-read it. "Stafford House, Bed and Breakfast. Just outside of London. Enjoy the quiet and restfulness of our little town. He studied the pictures, then placed it in his case along with his passport and identification. He closed his suitcase, took a deep breath, and sighed; I am ready. Tomorrow was the big day. Look out London, here I come. Marvin now thought, "What have I forgotten?" Not one thought of the letter he had written.

Meanwhile in London, the Prime Ministers readers were going through a large pile of letters. As they were sorting them, they placed them into different piles. Important, less important, and not important.

One of the young readers held up a letter and hollered, "Hey, guys, look at this one. It came from Arizona, USA. This guy wants an appointment with the PM. He must think he is special." After they looked at it, he asked, "Where I should place it?" They all agreed, "Not important file." He placed it down without looking, not knowing he was placing it in the important file, and it was soon on its way to the PM. This pile of correspondence would be on the PM'S desk in the morning.

Late that afternoon, Marvin was arriving at the B & B, looking forward to a good rest. thinking these old bones need sleep. The Stafford House was an older, beautiful residence. He was glad he chose this one. As he got into the bed the image of his letter came to mind. Marvin wondered, has the PM ever read it. He remembered her picture, her look of sadness, and the flashes of happiness he saw. He said to himself, "Well Amanda, I pray that the happiness I saw wins out because you deserve it." His last thought as he was falling asleep was, "I sure wish I could have talked with you."

The next morning the PM entered her office and on her desk were the usual letters for her to read. This morning there were only seven letters, and she thought, good, it will be an easy morning. The Prime Minister read the first two and thought, why did they put them in the important pile. Then she picked up the third one, glanced at the envelope thinking strange. It came from Arizona, USA, from a man named "Marvin Malloy." What in the world is this?

Amanda began reading the letter and became intrigued with-its contents. Here was a man, a Mr. Malloy, who was concerned for her feelings of despair of losing her husband. She re-read the letter three times and made the decision to find this man. The Prime Minister wanted to have a conversation with him.

She buzzed her secretary, a Mr. William Jones, to come into her office. She told him, "Find this man and have him here tomorrow morning at Ten o'clock for a thirty- minute appointment." The secretary was perplexed but knew better than to ask why, he said, "Yes Prime Minister," and went out the door. The Prime Minister had a big smile on her face knowing full well the secretary could not figure out why she wanted to see this person.

The secretary sat there and said, "How am I supposed to find this person and who is Marvin Malloy anyway? I dare nor ask, just do it." Trying to think who to call, he decided to go to the top. He picked up the phone and called the "Director of MI6." If anyone one could find this man it would be them. The Director said, "They have more important things to do, but if that is what the Prime Minister wants, she will get it." The secretary's phone rang 30 minutes later, and he heard them say, we found your man.

Now what to do? He called Scotland Yard and asked for "Mr. Livingstone and explained to him that they should bring Mr. Malloy to them in the morning for a 10AM appointment."

Just then the PM rang him and told him, "Change the appointment from her office to her residence." He then relayed the information to Mr. Livingstone.

He rang the PM and asked, "Do you need him to be present at the meeting?" When she said no he thought what in the world is going on.

Mr. Livingstone was shaking his head as he hung up the phone. Thinking to himself, well Madam PM, what now? I have got much more to do but he knew better than to pass it on to a Jr. officer, so he planned to have a car ready in the morning to pick up this Mr. Malloy. He shook his head thinking oh what we do for our country.

Evening was approaching and Marvin was taking his evening walk, enjoying the sound of the birds and the fresh smell of evening. As he looked around he thought, I love it here, so quiet, so friendly. He took a few pictures with this new phone wondering, "What will they think of next." He thought of his Dick Tracy wrist radio of his youth and said, that is next. Little did he know it was already here and called, Fit Bit.

He looked up and saw a young man getting into a big black limo in front of the B&B and guessed it must have been someone important. As he came through the door Mrs. Stafford said, "Oh Mr. Malloy this letter just came for you;" She was handed it over to him. He looked at it and on the front it read, "From the Office of the Prime Minister," and it had a wax seal on it. He could tell Mrs. Stafford was just as curious as he was, so he said to her, "I think we should open it."

Inside was a handwritten note from "Amanda Watkins, Prime Minister. Mr. Malloy, after reading your beautiful letter I became intrigued and decided to give you that thirty-minute appointment. Your concern for me was genuine so we will meet tomorrow at 10:00 AM. A car will pick you up and I look forward to meeting you. In advance, I thank for your concerns about me, and I feel that we have much in common. Until tomorrow, Amanda Watkins."

Marvin's hands were shaking, he looked at Mrs. Stafford and said, "It seems that I have a meeting with your Prime Minister tomorrow morning at Ten O'clock." The look on her face was priceless and he wished he would have taken her picture to show his daughter. His excitement level was at an all-time high, he didn't know if he was going to be able to sleep.

Chapter 3

S LEEP WAS SLOW IN COMING but he began to dream. "He and Amanda were in the garden, music was playing, they began to dance. Around and around they went, laughing, holding on tighter and tighter. Suddenly, he leaned down and started to kiss her, he woke up and it was morning.

As he got up to shower he thought, wow, what a dream. As he dressed he thought, shall I go formal or casual. This is a casual meeting, so he put on a royal blue turtleneck with light brown slacks, brown loafers, and a navy-blue jacket. He looked into the mirror and liked what he saw and declared; I am ready. As he looked at his watch and saw it was 9:35, he heard Mrs. Stafford shout, "Mr. Malloy the car is here." As he came outside he saw the same young man that he saw yesterday, and he said, "Good Morning young man."

"Good morning sir, I have the pleasure of being your driver this morning." Marvin asked, "Where are we going young man?" The young man replied, "I think you will know the address sir."

They were driving and Marvin was enjoying the scenery, they turned, and he saw that they were on Downing Street and stopping at number Ten. He thought how many times he had seen on TV, number Ten Downing Street, and there it is. His driver jumped out and opened the door for him and said, "It's been a pleasure sir."

Marvin asked his name, he replied, "Tony sir." Marvin shook his hand and slipped him a new crisp 20-dollar bill and said, "Don't argue Tony, don't argue."

He walked to the door and before he could knock, the door opened and there stood a woman whom Marvin knew was "Amanda Watkins." He looked at her eyes and he saw them dancing with happiness and he knew instantly that they would become more than just friends.

She looked at him and said, "May I call you Marvin," he replied, "Only if you let me call you Amanda?" They started down the hall when they came to a painting hanging on the wall.

She stopped to show him and explained that this painting was her favorite. She told him that, "Every day I would stop and look at it and it brought her peace. You can almost see the tall grass moving with the gentle breeze, heard the birds singing, and see the clouds moving along."

As she was describing it to him, he was thinking, "I wondered where this painting would end up. I felt the same way when I was painting it as she does when she looks at it."

Just then a young man of college age is coming through the hall, and he says, "hello grandma." "Well hello Jeremy, here I would like to introduce you to someone. Jeremy, this is Marvin Malloy from Arizona, USA. Marvin, this is my Grandson, Jeremy O'Dell who works as one of my readers, sorting the mail."

As they shake hands Jeremy recalls and says, "Mr. Malloy I read your letter and I am sorry to say that I put it into the no-good pile." About then, Amanda says, "Well Jeremy you must have placed into my file because it ended up on my desk. Oh and, I am certainly glad it did."

Just then Jeremy's eyes begin to dance, and he looks at Grandma and says to her, "Do you know who this is," pointing at Marvin? She replies, "Do you mean Mr. Malloy?"

"Yes, do you really know who this is?" Amanda says, "Well yes, he is the one who wrote the letter." Jeremy says, "No, no, he is the one who painted this picture."

She says loudly, "What," and then looks for the artist signature. Amanda puts on her glasses and reads, "Marvin Malloy." She turns, looks at Marvin and says, "Why didn't you say anything?"

Marvin smiles, "You were enjoying it so much I did not want to spoil the mood. When I painted this in 1985 it brought the same joy to me. I stood up on the hill, looking down, and on the porch was my wife and began painting. We were living in that house at the time, and we did not have too much money so reluctantly, we sold it. It gave us enough money to last through the winter. When I heard you describing it, I did not have the heart to say anything. It makes me so happy that my work gives you peace and Jeremy, I am so happy that my letter was placed on your grandma's desk, thank you."

Jeremy spoke up and said, "Well sir I guess it was a good thing I did not pay attention where I set it. It has been a pleasure meeting you sir," and walked away. Marvin turned to Amanda, looked into her eyes, and commented, "Nice young man." Amanda still had that look of surprise on her face and said, "Let us go to the sitting room and have some tea." He said, "After you my dear."

When she heard that she could feel goose bumps up and down her body and it shook a bit and to herself she managed to say, "Oh my." Their thirty- minutes went by so fast; they began to get interrupted by her secretary. She became annoyed, picked up her phone, dialed him and said, "Mr. Jones, cancel all my meetings until tomorrow, Mr. Malloy and I will be unavailable the remainder of the day." The secretary knew she was upset because she never called him Mr. Jones, she always called him William. He tried to figure out what she was doing but could not pinpoint it. Oh well, I will find out tomorrow.

Amanda's and Marvin's time together was flying by, their variety of subjects was endless and not one word of politics. They looked at the clock and couldn't believe it was 5 PM. Amanda says, "Marvin I am hungry are you?" He answers, "Yes I am. You know I would love to dine with you and then go dancing." She blushes a little and says, "I haven't danced since my husband died," and he shakes his head and says, "I haven't either since my wife passed, maybe it's time we danced again?"

He looks into her eyes and says, "Amanda, I have this feeling that this is only the beginning between us and the ride we take is going to lead us to a level that we did not know we could ever get to again". She nodded her head and quietly said, "I feel the same and don't know why, but I must warn you, the press is going to be all over you, they will let nothing stop them. Your picture is going to be all over the world and the headline will read M&A, who and why?" Marvin laughed and said, "Let's do it."

Amanda picks up the phone and presses key #3 and her security chief answers, she informs him that, "She and Mr. Malloy will be going to the

Editors for dining and dancing. Please make the arrangements and we will be leaving in thirty- minutes. She heard him say, "Yes Madam everything will be taken care of." She hung up and Marvin asked who was that? "Oh that, just my security detail, they are just like your secret service. They watch over me and I cannot go anywhere without them, well maybe to the loo but they do have female members."

Marvin laughed, "Stated that he did not even think about them." She warned him, "They will be watching him closely, so no funny stuff." He grinned and said, "Will they be dancing with us also?" Amanda broke into a large grin and said, "They better not. Now I must go and change, I'll send in Jeremy in to keep you company," and left the room.

A minute later Jeremy walks in and says, "I understand you and Grandma are going to dinner and then dancing." Marvin was studying Jeremy and said, "Yes we are. So tell me Jeremy, I understand you are in college, what are your interest?"

"Well sir when I was younger my father was pushing me toward a career in politics. I never got the chance to tell him that wasn't for me. He did know I loved to draw and paint but always said that was for sissies, and it made me feel sad. After the crash, grandma took me in and told me artists are the keepers of our history, and it is a noble profession. Do you feel that way sir?"

Marvin looked at him and saw himself at that age. He spoke up, "Jeremy, your grandmother is a wise person, you should be thankful that she is looking after him. Son, if I am here I will be happy to help you in any way. There is nothing that gives me greater joy than to help young artists, I think we can put together some excellent work. I will talk to Amanda tonight; I am sure she will like the idea."

Amanda walked in and said, "What will I like?" Marvin smiled, "Your grandson and I are going to collaborate with each other doing artwork, maybe I can learn something." Amanda and Jeremy both laughed at that statement and said wonderful.

Chapter 4

Amanda grabbed Marvin's hand saying, "Goodnight" to Jeremy and headed for the door. Marvin was on cloud nine and could not resist squeezing her hand saying, "Look out London, here we come." They opened the door and to Marvin's surprise, two big black limos were there with six people standing at attention. Four men and two women dressed all in black. Amanda leaned over to him and said, "Just security." Marvin was impressed when Amanda went over to each one and greeted them by their first names. She turned toward Marvin and said, "Are you ready?"

The guard opened the door for them, and Marvin let her enter first. As the door closed he saw across the street about twenty people with cameras and asked, "Is that the press." She laughed and said "Tomorrow morning your picture will be in all the papers so your privacy will be gone. Just stay calm and in time they will respect you. Be patient. The M&A boat is leaving the dock and they will dig up all your history, so beware."

It was only a 10-minute ride to Editors, but when they got there they saw many customers standing in line to get in. The customers did not know that they had to wait for the Prime Minister to arrive before security would let them enter. As they got out of the car the customers broke into applause and she waved at them saying, "Sorry you had to wait," and of course when they spotted Marvin you could hear a buzz in the crowd. Amada laughed and said, "Oh they are talking about you now. Marvin, tomorrow morning you are going to be a big celebrity, but I guess you are use too that, Mr. well known artist."

Marvin began to laugh, and they entered and Edward the owner of Editor welcomed them and said, "Your table is ready, and everyone knows, no pictures as you requested." The table was in the corner facing the door so security can see who is coming in. It was a nice cozy table for two. Amanda tells Marvin, "No need to order, I had them prepare the special they are known for." Just then the waiter brought a bottle of wine and had Marvin test it for approval. He nodded his head yes, then he filled both glasses and began a toast.

"Amanda, when I first saw you I knew instantly that we would become close. I could feel that you were feeling the same. I composed a little poem, so here goes. Roses are red, violets are blue, God said Marvin, what can I do, so I said, please send me you."

Amanda blushed, "Marvin, I too felt giddy when I first saw you and I truly want to get to know more about you, in other words, let's explore and get to know each other." She reached over and squeezed his hand and at the same time the waiter brought over their food. Marvin looked and saw pot roast with new potatoes and fresh peas with a rich gravy for the roast. He looked at Amanda with surprise, shook his head, "How did you know this is my favorite meal?"

Amanda smiled, "Prime Ministers secret." Marvin spoke, "Do you mind if I say a prayer?" "Goodness, I would love that." He began, "Almighty God we thank you for bringing us together today and we look forward to doing your will together. Amen."

Amanda looked him in the eyes, "Marvin that was so special, thank you, I needed that." They continued their conversation during dinner, just getting to know you talk, never once checking the time and enjoying each other. After dinner was finished Marvin said, "While we wait for desert let's dance. Amanda's eyes lit up, she smiled, "I haven't danced in ages." Marvin looked her in the eyes, "Well it's time you started again.

As he walked her to the dance floor he took by the arm and led the way. When they got there they turned toward each other, looked in each other's eyes, and both saw what looked like future romance. He took her into his arms and pulled her close. He could feel a resistance at first then she relaxed and leaned into him. As they went around the dance floor they could feel the other diners watching them. He leaned into her ear and whispered, "Let's give them a show." She got a big smile saying, "Let's do it." They swirled around and around, he pushed her out and then twirled her and when he pulled her back, he dipped her and then pulled into him, surprised her, and kissed her. When they stopped she was breathless and sighed, "Oh Marvin!" He smiled at her proclaiming; "Gee desert was wonderful."

As they walked back to the table Amanda said "Marvin, you sir are a joy." They reached the table, the desert awaited them, Amanda said, "Oh look the real desert." Marvin burst out laughing, drawing attention of the other patrons, who themselves were smiling.

Spontaneously the other patrons burst out with applause. Amanda acknowledged them and sat down. "Marvin, you can sit down now." Desert was a sweet lemon cake. After Marvin's first bite he leaned over and in a muffled voice declared, "Just as sweet as that kiss."

Amanda felt her body shiver a little bit thinking, "I sure am glad I read his letter, I haven't had this much fun since," and then felt a tinge of remorse. They danced quite a few more dances, then Amanda said, "We had better leave because I have some important meetings in the morning." She stood up, said good night to all the other patrons, and in unison they said, "Good night, God Bless."

When they were in the car, Amanda thanked Marvin for a lovely evening and Marvin replied, "You are the one who made it special." They reached Ten Downing Street, got out of the car, she told him that the driver would take him back to Stafford House and then she said, "As Prime Minister, I demand that we meet again and again so we can know more about each other."

All he could say was, "Yes madam." She walked to the door, turned, and watched him get into the car, and her thought was, "I need to get to know this man because my feelings are a big surprise."

He watched her go into the house and his thought was, "I need to know this woman better because my feelings were a big surprise."

It has been three days since he was with Amanda, so he decided to contact her again. As he was about to call his phone rang and Amanda's name was on the caller ID. He answered and a male voice said, "Hold for the Prime Minister please."

He heard; "Marvin this is Amanda, I am so sorry I haven't called sooner; I have been busy with another world crisis, but we worked it out."

Marvin spoke, "Amanda, no need to apologize." She continued, "I will take the whole day and night off Friday if you want to spend it with me."

Now Marvin paused just enough to make Amanda wonder, then he said, "I would love to spend that time with you."

"Oh good, there is a favor I need to ask but I will wait until we are alone together. I must go now, till Friday."

She hung up but Marvin could swear he heard 2 clicks hanging up. What did I just hear? Should I tell Amanda? I think I'll wait to see if it happens again.

At that same time, Amanda's Secretary, William Jones, had hung up his phone not knowing that it was slightly later than Amanda's. He sat there and thought, where is this going and how is it going to affect the Prime Minister. I think I had better keep my eye on him. Something just doesn't feel right to me.

Meanwhile, Marvin thought, wondering what favor Amanda wanted. He then decided to stay in London for at least 6 months, so he went to talk to Mrs. Stafford. He sat down with Mrs. Stafford for lunch and explained, "He wanted to stay in London and would need a flat with a space for an art studio."

Mrs. Stafford said, "Since you were with the PM the press is going to be hounding you, and I can't have them here bothering my guests. It just so happens my late husband had a flat about 2 streets from here with just the space you might need. I will give you the address and key and you can look at it to see if it meets your needs. The rent would only be 400 pounds per month which compared to all the other places, is low."

He thanked her, I will walk over this afternoon and see it." She gave him the key, he said "He was sorry that the press would be a nuisance and he certainly didn't want that to happen." She said, "It's ok and now tell me about you and the PM."

He told her a story first about when he was small, "I thought I was German and a few years ago I had his DNA checked and learned that I was Fifty-five percent English, 25 percent Scot and Irish, and seventeen percent Eastern European and three percent unknown. All those years being German and not one ounce of German blood, so I feel at home here.

Mrs. Stafford smiled and said, "Welcome home Mr. Malloy." He then proceeded to tell her, "When he first saw the PM, he knew that they would become friends and he wants to pursue the friendship."

She smiled and remarked, "Are you sure it's just friendship?" He looked at her and thought this is a smart woman. He smiled at her and walked to the door saying, he was on his way to see the flat.

The day was beautiful with a gentle breeze and a hint of fall in the air. His favorite time of year was fast approaching. As he walked, the people he passed would say hello and he thought, how nice and friendly. I think I am going to like it here.

He saw the flat Mrs. Stafford spoke of and was impressed. He unlocked the door and entered. It smelled stuffy but he knew that was no problem, so he opened the window to let the fresh air in. The flat was still furnished and looked very comfortable. He inspected the kitchen and saw it was very well equipped. He was already thinking about living there. On to the bedroom which was quite large with a queen-sized bed, nice closet and two large dressers.

Now on to the space that may become his studio. He has not been painting in a long time but was getting excited about returning to it. He opened the door and couldn't believe how large it was with skylights that let in natural light. His first thought was, "Wonderful" and then he remembered Jeremy.

Wondering if he might like to work with him. He decided to take him under his wing and become his mentor. After seeing his artwork, he was impressed and especially his portrait work. With a little more training he could become very popular. He made up his mind then and there and couldn't wait to tell Mrs. Stafford.

His walk back to the B&B was a little brisker, there seemed to be happy back into his steps. He stopped so he could make a phone call to Amanda. He rang up her number and her secretary answered but told him, "She could not be disturbed." As the secretary was hanging up, Amanda came out of her office, "Who was that?"

"Oh that was nobody, just someone wanting to sell us something." Amanda just shook her head and said they will try anything. "Good night William, tomorrow is another day."

As she was walking to the car she couldn't understand why Marvin hasn't called. Well I think I will call him, so she did. She heard him answer, "Marvin how come you haven't called?"

He told her he just did but your secretary said, "You couldn't be disturbed." She got a puzzled look on her face. Why would he do that and then say someone trying to sell something. She told Marvin, "I want to see you again," and she could almost feel him smile. Even being apart they had already developed a closeness, it seemed she could feel his moods, his thoughts. She needed to see him tonight, so she asked about dinner. She could feel the excitement he was getting, and he said give me about 20 minutes and I will be ready. She exclaimed wonderful; I will pick you up, bye for now.

She called her housekeeper Molly and asked, "Can you prepare a picnic supper for two?" Then she remembered to have Molly include a blanket.

Molly replied, "Well now silly, how could you have a picnic without a blanket? You must be smitten with this man; I think I should meet him for my approval."

Amanda laughed because Molly had been with her for the last thirty-four years and she watched over her like a sister. "Oh Molly, what would I do without you," and she heard, "You better never find out."

I will be there in 5 minutes, meet me at the car." Molly replied, "Miss, sometimes you are more trouble than you are worth," and they both broke into a laugh. In the meantime Marvin was rushing around, he knocked over his after-shave lotion, grabbed it quick so not too much spilled. He almost ran down the stairs and Mrs. Stafford yelled, "Slow down before you kill yourself. You look like a young man going to meet the girl's father for the first time."

Then he remembered to tell her he was going to rent the flat. She said, "I knew you would and by the way my name is Delores not Mrs. Stafford." Just then he saw the car pull up, "Got to go Delores." She smiled and said, "Have fun!" He almost ran out the door, almost tripped, his excitement getting the better of him.

Chapter 5

MANDA WAS WATCHING, GRINNING AND when he opened the door she was laughing and said, "Slow down Marvin."

He sat down and said to her, "Oh my lady, you are so beautiful I wanted to be with you as quickly as possible."

She smiled, "Your slick Marvin, your slick." They both laughed knowing they could tease each other. Amanda knew it was going to be a good evening.

Marvin looked into her eyes and said, "I have news; I am going to stay in London for at least 6 Months and am going to open a studio and I am going to call Jeremy and ask him to work with me."

This made Amanda so happy that she hugged him tightly then kissed him. When they separated, she explained, "We are going to go on an evening picnic." They drove to the country and stopped at a meadow with some beautiful trees and Amanda told him, "I own the land, so we won't be trespassing."

Marvin looked so happy as they got out of the car. He looked around and saw the security people and knew they would never be alone. He wondered how she did it. Just part of life I guess. He spread the blanket and she opened the picnic basket and removed the utensils and food and a bottle of wine. She handed it to Marvin along with an opener and he popped the cork. As she set out the food, he poured two glasses handing her one.

He asked, "What shall we toast," she replied, "I will do it." They wrapped their arms around each other as people sometimes do and she said, "We give thanks that we have been brought together so we may become closer. Marvin, I salute you for having the courage to write that letter to me, I am forever grateful to you, for you have brought excitement back into my life."

As they clicked their glasses she could see tears flowing from Marvin's eyes, she pulled him close and hugged him and felt him shiver. She released him knowing this man is sensitive and kind, I could fall in love with him. When she realized this, she thought I didn't think I could ever find someone to make me feel this way again.

He looked into her eyes and remarked, "Amanda, you make me feel young again, a feeling I thought I would never feel again. I was married for over sixty years, and I am amazed how you make me feel. If you were not the Prime Minister, I would ask you to marry me right now even though we have only known each other such a short time."

Amanda looked him in the eyes, and he could see tears, so he hugged her, and she whispered, "If I were not Prime Minister I would accept, but I will tell you this, which no one knows yet, I am retiring in three months."

He looked at her with surprise saying, "Why?" Amanda hesitated, wondering if she should tell him she had Breast Cancer. She decided not to, so she said being Prime Minister has made me tired and it is taking my energy away, I need to step down and recover my energy.

"After I do, ask me that question." Marvin had the biggest smile and promised he would. They both said at the same time," Let's eat." Later they were looking at the stars and Marvin could see five security people around the hill. He leaned over to Amanda and in a quiet voice wondered, "Will they be in the bedroom for their honeymoon?"

Amanda burst out laughing saying, "They better not be." She looked at Marvin saying, "I love you, I can't explain it, but I do. How do you feel?"

Marvin thought for a moment then declared, "The first time I saw your picture on that magazine cover, I knew that I must come here to meet you. The attraction was so strong I bought the ticket with an open return ticket. Amanda, I want to be with you here and now, but I would be afraid your people would think I was hurting you, so I will wait for another time."

She smiled saying, "Time to go, shall I drop you off or would you like to come to my place?" Marvin spoke, "Amanda what do you think I will say?" She was quick to reply, "I believe we are going to my place." "Oh you are so right," and he grabbed her arm and led her to the car.

Once in the car Amanda told the driver whose name is Edward, to hurry up to the house. Marvin was smiling as he whispered, "What is your hurry?"

She gave him a shot in the ribs with her elbow and he was laughing aloud now. He grabbed her knee and said, "Nice," she was about to give him another shot, but changed her mind, instead she grabbed his thigh and squeezed.

The playing had begun. They got to the house in record time because Edward knew they needed to get there to be alone. He thought, "Good for you madam," as he brought the car to a stop and they both exited the car in record time without Edward opening the door for them. As he said good night to them he was thinking, "Love is a wonderful thing," and they disappeared into the house.

When inside she saw a note from Molly, she picked it up and smiled. Marvin said, "What is it?" She handed it to him, and it read, "Amanda I knew you would want some privacy tonight, so I went to my sisters. See you in the morning."

Marvin looked puzzled, turned toward Amanda, and said, "How did she know?" Her answer was, "She knows me like a sister. Let me show you the upstairs," grabbing his hand and leading him to her bedroom.

It was a room fit for a queen, four poster king size bed. The carvings were beautiful, the room was extreme comfort. Marvin had to excuse himself and she showed him to the loo. Once inside he marveled at how exquisite it was. After he finished he noticed a medicine bottle on the sink, so he picked it up and read what the contents were. Upon reading it he turned pale and knew why she was going to retire. It was the same medicine that his wife had to take for her breast cancer.

He debated whether to say anything or whether to say nothing. He decided to say nothing, letting her get the chance to tell him. Now he must act normal, so she will not suspect anything. He returned to her side and leaned into her "Amanda, I love you and want you now." She caught her breath, "I want you too."

And so their love began, and both knew it was going to grow. In the morning, Marvin looked around and Amanda was gone. He dressed and went down the stairs and there stood Molly. She saw him and said, you must be Marvin, "If you hurt her you will have to deal with me."

Surprised, Marvin looked Molly in the eyes and told her that he wanted to marry Amanda when she retired. Then he wondered if she knew. Molly smiled, "I know about the retirement so I will be watching closely, breakfast is ready, and the driver will be here in thirty minutes to take you back to the Stafford house." She knew everything and this is the first time she ever saw him.

As he sat down to eat, he asked her, "How do I get ahold of Jeremy?" She said that she would make sure he would contact him. He thanked her, wondering does this woman know everything? I bet she knows the color of my underwear.

Just then she says, "I know everything except the color of your underwear." They both broke into a laugh, she said "Hurry up the driver will be here soon.

Chapter 6

MARVIN RETURNED TO STAFFORD HOUSE. Delores was busy cleaning and straightening things up, said to him with a grin, "Hello night owl." Of course she knew who he was with, so she mentioned that the press was poking around this morning, but she shooed them away so be aware.

He told her, "I am going to move my things this morning and start living in the flat. Is there anywhere he might find a car so he could be more mobile?" She gave him directions and it was not extremely far away. His phone rang and he saw it was Jeremy. "Hello young man, I was going to call you. How would you like to collaborate with me because I am going to open an art studio and I would love to help you?"

He could hear Jeremy sigh and he knew it was going to be yes. "There is an extra bedroom if we are working late." Jeremy responded with a "Yes, when do we start?" "I will be moving in today so how about Monday?" Jeremy thanked him and said see you Monday.

Marvin went about the task of packing up and moving. He did not have much, but he talked with his daughter, and she was shipping him art supplies he needed and the rest he would purchase here because supplies were expensive to ship. He realized that he would now have 2 studios, maybe I can get something done. His thoughts turned toward Amanda, so he called, and the secretary answered, told him she was not available and hung up.

About 2 minutes later Amanda rung him up and said she was sorry she was not there when he got up, but duty called. He commented that he just called and was told you were not available and then the secretary hung up. Amanda was getting upset, "I will investigate this. I just wanted to say, last night was the best night I have had in ages, and it was because it was with you. I love you Marvin. Oh, did you meet Molly?"

Marvin started laughing and said, "Boy did I ever meet Molly. She told me directly that if I hurt you, I would be sorry." He could hear Amanda laughing, "Yes you did meet Molly. She is my absolute best friend looking out for me. Well Marvin I must go, things to do, how about tonight?" Marvin said, "I would love it, call me with your plans, Goodbye, love you!"

As he was hanging up, he heard her say, "I love you too." She touched the number three on her phone and the secretary said, "Yes madam."

"Please come in here now!"

As he walked in he could tell, something was not right. He started to sit when she said, "Stay standing." She then stared at him for a few seconds and then started in saying, "Just who do you think you are? When Mr. Malloy called, you said I was busy and could not be disturbed." Her voice grew louder as she talked, "Since when do you decide whether I am busy?" He started to speak but she held up her hand and he stopped. "Also when he called the other day you told me it was just someone trying to sell us something, but you made a mistake, because when you hung up Mr. Malloy heard 2 clicks. How dare you listen in on my conversations. If you ever do that again I will have you arrested for espionage. Do I make myself clear!" He nodded his head yes. "Now get out of here, you are suspended 5 days without pay. Your last duty today will be to call the pool and have them send me a new secretary. Understand?"

As he was leaving she heard him say yes, his head was down, and she could see him shaking. He closed the door and Amanda was wondering if she should have fired him. Well I think he needs another chance so I will give him two weeks to shape up.

Her phoned buzzed and there was a new voice, a female voice saying a representative of the royal Family was here. She acknowledged by saying, "Send him in."

The door opened, and she could see Secretary Jones was leaving the office, his head hanging down, shoulders slumped, she thought he just learned something. She made a note so she would remember to have a long talk with him in a week.

Now, "What does the Royal Family want now?" Out in the outer office Jeremy entered, seeing a new secretary who happened to be very good looking, "Well hello, and you are?" "I am Jennifer, Madams temporary secretary. How may I help you?" Jeremy was a little flustered, "Well I came to see my grandmother."

"Oh, she is with someone from the royal's office." He looked at her left hand, saw no rings and nervously said, "Would you like to have lunch with me?" She looked into his eyes and saw sincerity, so she accepted. "Come back in 2 hours, we can go to the cafeteria." Jeremy smiled, "Fantastic I will return, and I look forward to it." He left and she felt tingling, "Wow I am sure glad they sent me here." As Jeremy was leaving, people were watching him, and it seemed like he was dancing as he walked. They all knew that something or someone touched him. He made the whole room smile.

He remembered he needed to call Marvin. He felt privileged that Marvin wants to help his career. He thought of his father, and how he did not want him to be an artist. He silently said, sorry father but I must do it my way. He stopped walking and rang up Marvin. "Hello Marvin, I would love to work with you, I will be there Monday around 11 AM."

He signed off and his thoughts went back to Jennifer. Must be my super lucky day, first offer from Marvin and then meeting Jennifer. God is wonderful! He saw William standing next to the light pole, so as he approached he knew something was wrong. Will, what's wrong? He turned, saw Jeremy, "I screwed up royally. I listened in on Madam's conversation with Mr. Malloy, trying to see if everything was ok and then, this morning when he called I told him she was busy. I just want to make sure he was on the up and up. She chewed me out big time. She was almost yelling. I have been suspended for five days without pay. Jeremy, I feel terrible."

"Well Will, welcome to my world. Grandmother can be very tough but in the end she is always right. When you go back let her know how bad you feel and learn from this, always be honest. Grandmother will forgive you because that is her way."

"Thanks Jeremy, I will follow your advice, but it hurts for now." "And that my friend is how grandmother works, and she knows you will learn from it." As they parted, Jeremy knew how William felt because grandmother had come down on him the same way. It was a hard lesson, but it did work. As he remembered that day he silently said, I love you grandmother, thank you for loving me. The vision of Jennifer entered his mind and he thought he should thank William, because if he did not screw up he never would have meet her. Time for lunch so he returned and met with Jennifer.

Chapter 7

M RS. STAFFORD WAS CLEANING HER house when she thought of Mr. Malloy. She smiled and wished someone like him would come into her life. She was married for forty-two years when her husband passed from heart disease. She was only sixty-two and would love to feel needed again. She looked into the mirror and decided she needed what they call a make-over. She thought for a moment and decided to talk to Mr. Malloy, him being a man of the world, about what she might do. They had become very close in the short time of knowing each other.

She stopped what she was doing and walked over to the flat. She rang the bell and Marvin opened the door, "Delores how nice to see you, come in." She looked around and already Marvin had made changes and they looked good. She said to him, "Marvin I need your help. I saw how you reacted to Ms. Amanda, and I was wondering what attracted you to her? I am only sixty-two and I would love to have a man look at me the way you look at her."

Marvin was amazed she would ask him but since they were friends he thought he could help. Marvin looked up and then moved down. He saw a woman who was attractive but needed something more to make her standout. "Delores, what I think should be done first is your hair. You have streaks of gray and that detracts from that reddish brown look. You need to have it colored. Then I see your complexion and you need instructions in how to apply makeup."

Just then there was a knock on the door, he said excuse me, he answered it and there stood Amanda, smiling when she entered and saw Delores. She said hello and Delores was flustered to be in the presence of the PM. Delores nervously said "Hello," when Marvin explained that Delores was his landlady, and she was asking him for advice. Amanda asked her what kind of advice and Delores was starting to feel more comfortable, so she said, "I have seen how Mr. Malloy spoke of you and how he looks at you, so I asked what I need to do to have a man look at me that way?"

Amanda turned to Marvin, smiled, and spoke, "I did not know you were an expert in love matters." He replied to her that, "Delores was asking how to change her look so the men would see that she was indeed, a very attractive lady."

Amanda turned to Delores, "Well, let Marvin and I help you; it will be fun." Delores could not believe what she just heard. The Prime Minister and Marvin going to help little old me. Marvin asked Amanda, "Do you really want to do that?" She said, "Of course, a friend of yours is a friend of mine, now where shall we start?"

Marvin was amused and said, "I have already advised her to color her hair to bring out the reddish highlights and to get advice in how to apply makeup." Amanda looked at Delores for what seemed like a long time, pulled out her phone and hit call and said, "Andre, I have a new friend that needs your expert help. Can you work her in tomorrow at Ten O'clock?"?" She turned to Delores and asked, "Is ten ok?" Delores shook her head yes; "Andre is ten ok? Fine, see you then."

"Now Delores, my car will pick you up at 9:30 to go to your appointment with Andre. What address should I send the car to?" As soon as she said Stafford house Amanda said my driver knows that address. She turned to Marvin, "You should come along because this is now our project." Marvin began to laugh, "My, my, you sure do like to give orders, don't you? Of course I will go, this is going to be fun."

Delores thanked them both so much, see you tomorrow and left. Amanda looked at Marvin with a come here look, they met in the middle, hugged, and began kissing each other. When they separated he said, "Oh this is going to be fun." She spoke up, "Which part are you talking about? I took the afternoon off, what would you like to do." He got that look in his eye, "Oh, I will think of something. Let me show you the flat." He purposely did not show her the bedroom until last and they lingered there.

Later they were in the kitchen when her security chief notified her that the President of the United States was calling. Marvin piped up and said, Tell Richard I said hello." She looked at Marvin in surprise, whispered, "You know the President?" He nodded yes. She picked up the phone her security chief gave her and said, "Richard guess what, I am sitting here with a man who says he knows you. His name, it is Marvin Malloy. You do? Small world. Oh I forgot, our picture was all over the place and yes we had an enjoyable time, now why are you calling me?"

As she spoke to the President he could tell it had to be serious. He heard her say that "Yes we should have a meeting, do I come over there or will you come here? Ok when? I will make the arrangements and for public consumption we will have a formal dinner and we will tell them that we were talking trade, to not alert them of the real subject. Well Richard, we will see you next Tuesday. Yes I will tell him, goodbye."

She hung up looking at Marvin. "Marvin this phone call never took place, understand?" He saw the serious look on her face, so he answered, "What phone call?" She knew then he could be trusted but she knew that anyway. She told him that Richard said good choice, and what did he mean by that?

Marvin smiled, "Before he became President, he was at his ranch in Montana, and I was doing a painting of the ranch for him, and we became good friends. It was just after my wife passed and Richard and his wife were a great help to me, and we have been closed ever since. He calls me periodically to check on me and what he meant by good choice was that you and I are seeing each other."

Amanda blushed a little, smiled, hugged him whispering, "You did make a good choice. Now Marvin, I want you to join me when we have that dinner with the President and his wife. There will be some who will object about you being there, but this is my life, and I will live it my way. So is it yes or no?"

"Amanda, I would walk to the moon if you asked me too. Yes I will be there at your side if that is what you want, or I will stay in the background if needed." Marvin had a serious look. Amanda looked him in the eyes and stated, "I want you at my side because when I retire I want to be with you always. Marvin do you think we are moving too fast?"

He started to shake his head but then he said, "I don't think we are moving fast enough. I know it has been fast, but when you know it is what you want and need, you cannot move fast enough." Amanda received another call from her chief, said OK and turned to Marvin saying I must go back to the office and set-up the dinner plans for Tuesday. "I will see you tomorrow with Mrs. Stafford at Ten O'clock, it should be fun." She kissed him goodbye and left.

Marvin was amazed at how this whirlwind romance was progressing. He thought of the picture he first saw of her and marveled at where they were now. It was just meant to be. He thought for a minute, then called Delores and asked her to dinner so they could make more plans, she was excited and could not believe that the Prime Minister was going to help her. Marvin asked if six-thirty was alright, and she said of course. Marvin placed a canvas on the easel and started a portrait of a woman from memory and how she might look. Delores will be surprised. Such a good person, she needs excitement in her life, and he hoped he could help her achieve it. When he and Amanda were done with her the fellows won't stand a chance. Oh, it certainly is going to be fun.

Marvin knocked on Delores's door and he heard, "Come in," he entered and waited by the door. Delores came into the room, saw her, and marveled at her look. His thought was, it's not going to take much work, she looks fine. She thanks Marvin for being so kind and asking her to dinner, "I haven't been out in ages." Marvin smiled, "Delores you need to go out more often and let all the men folks see what they are missing." Delores blushed, "Oh we can go to the pub down the block, they have very good food, and a lot of our neighbors will be there. Lead the way Marvin."

As they walked down the street it almost looked like Delores was dancing, she was so happy. She held on to Marvin's arm letting Marvin know how she felt and so looked forward to tomorrow. As they walked into the pub all eyes turned and looked to see who was entering. Most already knew who Marvin was and they began whispering, who is he with? When they realized it was Delores, you could hear them say, she looks different. Marvin happened to overhear them and thought, wait until tomorrow fellows, you will be standing in line. They both ordered their food and got a glass of Mead and started to make plans for tomorrow. All the while they were talking, Marvin could see Delores's eyes dancing around the room, as if she was scouting for a man. She looked back at him, and he smiled, she knew he had caught her checking things out and a blush gave her away. He whispered, "Having fun Delores?" She shook her head and Marvin could already see a change in her already. He picked up his glass of mead and proposed a toast, "Tomorrow is going to be Delores's day and may all of the surprises be happy ones."

As they were leaving they heard one of the gentlemen say, wow she has changed, she looks good. This made Delores stand a little straighter and walk prouder as they were leaving. She turned to Marvin saying, "I am so happy you decided to come here, and I am so glad I got to meet you and become friends. My wish for you is that you and Ms. Amada become one, and as the press has said of you two, M&A. Good night Marvin, sleep well."

Walking back to the flat he felt at home here and enjoyed all that was taking place. He looked at his watch and decided to call his daughter back in Arizona and describe all that was taking place. He knew she had seen the picture of him and Amanda, so he would tell her of his intentions for the future. Just then the thought of Amada's breast cancer came to mind. Well I will have to figure a way to approach that subject. He turned on the lights in the kitchen, looked down and saw the first sign of Amada's problem. There on the floor was a small clump of hair and it matched Amanda's. He remembered his wife's ordeal and knew that Amanda's was just beginning. He was going to have to deal with it sooner than expected, tomorrow. Tomorrow was not going to be as much fun as he thought.

Chapter 8

TOMORROW ARRIVED, HE SHOWERED, SHAVED, looked into the mirror, and wondered, how a goatee look would? Nah, stick with a smooth face. He dressed and it was off to meet with Delores, then the car and on to Andre's. When they arrived Delores was nervous, slightly shaking, grabbed Marvin's arm, and held on tightly and were greeted by Andre himself standing along with Amanda. Andre turned on the charm and spoke, "You must be the Delores I have heard so much about. Looking at you I can see, there will be truly little we will have to change. Delores, you are a beautiful woman. Come let us begin."

They all walked into the salon and Andre announced, "Ladies, this is Delores and today we are going to turn her into a new woman and when we are through all the women will be jealous and all the men will want to be her lover."

He clapped his hands, and they took hold of Delores and disappeared through the curtains, telling Amanda to come back in three hours and you will see a new woman. Amanda took Marvin's arm and asked, "What shall we do for the next three hours" Marvin had a serious look about him as he told Amanda that they needed to have a serious talk. Andre had a conference room, so they went there and were served coffee, tea, and biscuits. Marvin looked into Amanda's eyes, and she knew that something serious and important to him was about to be talked about. Her husband used to get that same look when it was serious.

He started, "First I want to tell you I talked to my daughter last night and the main topic was you. She is so excited that I have found someone genuine and real as you, and not someone who was replacing her mother, but someone who is an addition to her mother." Amanda smiled, "What a beautiful way to say it, I look forward to meeting her."

Marvin's looks turn more solemn, he reached into his pocket as he spoke, "Amanda, my wife died of breast cancer, so I know what happens when treatments are administered, and I found this on my kitchen floor." He opened his hand and she saw the clump of hair. He went on, "I know it is yours and I also know you have breast cancer. The other night when I went into the loo I saw your medicine bottle and read what sort of medicine it was and knew it to be for breast cancer. It was the same that my wife had to use."

He noticed Amanda, she had turned pale and was nervous as she spoke up. "Marvin I was going to tell you after the Presidents dinner, now you know the reason for my retirement. I can't do my duties much longer, my body is getting tired. I am so grateful we met and so grateful for our love, but I believe that we must part, you do not need to go through this again."

Tears were falling in abundance now as she spoke, he embraced her saying, "My darling, I am not going to walk away just because you are having a problem, I am here for you now and forever and I know if I had cancer, you would be doing what I am going to do, stand by your side."

She put her arms around him and held him tightly thinking, I love this man, I do wish we were married. Marvin stepped back, looked into her eyes, and made the decision, "Darling let's get married now!" Amanda had a look of happiness and said, "I will announce to the ministers next week of my coming retirement and we can plan the wedding for that very same day, how does that sound?" Marvin gave it some thought; "I like it on one condition." Amanda had a surprised look and asked, what is the condition? Well Amanda, "We must be together tonight and as many nights as your schedule will allow."

"Oh Marvin, I do like how you think, and I know I like how you paint. I think we have just negotiated an agreement we can both live with. Let's go have some lunch." They left the conference room hand in hand, saw Andre, told him they would return in two hours and out the door they went, hopped into her limo and went back to her house for lunch and whatever else they might think of, laughing and giggling like two love struck young lovers. Marvin then remembered her words from yesterday, it was going to be a fun day. Just then Jeremy came down saying, "Well look at you two. Marvin, I will be at your flat Monday morning ready to work with you. I have some ideas what I can start with." Marvin told him he looked forward to it and out the door Jeremy went.

Amanda spoke up, "Alone at last, alone at last. Shall we start with lunch or," and Marvin spoke up saying, "I like or." Off they went up the stairs hand in hand. Marvin spoke, "I like this walk." When they came back down they did not have time for lunch, they had to hurry back to the salon. Both came through the door holding hands and Andre saw them and gave them a look of approval.

He said, "Are you ready to see Delores?" At the same time both said yes. They watch as the door opens, out came Delores and they could not believe it was the same woman. New hair color which fit her, new style which looked amazing, the bangs coming lower on one eye. Marvin quipped; "She reminds me of Rita Hayworth. Reddish brown hair with a perfect style to fit her face and personality."

Andre had given her a new dress that showed off her figure. They looked and had no idea her figure was this beautiful. Marvin whispered into Amanda's ear, "It's a good thing I saw you first." Andre took Delores's hand said to her, "Darling if I put your picture in the paper stating, looking for a man, the line would go all the way around London." She looked into the mirror, smiled, turned, and grabbed Andre and squeezed the air right out of him. Amanda walked over to her, took her hand, and said, "Delores, I am having a dinner for the President of the United States Tuesday evening, and I want you to attend. There will be quite a few eligible men there and I want to present you to them. You will love the attention, trust me." Delores was speechless but then she managed, "But madam I am only," when Amanda put up her hand saying, "You my dear are my new friend and I want the world to see what they have missed." Delores managed to say yes, I will come. She turned to Marvin and thanked him for this wonderful day, it was more than I could have hoped for.

Amanda announced she was hungry because she missed lunch, let's all go together. They bid Andre farewell and off they went with all the security guards as well. They stopped at a place called "The Bellows". As they were entering Amanda proclaimed, great food. All Delores could say, "I know of this place, but I never thought I would be eating here, especially with the Prime Minister." Amanda laughed and told Delores; "I am just a woman, just like you are dear."

They could hear the phone camera's going off and they all knew it would be on the internet before they could sit down. Amanda took pleasure in ordering for everyone, and Marvin leaned over to Delores saying, "There she goes again, giving orders." Delores looked at Marvin saying, "How am I supposed to act at the dinner party?" All Marvin said was "Just be yourself Delores and everyone will love you."

Lunch arrived and Amanda stood and said for all to hear, "Delores my new friend, I admire your spunk and I will tell all who will listen that you are the best example of how the English women should be. God bless." The other patrons could be heard saying, here, here. "Let's eat, I am hungry!"

While they were eating he look over at Amanda and he could tell she was in pain. Her eyes gave her away. Just then he watched as a very small clump of hair floated down to the floor. He leaned over to her and told her, and he saw the concern she had. She told him thank you and announced that she must return to the office and her car would deliver them home. She stood, hugged Marvin and Delores both, thanked them for a wonderful day and left. She got into the limo, broke down crying, and bent over in pain. No one saw and that is how she wanted it. She thought she might not last three months until retirement. The idea came to her that she might step down right after the dinner Tuesday. She felt that the public did not need to watch her suffer through the treatments and the losing of her hair. Her security people already knew but they were sworn to secrecy. I think I will tell the Ministers Monday Morning and the public Wednesday. We have a busy day Tuesday. The real meeting in the morning was about those Russians. Why do they have to keep raising trouble?

Chapter 9

MONDAY ARRIVED AND AMANDA WAS having second thoughts about telling her Ministers so she decided she would wait until after she talked to her great friend, Richard Mackenzie, President. She had a lot on her mind and right now breast cancer was not one of them. She hit number three on her phone and ask the secretary to come in.

Jennifer knocked and entered. "Good morning madam how may I help you." Amanda smiled, she was very pleased with Jennifer and decided to keep her aboard with her. "Secretary William would be back Wednesday, but he was on shaky ground."

Amanda explained that President Mackenzie would be in tomorrow morning for a private meeting, and she would like her to make sure they would not be disturbed even if the Queen herself showed up. With that information, Jennifer knew she meant business.

Jennifer was nervous but decided to tell the PM. "Madam I am having trouble with one of the cabinets, I can't get it opened. I think there has been different locks placed on it." Amanda arose and with a commanding voice remarked, "Well let's go and look!" Jennifer led the way and pointed to the cabinet saying, "It also has no identification slip on it." Amanda inspected it, grabbed her phone, called maintenance, and asked for George. He answered yes madam, she told him to bring his lock tools to her office right away.

As they were waiting Amanda spoke to Jennifer about staying with her as her assistant. Jennifer was thrilled and almost screeched a yes, "Oh thank you so much," and hugged Amanda catching her by surprised. Jennifer apologized and Amanda said that's alright. George walked in thinking something was wrong, but Amanda held up her hand, so George knew everything was ok. George said, "Just what do you need?"

"Well we have a cabinet that we can't get opened. We think the lock has been changed." He looked at it and said, "This one has a U-thirty-two lock and all the others have C-thirty-three locks. Somebody did change the lock, but I happen to have a key for the U-thirty-two." He inserted it and it clicked and opened. Amanda asked, "Can you get me a key for this cabinet." He told her, "Here keep mine, I have others in the shop." She thanked him and he left.

"Well Jennifer now that it's opened let's have a look." In the top drawer the first folder had the name of Charles Watkins, her husband. The second folder had Molly Bradley, her best friend, and the third folder had the name of Samantha Bernard and Allison Maureen Bernard. She had no idea who they were. She looked through her husband's folder and was disturbed by what she saw. She investigated the other drawers and found papers from Private Detectives. She saw that they were addressed to William Jones. She felt she discovered important information and asked Jennifer, "Please copy everything and to be sure to place it back into the folders the same as is now."

Jennifer realized that the PM was serious about this and promised she would do as she asked, and she would lock it back up and give her back the key when finished. Amanda told her that she trusted her very much and knew she was right in picking her as her new assistant. Jennifer went to work and was very careful the papers went back into the folder the same as they came out. There were many papers, so Jennifer put the copies in order in the new folders. It took her about one hour to do the job and she took them into Amanda's office and placed them in her drawer so no one would be able to look at them. She placed the key in the small compartment in the top drawer. She made sure there were no markings on the folders so if someone was in the office they would not know what they were. Jennifer was very efficient. When Amanda came back to the office, she would show her where everything was.

While all this was taking place, Jeremy was arriving at Marvin's flat and started unloading his current paintings. Marvin looked out the window, saw him and came out to help. They carried them to the studio and placed them so Marvin could look at them and study them.

After they finished unloading the car they went inside and set-up Jeremy's supplies so they could begin working. Marvin asked Jeremy to sit down, and he would look at each painting. As Marvin was looking he was making comments, nice, needs a little more shadow, perfect, this one needs a better focus, and so on. Marvin in general was very pleased with what he saw. When he came to the portrait of a young woman, he stood back, studied closely for a long time. He turned and began, "Jeremy, you have enough here to have a show. These are magnificent and this one is your show piece."

He was holding up the portrait of the young lady. "I can tell you painted her with love. It shows and it doesn't make a difference what angle you look at it, you can see the love you put into it. I see you called it Sammie, is that her name?" Jeremy answered yes, "I was in love with her, thought she would be my forever person, but she disappeared, and I never saw her again. That was five years ago. I still miss her."

Marvin could see the tears so he spoke, "Jeremy, love can be hard, and I feel that she had a good reason she left. I would like to tell you, do not give up she may reappear. Let's set-up the show and just maybe someone will know where she is." Jeremy asked, "Are we dreaming Marvin?"

He answered, "Well look what happened to me. A lonely man and I discovered a woman who was meant for me, so do not give up! I believe that your grandmother and I will be together for a long time."

Jeremy remarked, "I sure hope so, you and she are a match and I love seeing you two together. How soon can we have a show?" Marvin laughed, "You are your grandmother's grandson, great at changing the subject. She is a master at it. Now speaking of a show, we can have it ready in a month to maybe six weeks. I know most of the dealers here so I know one of them will be happy to accommodate us. You let me worry about the show, you get ready and if you had any ideas for a new painting I would love to hear about it."

Jeremy spoke up, "I would like to paint a portrait of my grandmother." Marvin thought and then said, "Why don't we let her believe that I am painting it and then surprise her when she finds out you did it. She would be so proud." Jeremy liked it and said, "let's do it." So the first day together started off with a big bang. A show and a new painting.

Meanwhile Amanda was sitting at her desk looking at the folders wondering just what was in them. She opened the one with her husband's name on it. As she read she discovered that Charles met with a woman named Samantha Bernard and she had a child named Allison Maureen Bernard. Amanda could not figure out what all this meant. She read further and discovered that Jeremy was the father. She sat there thinking, why hadn't my husband ever told me of this.

She continued and discovered that her husband had paid $250,000 American dollars to this woman to disappear and in the event of his death, there was an insurance policy in place for one million dollars. She sat there trying to believe what she was reading. She picked up her phone, called her driver, and asked him to come to the office.

She set that folder aside and opened the one that said Molly Bradley. As she began reading she learned that Molly and her husband were lovers for many years before her marriage and even after. She found out that when her husband died they were still lovers. She saw proof that there was another insurance policy in place. This one for 500,000 Pounds. She sat there in disbelief.

Jennifer had placed a note in the folder explaining that there were pictures in that folder. She went out and Jennifer handed her an envelope saying, "I thought you might want to see these; I will put them back when you are through." She returned to her office, her hands shaking, she sat down and looked. So many pictures, someone must have been blackmailing him. In one picture there was a reflection. The picture must have been taken through a window. She got out her magnifier and looked at the window. She made out an image, studied it and realized it was William Jones. She thought about it and surmised that William had taken the recent pictures but someone else had to have taken the earlier ones. There were many different poses taken.

Amanda was livid. She wanted to go home and grab Molly and throw her out the window but then thought about asking her who the blackmailer was. Yes she would do that.

Jennifer rang her telling her the driver was there. He came in and she told him there was a confidential job to do. He was to locate a Samantha

Bernard to see if she was still in London. She told him she was an American and she had a child, possibly four-five years old. This was a secret job, and he was to tell no one. He agreed and asked if there was a deadline. She told as soon as possible.

He left and Amanda took the photo's back to Jennifer and told to place them back in the folder. She told Jennifer she was going home if she needed to be contacted. She knew Molly would be there but not for long. Her driver dropped her off and told her that he would begin the search right away. He drove off and Amanda walked toward the door regretting what she was about to do.

She entered and Molly was all smiles, greeted her with a big hug. Amanda being a woman who did not like to play games said, "How many times did you greet my husband that way or did you give him a big sloppy kiss with or without clothes?" Molly looked flustered and realized Amanda knew of her affair. She did not know what to say. She started to say sorry but stopped because she knew that saying sorry was meaningless. She looked Amanda in the eyes and said, "We loved each other but he was married to you." Amanda burst out "You are lying; you were lovers before I married him. I've seen pictures! The one thing I want to know is, who is blackmailing you!"

Molly could not believe what she was hearing, "How did you find out." Amanda said, "It does not make any difference how I know; I want to know who."

"I do not know. I send the money to a postal box each month, 1,000 pounds."

Amanda asked, "How long have you been paying, and she said, "Where will I go?" Amanda looked at her and with a smirk on her face she said, "I guess you will have to spend some of those 500,000 pounds you got when Charles died. Did you make that plane crash? Get out! Get out now! When I come back down you had better be gone."

When she got to her bedroom she called Marvin. He answered with an upbeat voice and heard her say, "I need you now." He instantly knew something was wrong, "I am on my way." He told Jeremy he had an emergence and left. He ran back in saying I forgot I do not have a car, take me to your grandmothers.

Jeremy asked, "What's wrong?" "He replied, "I don't know but she said she needed me now." "I will drop you off and if you need me, call me." Marvin got out of the car just as Molly was leaving. "Where are you going?" She looked at Marvin saying, "ask her."

Marvin went through the door, yelled Amanda, and heard her response, "I am up here." He almost ran up the steps, raced to the bedroom saw her, "What's wrong?" She came to him, wrapped her arms around him and began to cry. Her crying soon turned into sobbing, and she couldn't stop. He asked is it your cancer and she shook her head no. He let her get it out and waited. After about Ten minutes she stopped, apologized, thanked him for coming.

He looked at her, said, "You don't need to apologize because I love you, when you hurt, I hurt and never thank me for coming, I will always be there for you. Now tell me, what's going on."

Amanda started from the beginning, "Her husband paid off a young girl to leave because she was pregnant with Jeremy's child. He did not want her to interfere with his career in politics. She had a daughter named Allison Maureen Bernard. He paid her $250,000 American dollars and when he died she received 1 million dollars insurance money.

That's only part of the story, he also was having an affair with Molly from before we were married right up to the end. They were both being blackmailed. I found the information in folders in my outer office cabinet placed there by William Jones."

Marvin sat on the bed, "My goodness, what are you going to do? Before you answer, do you know the name of the girl?"

She shook her head yes, and in a soft voice she said, "Samantha Bernard." Marvin then asked, "Would she be called Sammie?"

Amanda thought yes that could be her nick name. Marvin then told her, "He saw her picture today. Jeremy painted a portrait of a beautiful girl and said he was in love with her, and her name was Sammie."

Amanda was surprised, "What did Jeremy say?"

"Well, he said how much he loved her, thought she was going to be the one but then she disappeared. He has been heartbroken ever since."

Amanda told Marvin; I have had my driver searching for her to find out if she was still in London. I don't know what I will do if she is. I guess I will just figure it out when I get the information. Now Molly is a different matter. There were pictures in her folder, and I am sure you can guess what kind. How could they carry on all this time, and I not know? I guess it is true, the wife is the last to know. Oh Marvin, what shall I do?"

Marvin hesitated, he could see the hurt in her eyes, and he felt it too. This magnificent woman has just been hurt beyond belief, so he knew he had to remain strong. He pulled her into his arms, held her close, kissed her, wiped her tears away and said with all the love he had, "Daring I am here with you now, I love you with all my being and I promise I will always be at your side. What is past, even though it hurts, is in the past. We need to concentrate on the now. If you need to investigate further I will stand with you. I believe you need to figure out how much William had to do with the blackmail.

Also, you need to sit down with Molly and learn more. She knows more, but I do not think she wants to talk, but you must confront her, force her to talk. That is the only way you will discover what really took place."

"As for the girl, find her because she is the mother of your great grandchild and Jeremy still loves her." He could feel Amanda shaking. She looked into his eyes, as she trembled she asked, "Would you help me?" Marvin lifted her chin and with a soft tender voice whispered, "Darling I will be at your side whenever you need me to, I love you."

Amanda smiled at him, mouthed the words, thank you, I love you too! Marvin let out a big breath, "What do you need to do now?" Well Marvin, "Can I call you Marv instead of Marvin?" He laughed; "Darling you can call me mud if you want to. Should I call you Mandy?" She answered fast, "NO! My husband called me that, I don't want to hear that ever again."

Marv understood that real fast, "Maybe I will call you pussy cat." He received another famous shot to the ribs. He grabbed her, "I think I should have you arrested for abuse." They both laughed at that.

Amanda thanked him for bringing her out of depression. She told him, "I must go back to the office to prepare for tomorrows meetings with Richard."

He understood, "Shall I come back this evening?" "Yes, around 8:00." He nodded yes, got to the bottom of the stairs, turned and in a loud voice, "See you later pussy cat," and out the door he went.

Chapter 10

AMANDA LEFT; MARV HAD CHANGED her mood to a playful one. She got back to the office, saw a note on her desk from the United States Ambassador about when the President would be available. He was going to be there by 8:30 AM. She thought good, he and I can have a private meeting with no one present. All the others won't like it but too bad.

She called in Jennifer, "You got any ideas about William?" Jennifer thought and started by saying, "I think we should let him come back and maybe trap him. I suspect he is recording you trying to get something he can blackmail you with."

Amanda raised her eyes, "I think you are right, and I think we can place some false information which should give him reason to try and blackmail me. Such as stashing money aside for my retirement. If he is recording us, then we can trap him.

The only person we can tell would be my Security Chief. I think he might record William, trying to catch him at something. Call the Chief and have him come to the office now so we can set things in motion."

About 20 minutes later Chief Stanley Michaels entered saying what's up? He and Amanda are very close friends; the Chief had been with the PM for many years. "Well Stanley, I believe that my secretary has been recording my conversations trying to get incriminating material to blackmail me. I have found evidence that he was blackmailing my husband and my friend Molly Bradley. I will give you my copy of the file he has locked in the cabinet in the outer office, look it over and think of any way we can trap him and have him arrested."

Chief Michaels could not believe what he just heard but knew that the PM would not make it up. "Well Madam, I will look it over and by Wednesday I should have a plan."

Amanda continued; "Well, William will be back in the office Wednesday, so I can meet you in your office, so we won't have ears listening to us." The Chief affirmed the plan and left with the folder.

Amanda's thoughts then turned toward the meeting with the President. She believed that the two of them were thinking the same, they would call a meeting of NATO and put the pressure on the Russians to back off. She did not really like giving the press false information, but in this case, they had to. They did not want to tip their hand, although she was certain the Russians already knew what the real meeting was all about. The Russians loved to push just to see how you were going to push back. Reminded her of two children playing games.

She's been the Prime Minister now for seven years and she was glad retirement was going to be soon. She's had enough of this nonsense. Then she felt a pain and was reminded of things to come. She wiped her forehead, and a small piece of hair came out. She then knew she would have to start wearing a scarf. She had 4 more treatments to go and so far it was not too bad, but now it was getting worse. She knew that soon she was going to have to tell the public because she couldn't hide it much longer. She was dreading releasing the news, but it was something that couldn't be stopped.

Her phone rang, she saw the ID and it was her driver. She quickly answered, she heard him say, "The girl you seek is still in London and I have her address." She felt relief and then told him, "Meet me out front." She knew the security team would have to go with them so when she got to the car she talked to the agent in charge and said that "This was personal, and I need you to be indiscreet." They had done this many times, so the PM had nothing to worry about. They drove for about 25 minutes when they stopped and could see a large white house, with a large window. Through the window she could see a little girl dancing for a young woman, whom she guessed was the girl's mother. The girl turned toward the window and Amanda sucked in a deep breath. The girl looked exactly like her deceased daughter, Maureen. Her eyes filled with tears and the crying began. She knew that she was going to have to meet this woman called Samantha and her daughter. As they drove away the realization that she had a great granddaughter hit her. How was she going to let Jeremy know he has a daughter? She then felt a peace, my daughter lives through this girl. This is the only thing that the files held that was good. She said a silent prayer asking God to help her bring the family together. As she said Amen she felt happiness within her. First Marvin, now this. Thank You God. She told her driver to take her home and even though she has never met the girl, she loved her already.

Chapter 11

MARVIN WAS TALKING TO JEREMY about shadows and colors. They were going over some landscapes Jeremy had painted. He pointed out how on one side of the painting the shadows were correct but the other side they were off slightly. He had Jeremy step back five paces, turn and look quickly, then turn back. "Did you see it?"

Jeremy was amazed, it seemed to jump right out at him. Marvin told him, "I learned this trick many years ago, so do it with every painting. Even do it many times while you are still painting so you can correct it if needed. This never fails because when you turn around your first impression is always correct."

Jeremy started doing it for every painting he had brought. Marvin chuckled; well he got his first lesson. He looked at his watch and told Jeremy to call it a day. "Come back tomorrow and start your preliminary drawing of your grandmother's portrait, I won't be here, I will be with you grandmother most of the day and evening. Here is a key, keep it, come, and go when needed. Oh, if you want to move in there is a bedroom up in the loft."

Jeremy was surprised and said, "He would consider it." Amanda's driver picked Marvin up to go to her place. He and the Edward were becoming friends. Edward asked how the studio was coming along so Marvin said, "You should stop in when you are free." Edward smiled saying, "Madam keeps me busy, day and night, but I do love my job. I must be available at all hours. Are you staying the night sir?" Marvin did not know; "I will let you know."

Arriving Marvin got out, "Goodbye Edward," headed for the door. It opened just before he was going to ring the bell, there stood the beauty he loved. She had a look of contentment, Marv hugged her, and she whispered, "The cameras are clicking." He stepped back, walked in, "Sorry I forgot. When I see you, I see nothing else? Oh pussy cat," and before he could say another word he got the famous elbow treatment. He loved to tease her. "So, how was your day?"

Amanda led him to the sitting room where she had two glasses of fine wine ready, "Let's sit here next to the table, I have a few pictures to show you." He picked up his glass, "let's have a toast first." She picked up hers, "What shall we toast?"

"I know just the thing. May tomorrow be a good and successful day." Amanda spoke, "I'll drink to that." They sipped and she lifted the photos to show him. He saw a young girl swinging and in another, she was playing with a dog. Then Amanda set them down, now look at these. A young girl was skipping along the sidewalk and in the other she was sitting on the porch steps with a young woman.

Marv commented that they were the same girl. Amanda smiled, picked up the first ones again and explained, "These two were of my daughter Maureen, Jeremy's mother." She put those down, retrieved the other two and explained, "These are of Jeremy's daughter."

Marvin studied them and finally said, "I cannot tell the difference, amazing. What is your plan Amanda?" She hesitated for a second, then said, "Wednesday I am going to go to her house and try to convince Samantha to become part of the family. I am not sure how, but I will think of something. Also, my security Chief is going to collaborate with me to trap William. He is going to bring me a plan in a few days, also Molly is coming to the office Thursday to talk. Thanks for advising me to see her. Wish me well."

Marv picked up his glass, handed hers to her, "I toast to your success." They clicked glasses, drank the wine, then embraced. "Amanda whenever I hold you I feel so good, how do you do that?"

She looked him in the eye, "Marv you bring out the animal in me. Grrrr!" Her security Chief interrupted them saying "Madam the President and his wife are on their way here for an impromptu visit. They arrived in London early and requested a meeting." She asked, "how soon?" The Chief said in about twenty minutes.

Amanda turned to Marv, "I am going to go upstairs to change." She had dressed for Marvin, not the President. As she was leaving to dress Marv asked, "Do you need any help?" Laughing, Amanda said, "Not this time, maybe later," and up the stairs she went.

The security Chief was not sure if Marvin should be there, then Marvin told him that Richard and Ellen were old friends. He has known them for a long time. Just then his agents voice, who was inquiring about Marvin, told him what Marvin just told him. The Chief grinned said, "You pass."

He leaned closer to Marvin and in a deep voice said, "Sir I am glad you and Madam have become a couple and if you tell her, I will deny it." Marvin thanked him, "Mums the word."

Amanda came down after five minutes had gone by, the Chief said, "They will be here in five minutes." Amanda was wearing A pale blue dress with a white belt accenting her waist. She also had a neckless with a round black pearl and gold chain. She chose to wear flats because she had been wearing heels all day. Marvin noticed that she had removed her wedding ring. He guessed it was because of the information about her husband that she discovered.

The doorman opened the door and the President of the United States, and his wife Ellen appeared. Amanda and Marvin greeted them, hugs all around. Richard said, "Amanda sorry to bust in early, we left to beat the weather. They told it is going to be nasty." With a gleam in his eye, "I hope we did not interrupt anything." Ellen started laughing, grabbed Marvin's arm, "darling so good to see you again, we have missed you and your sense of humor."

"Amanda, you will have to tell me how you landed this hunk who still looks so young." Amanda led them into the sitting room when they passed the painting Marvin did and stopped, admired it, Richard spoke up, "Isn't this the one you told us about when you were at the ranch painting ours?" Marvin replied, "Yes it is and I was surprised to see it here. Amanda loves it and her grandson had to tell her I was the artist."

Amanda had a sudden pain that gripped her, and Ellen noticed, "what's wrong?" Amanda tried to fool them by saying gas, but Ellen knew better.

Amanda started to cry, and Marvin hugged her asking, "Shall I tell them?" She shook her head yes, so he looked at them and said, "Amanda has breast cancer, she has four more treatments, and we are praying she will go into remission." Richard asked if they could do anything for her.

She replied, "Please keep my secret until I make it public. I plan to retire after our meetings." You could see the look of disappoint on Richard's face. "It is going to be tough to replace you. I will say this, the Russians will love it. You have always been a tough opponent." The pain subsided and Amanda remarked, "I sure will not miss them and their foolish ways."

Amanda changed the topic; she told them how her and Marvin came together. Ellen shook her head, "Are you saying all because he wrote you a letter?" She nodded yes and Ellen said, "I need to start reading Richards letters."

Marv and Richard got a big laugh from that statement. They talked for two hours then Richard and Ellen left. Amanda and Marvin waved goodbye and came back in. Amanda was tired and Marv could see it. She asked him if he wanted to stay or go home?

He looked at her and she could see that he was worried, "I want to stay and hold you as you go to sleep. I want to be by your side always so when you need me all you must do is roll over."

She was suddenly filled with love for him, let's go to bed. He smiled, "lead the way." They both got ready for bed, climbed in, snuggled together and Amanda was asleep within five minutes.

Marvin thought this disease is starting to take its toll. He started to pray, God, please watch over Amanda, she needs your help. Amen! Marvin woke up hearing Amanda in the shower, so he got up and went down and began breakfast. He fixed English muffins, looked in the pantry saw what looked like oatmeal, fixed that, and brewed her some tea. Put it all on a tray and went back up to the bedroom. Amanda was sitting at her makeup table putting on her makeup when she noticed him walking in. "Oh you did not have to do that."

He answered by saying, "You are going to have a big day today, you need something to give you energy." He placed it in front of her then pulled a chair over and sat next to her. He knew her appetite was not good, but she did need to eat it. He spoke up, "If you do not eat it I will force feed you."

She turned, "My, my, bossy this morning. I sure hope you are not this way always. My driver will be here in twenty minutes so I will eat it all my love, you worry too much." Marvin spoke, "I will do the worrying for both of us, you save the world."

She snickered; "I think I have the easier job". She finished her food, slipped on her dress, kissed him, "Thank you darling, it means so much to me that you stayed last night."

Marvin could feel concern building, tears filling his eyes knowing that the breast cancer was starting to take its toll. "If at any time you just need to talk today, just call, I will be there for you and try not to overdo at your meetings with Richard. I asked him last night to watch you and stop the meeting if he sees you getting exhausted. The hell with the Russians, you come first in my book."

Smiling she placed her hand on his cheek, leaned down, gave him a lingering kiss, whispered, "I love you," and left. As she is going down the stairs she hollered, "Hey pussy cat, get dressed," laughing all the way down.

When Marvin stopped laughing, he showered, dressed, and left. He was pleased that the driver Edward came back for him. He said, "Good morning Edward, we are heading to James's Art Gallery." Edward informed him that Madam instructed him to stay with him for the rest of the day and off they went to the studio. Once they got there he told Edward to come in with him. Edward said, "No I must stay with the car."

"Nonsense," replied Marvin, "Today is your education day. Learn my boy, learn!"

As they approached, James greeted them, "Marvin so good to see you again, how can I help you?" Marvin introduced Edward as his assistant which put a look of surprise on Edwards's face, "I have a proposition for you. I am mentoring young Jeremy O'Dell and we are going to put together a show and we would like you to set it up for us one month from now."

James had a strange look on his face, "Yes I know of young Jeremy, a very promising artist but don't you think we should give more time to develop a following?" Marvin knew he was right, "Yes you are right but for reasons I can't divulge now we don't have time. If it will help I have had many of my recent paintings sent over and we could put together a dual show and call it Jeremy and Marvin. What do you think?"

When he added his own name, James was all in, as they say in poker. Marvin gave him his address, "All the paintings are already at this location, except for one, which we are still painting. I and my new assistant Edward here, will work with your people to set things up." Edward looked at him with disbelief as Marvin leaned over and said, "I just stole you from the driving game and I am going to teach you about the art game, you will be making a lot more that you do driving. I will straighten things out with Amanda. Deal?"

Edward did not know what to say, so he said, Deal! "We will talk details later." He turned back to James, thanked him, and left. When they got back into the car, Marvin quipped, "Since you no longer work for the Government I suppose we should take their car back. Do you have a car there?"

Edward said yes and off they went. "Oh Edward, now that you work for me, what is your last name?" "Brooks sir!" Marvin mused, Edward Brooks, now that name sounds strong, regal, you're not a royal are you? Edward laughed, afraid not sir. As they drove on, Marvin said, "Do not call me sir, call me Marvin or Marv but not sir. I will call you Ed, is that ok?" Ed said, yes that is ok.

The one thing no one knew was just how rich Marvin was. Let's just say, he never has to paint another painting again, but an artist never stops creating. Every month he gets residuals more than $50,000.00 Per. They dropped off the car, jumped into Ed's car and Marv said, "Let's go buy a real nice car, try Rolls Royce first." Ed heard that and knew he was going to like this new job.

Chapter 12

As Marv and Ed were having fun, Amanda was in the conference room with the President and all the others. Amanda arose and said, "clear the room, the President and I are going to have a private meeting, and on the way out turn off all recording devices, which is an order, make sure it is carried out." Once the room was cleared they could talk personally.

"Richard, I am thinking of retirement right after this meeting, what do you think?" Richard thought, then proceeded to tell Amanda she was making a mistake. He felt she should wait two-three months before doing it and don't announce it until just before leaving office. With the Russian thing it would better. That problem could be solved before then. She gave it some serious thought and agreed with him.

She then asked if she should tell the public about the breast cancer. He replied, "Yes you should, and tie it all in with a Cancer Campaign, it will help research worldwide. She smiled and said, "Richard I always knew you were smart." He laughed out loud, "He and Ellen talked of this very thing last night and it was her idea to tie it all together. I must confess that most of my ideas come from Ellen." Amanda kidded him asking, "Is Ellen going to run for President?" "I hope not, once was enough, when my term is over, we're done. Say, how about you and Marv come to the ranch for a much-needed rest?"

"Richard, I can tell you now that Marv has asked me to marry him, and I accepted. Told him that we would after I retire. He wanted to do it today." Richard says, "Let's plan, my term is over in January, why don't you come over in, let's say June and stay for at least a month?"

Amanda was happy it sounded perfect and when they were in the States she could meet his children. "Well let's call everybody back in and plan on giving those Russians a piece of our minds." "Well said Amanda, well said!" Everybody came in wondering what was talked about and they got down to business. The meeting lasted for 6 hours, they had lunch brought in but in the end they drafted a statement that said if the Russians did not back off they would deploy the NATO troops that were in the area and would send in many more by Friday and because England was hosting the meeting it was to be delivered by Amanda and by the tone of her voice the Russians knew that they were serious. In a matter of hours the Russians began a pull-out hoping that one day in the future, NATO would be weaker.

After the meeting the pains came back, and they rushed Amanda to the hospital causing the press to scurry around trying to get information. They were told that the Prime Minister would be making a statement in the morning at Ten AM. There was much speculation about what was wrong, but the press held back on guessing, out of respect for the Prime Minister.

She was well liked by the public and that was a great help to her. She felt close to the public and they to her. She left the hospital a few hours later with new non-addictive pain pills and she contacted the Cancer people and told them her plans to announce about her breast cancer, and they said that they would be by her side when she did. She looked around asking, where is Edward. Oh, he left us this morning for a new job, someone named Marvin.

Amanda was speechless thinking just wait till I get home, hoping he would be there. Her phone rang and the ID said Stanley Michaels. Answering she spoke, "Yes Stan," he said, "I think I have a plan to trap our Mr. William Jones. Can we meet tomorrow?" She replied, "Yes we can, call Jennifer in the morning, no wait, William will be back tomorrow, call my cell and we will set it up, I will come to your office." "Ok I will do that, tomorrow then."

They arrived home, she saw this beautiful RR in the drive wondering whose it was. She entered and Marv greeted her, "Well hello pussy cat." She responded, "Don't pussy cat me, what did you do with my Edward?"

He laughed, "I stole him from you, and he is now my assistant. I offered him a chance to learn the artwork game instead of the driving game, in other words, I offered him a chance to learn and improve, he took it. We set up a show for Jeremy and me in 4 weeks and Edward will play a big part in it. Any more questions?"

"Now Mr. Malloy, don't give me attitude, I don't need it right now. I just came from the hospital." Marv was stunned, "I didn't know, I am so sorry luv, are you ok?"

"I am now, the pain was intense, but they got it under control." He hugged her, she melted into his arms, and they stood that way for what seemed like many minutes. They parted, "I talked with Richard this morning and we concluded that I need to tell the public of my condition tomorrow. I set an announcement for Ten AM. We also talked about you and I visiting them next June for a month and I thought that would be a good time to meet your children."

He looked at her with love in his eyes, "Did you just say we are going to get married?" She smiled; "I think I did." They hugged, kissed, and he said, "This is better than stealing Edward from you."

Once again the famous elbow in the ribs. "Dinner is ready your highness!" That almost got him another shot in the ribs. She thought about telling him about plans they might have for Willian but decided to hold off, instead talk about that beautiful car in the drive. "Oh that, I needed transportation, so I bought it." She said, "Where did you get the money? That car cost over 150,000 pounds."

He laughed, "You mean to tell me that your investigators did not tell you, I have more money than I can use. I just wrote them a check."

She made a note to check his assets. He told her all about the art show and when it will take place. He wasn't thinking when ran his hand through her hair. A large clump came out and he felt so bad. In its place was a bald spot the size of a ping pong ball. She looked into the mirror and made an important decision. She picked up her phone and called Molly, "Get over here immediately, I need you." Molly said, "Yes, right away."

Marvin knew then that she had already forgiven Molly. Affairs always involved two people; it was going to be her husband who she would not forgive. Molly got there in record time, Marvin answered the door, pointed to the sitting room, she's in there. Molly went in, closed the door and they didn't come out for one hour. Marvin decided to leave it alone, it was between the two of them. He heard the door open, and he saw them smiling and he knew they had resolved everything. They went to the upstairs bathroom and were there for twenty minutes. When they came down Amanda was wearing a scarf and Marvin looked puzzled. Amanda started to explain that tomorrow morning she was going to talk about her breast cancer and when she was finished she was going to pull off her scarf and reveal her shaved head. She pulled it off and all the hair was gone.

Marvin's eyes grew large, and he told her that was so brave, "I am proud of you," He embraced her, smiled at Molly, and broke down. He was remembering his wife and all that she went through. The grief came out with a rush, and he couldn't stop, and Amanda knew what he was feeling.

Spousal grief shows itself at strange times. He managed to tell her, "What she was doing would make all the people in the world who were suffering, proud of her courage for being honest."

The next morning Amanda was a little nervous, she made a lot of speeches but this about her retirement and breast cancer was altogether different. She sat at the breakfast table making some notes, outlining the direction she wanted to go. Of course the first thing on her agenda would be crisis that the Russians were trying to fabricate. She decided to be stern and let them know that the whole world is getting tired of their obsession with trying to control all that is happening in the world. She is going to tell them that if they do not back down and go home they will be starting the end of all things we all cherish and there will be no winners, only losers and the biggest losers would be the Russian People.

She decided to say that history has proven that leaders that choose war over love are foolish. Enough is enough! She put her notes in her briefcase knowing she was ready. She looked at Marvin and asked him if he would stand up with her? Marvin gave it thought and asked, "Do you think you fellow politicians would approve? Would they think I would be interfering? I don't feel at ease with this."

Amanda was disappointed but she did not want to embarrass him. "Ok, could you at least be standing down front where I can see you? Being able to see you will give me the strength I need to keep from breaking down and losing control."

He walked over to her, embraced her, "I love you and I will be down front for you; you have become my champion. Your driver is here, Molly and I will follow a little later. We will see you at the announcement."

Amanda left and Marvin turned to Molly, "I know you two have settled your differences but if you ever hurt her again I will see to it you will never get close to her again. You have a choice; be the friend she needs or never walk through her door again. It's up to you."

Molly seemed surprised that Marvin was so strong, but she could see that he loved Amanda, and nothing was going to come between them. She gained a new respect for him and told him, "She was going to be the best friend she needed." Marvin thanked her, time to go, God keep Amanda strong today.

Chapter 13

THE CONFERENCE HALL WAS FULL of the dignitaries from around the world and the press. The press was trying to push closer, but the security people kept them back. The room grew quite when President Mackenzie and Amanda walked into the room and the President stood before the microphone. He started, "Today, I asked my colleges from England if I could address you first and they graciously said yes. For many years now I have worked with Prime Minister Watkins and have become her friend. This lady is by far the strongest person among us today. Her leadership is an example for the peoples of the world to follow. Her ideals are examples for the world to follow. Ladies and Gentlemen, My dearest friend, Prime Minister Amanda Watkins!"

The audience stood and applauded for about three minutes and then the PM asked them to sit down. "Thank you Mr. President for your kind words but I must say, it is because you and I are so close that the world can rejoice the peace we have today. Now speaking of peace, I have a message for Russia. The time has come for you to stop creating trouble and go home. Provoking the free world will do nothing but cause your people great pain. You cannot win, only lose but the real losers will be the Russian People. If you love them as you say you do, let them live in peace. I am giving you a deadline, pull your troops back home within 24 hours or the suffering will begin. To the Russian people I say, your leaders are taking you down a dangerous road, stand up for peace."

The audience jumped up and cheered and clapped, they have never heard a leader say such harsh words before and mean them. The press was surprised, and they scrambled to get the story out.

After all was settled down the PM continued. "This morning I have further news that gives me sadness. Today I am announcing that in two months I will be stepping down as the Prime Minister. I have two reasons for doing so. First, I am getting tired. My body is running down, and I need to rest and get stronger. The second reason is I have a disease and its call Breast Cancer." When she said those two words you could hear the audience gasp.

"The treatments are making me tired and sick. Also because of the treatments I have consequences." She pulled off her scarf and reviled her bald head. The people were caught by surprise, the press started taking many pictures, and she looked into the camera and spoke, "To all the people who are suffering with breast cancer right now I say this. Let's be proud of who we are and let those who do not understand that you and I are fighters and with the help of the Cancer Society this disease can be cured. Thank you!"

Amanda went down into the crowd and straight to Marvin, embraced him and then kissed him. He whispered; "The cameras are watching, "Let them watch." As they walked out Richard and Ellen were with them. They retired to her office; William was back fussing over them. Amanda dismissed him and the four of them decided to go to Editors for lunch. She called her Chief Security Officer to see to the arrangements. She turned to Richard; "I think the press conference went well." Richard agreed and added, "The message to the Russians was strong."

Just then Jennifer came from her new office and handed to the PM reports of the Russian troops heading for home. Amanda remarked, "I thought what I said might be too strong, but it seemed to have the right effect." Richard added, "It was needed." They all agreed and gathered and left for lunch. On the way-out Amanda said welcome back William. They got into two limo's and left for Editors.

After they left William smiled, looked around then opened the cabinet to check the papers, checked them to make sure they were all there, looked good and he closed it back up. He thought to himself, it sure would be good to get something on the PM, then I could retire. Then he thought there is something I could hold over Mr. Malloy. He called the detective he used before and asked him to investigate Marvin Malloy, From Arizona USA. I'm sure they will find something.

Over at Editors, when Amanda and Richard walked in the patrons gave them a warm welcome. Amanda took off her scarf and they said Bravo to her. Marvin leaned over to her; "They love your courage." Richard leaned over, "You sure you want to retire." Ellen took Amanda's hand, squeezed it saying, "You are a strong lady." Amanda replied, "Oh I don't know about that."

The owner of Editors came over, took her hand said, "You and I have been friends for such a long time, I wish you a speedy recovery and I think you look good without any hair, are you trying to set a new trend." Amanda got a good laugh from that. They had a light lunch and good conversations, mostly about the trip in June to Richards and Ellen's ranch in Montana.

Marvin has been there, and Amanda said, "I wished I was there right now." Marvin piped up, "You know, we should get married there." Amanda's famous elbow came out. Marvin said, "Just kidding, I want to get married tomorrow." The four if them enjoyed a good laugh and then the pain hit Amanda again, but it went away quickly.

Richard and Ellen had to get to Air force One to head back home and Amanda and Marvin were on their way to see the house that Samantha and Allison lived in. While going there they talked about how they should approach them. Marvin could only say, be honest. He looked over at Amanda and could tell she was becoming tired. These treatments were wearing her down and he worried how much longer she could keep working.

The car stopped and they could see the girl on the porch. Marvin got a good look and he saw the resemblance. Amanda opened the door and was on her way over there quickly. Marvin hopped out saying "Wait."

Amanda kept going, reached the porch, said hello to the girl and asked if her mother was home. The girl went to the door and hollered, "Mum, a lady is here to see you." Samantha came to the door, saw Amanda said, "I have been expecting you. When I saw your car the other day, I knew you would be back. You have no right to be here, so please leave."

Amanda was hurt but she told Samantha, "I only found out about you a few days ago and I also learned what my husband did, paying you money to remove yourself from Jeremy's life. I am so sorry that he came to you and pressured you. Please believe me, I want you and Allison in my family."

She removed her daughter's picture and showed it to Samantha. "See, your daughter looks just like her grandmother Maureen. Also I can tell you that Jeremy still loves you, and no I have not told him yet about Allison, which will be up to you."

Samantha had to sit down, looked at Amanda telling her, "She had been following her ever since her husband died in the plane crash. Are you telling me the truth, you did not know?"

Marvin just stood there listening, this was between the two of them. Amanda spoke up, "Were you ever going to tell Jeremy about Allison?" Samantha sighed, "I have wanted to many times, but I thought that he knew and did not care. I believed that he had his grandfather come to me on his behalf and now you tell me he doesn't know. I always thought he didn't care."

Amanda turned to Marvin, "Tell her about what Jeremy is doing today." Caught by surprise, Marvin asked if she was sure, she nodded her head, so Marvin began. "Young Jeremy is an artist, not the politician that his father and grandfather wanted him to be. He is working with me and in a little over three weeks we will be having a show of our artwork. I need to tell you that his work is outstanding, you need to see it, and his show piece is a portrait of you. It is one of the most impressive portraits I have ever seen. Think about this and if you need help, Amanda and I will be happy to help in any way we can."

Samantha felt overwhelmed with it all, "I need to think about all this, and I need to prepare Alli for learning about her father."

Amanda spoke up, "Samantha, we will not tell Jeremy anything, this belongs to you." Just at that time Alli spoke up, "Why are you wearing a scarf, it's not cold?"

Amanda smiled, looked at her and said, "Do you know what cancer is? Well, it's a sickness and I have it and I wear this scarf because I do not have any hair." She pulled off the scarf and Alli laughed saying, "You look funny." Amanda laughed too remarking," I guess I do."

Marvin then said to all of them, "Leave it to a little girl to bring us all together." Samantha said she was sorry for all this, and Amanda said, "She was so glad you finally found out the truth. Now it is up to you Samantha to think wisely. We will leave you now but if you need to talk, call me at home or the office. Nothing I must do is more important than this."

Samantha looked at Amanda, "I saw your conference this morning, I have always thought you were a good person and now that I know the truth, I know you are. I promise to stay connected," and she wrapped her arms around Amanda, "I will pray for you."

As tears came to Amanda she thanked her and as she was walking away she heard Alli say, "Who was that lady mum?" Samantha answered, "That lady is your great grandmother." Amanda cried some more. Driving away Marvin put his arms around Amanda, held her and his thoughts were everything is going to work out.

Chapter 14

CHIEF MICHAELS WAS IN HIS office going over the plans to trap Mr. Jones. He had to create a story that sounded truthful and believable. He put together a story that the PM had a baby from a different father and the baby was adopted. He falsified documents that would look believable, complete with stamps of authenticity. He left the name of the father off but left clues who he was. A good friend who was retired from the security service allowed the use of his name. With the approval of the PM they would plant the papers in Amanda's office. Then they would wait and see.

When he heard the PM announce her retirement he was not surprised. He could see that the cancer was taking its toll on her. He always enjoyed collaborating with her and her leaving got him to thinking about retiring. This job did not leave enough time for family and that was why his wife left him ten years ago. Although alone, he felt the need to find someone to enjoy the autumn of his years. The image of Molly Bradley came into his mind. He has known her for a long time. On his note pad he suddenly wrote, why not and underlined it many times. He knew that William was extorting her, so he picked up the phone and called her. After five rings he had to leave a message for her to get back to him. He looked at his watch, decided to leave for the night. I will stop at the pub.

Molly saw his name on her phone and decided not to answer. She was puzzled as to why he was calling, if only he was calling for a date, that would be nice. She listened to his message, wondering what he wanted. As she sat there he came through the door, spotted her, and walked over to her, "I just tried to call you."

She looked up, "Yes I know, what do you want?"

He said to himself, go for it, "Well I was going to ask you to dinner."

Surprised, Molly smiled, "Well Mr. Michaels what brought this on?"

He looked into her eyes and said, "Call me Stan."

"Well Stan, I am hungry where shall we go?"

Stan smiled, "Let's go to that restaurant just down the street."

Molly stood up, took hold of his arm, "Let's do that," and out the door they went. Both seemed happy while walking there.

Jeremy was working on his portrait sketch of Amanda while he listened to the news conference. He looked and saw her removing the scarf. He did know about her cancer but was sworn to secrecy. Now the public knew and for some reason he was relieved. He looked up feeling like a burden was lifted, he turned, and he looked straight at Samantha's portrait.

It seemed alive, vibrant, and beautiful, all at the same time. He heard himself saying, "Oh darling, where are you? I miss you and still love you." Marvin is right, that portrait is alive.

He went back to studying Amanda's many photographs, picked the best one and thought I will have to use this one for her hair now that it is gone. He decided to start the actual portrait. The canvas was a 4ftX8ft. As he studied it he was choosing where to focus the face. He then decided that he was going to put her in her favorite evening gown as if she was ready to dance. That would make her facial expression the absolute best.

He grabbed his sketching pencil and started positioning her on the canvas. After numerous changes, he was satisfied with the positioning. He went to his paints and started to mix colors to determine the right mixes for skin tones and eye and hair color. He knew that this might take days to get the colors he had in his mind. You just do not pick up paint and start painting. Outstanding artistry comes from planning and details. He was mixing for the eyes, and he had mixed as many as 9 colors before he was satisfied. People just did not know that there are as many as five colors in the eye.

Now on to the hair. He had to mix actual hair color, shadow colors, highlight colors. He was not concerned about the skin tones. He would lay down the base and then start adding accent tones. He looked at the clock and realized he had been at it for 6 hours. Time to stop and rest. He went up to the loft, laid down and went to sleep immediately and began to dream of Samantha.

Chapter 15

A MANDA WAS IN HER OFFICE bright and early when her cell phone rang, and the ID showed that it was Stan Michaels. She said, "Yes Stan, what have you got?"

Stan replied, "You need to come to my office so no one will overhear our conversation." Amanda looked at her schedule and asked, "Is Ten O'clock ok?" Stan said, "Yes it is, see you then."

Just then William came in and checked with the PM to see if there was anything she needed. Then he asked, "Why did you hire Jennifer to be your personal assistant, wasn't he doing good enough."

Amanda looked him straight in the eye and said, "She will be managing all my business leading up to my retirement. I have many things that need to be done and you would not have time to do them and what I do is of no concern to you. You stick to my agenda's and make sure my appointments are in order and do not forget you are on shaky ground here for the time being. Dismissed!"

William turned and left the office shaking. He was not used to her talking to him like that. If only I had something on her she would change her tune. He looked up and saw the delivery person bring in a large envelope with his name on it. He knew it came from the agency that worked for him. He opened it and saw the subject, Mr. Marvin Malloy. He quickly placed it in his briefcase so he could look it over at lunch.

And who should walk in at that time, Mr. Malloy. "Is she in?" He thought, how rude these Americans are.

He was about to say she is busy when she came out, "Marv so glad you are on time." She turned toward William, "We have an appointment, if anyone calls just take the number and I will call them back" and out the door they went.

William did not know what to think, ever since that Malloy fellow came into the picture everything has changed. Well, we will see what skeletons are in his closet.

Amanda and Marvin were on their way to Stan Michaels office to work on the plans against William. After they arrived they saw the folder on his desk. He opened it and inside were official looking documents and many pictures of different sorts.

Stan spoke, "Here is what I have laid out for you. All these documents are false and the people who are in these pictures are actors who needed a paycheck and they do not know why we need the pictures. Now the story will go like this, earlier on in your marriage you had a baby with a different man, and you had her adopted out. No one in your family knows anything about it, that is your secret. We hope it will entice William to attempt an extortion and when you pay him off we will arrest him. Look these over and see if there is anything we should omit or add."

She looked them over and handed them to Marv and he looked also. They seemed to agree on them, so they handed them back to Stan.

Stan told them, "I want you to place them in your office where he might find them. I think then he will copy them and return them to where they were. Now if you place this black thread under the folder and it has moved, you will know he picked it up. That will tell us he has taken the bait. Then we wait and see. I do not think he will take long before he reaches out to you. Are you ok with this approach?"

Amanda said, "yes let's do it." As they were leaving Stan's office, Amanda said Let's go see Delores and see what has been going on with her and take her to lunch."

Marv smiled; "You are in for a surprise. I already know."

"What, tell me."

"No, I am going to let Delores tell you." Off they went. Delores was working on her flower beds this morning when her cell rang. "Oh hello Marvin, what she is coming here, I better go in and cleanup a bit, no, no, that's alright I look forward to lunch. When does she arrive, that soon, I better hurry, see you then?"

She scurried in, cleaned herself, changed into suitable clothes, and came down the stairs just as Amanda and Marv came into the house. The ladies hugged each other like old friends do and went off to the kitchen. Marv stayed behind because he already knew. While they were in there he heard Amanda say "Three suitors and how young was one of them, forty-seven you say, that's what, fifteen years younger? My Delores, you are doing good my dear. I am so happy for you."

They came back out, laughing and sounding like two teenagers talking about their first dates. Amanda looked at Marv, "why didn't you tell me?" Marv said, "What and miss all this fun? Let us go to lunch to pub down the street."

Amanda asked, "will there be room for my security detail." Delores said, "Yes."

When they walked in and they saw Amanda, they stood, and Amanda smiled at them and said, "Hello folks how is everybody today?" She then went to every table and shook everyone's hand and then she pulled off her scarf and said with a smile, "Do you like the fresh look?" At first they were shocked but then broke into applause. This made Amanda feel so loved she said, "Thank you, I love all of you."

Lunch was an exciting time. Everyone there came up to her and wished her well as they were about to leave she stood up, the room went silent, and she spoke. "I wish the people of the world could see us today. A room full of people from all levels of society getting along and laughing together, enjoying each other's company. God Bless England!" They all shouted, hear, hear!

As they left the conversations were about the PM coming to sit down with them. All the security staff was feeling good, and they were thinking they were going to miss her. Amanda dropped off Delores and Marvin at their respective homes and headed back to her office.

William was not back from lunch yet so she remembered what Stan said about the thread so she placed one on the cabinet to find out if he would open it. She went into her office and looked around to find a place to put her folder that was not too obvious. She investigated the corner and thought yes and placed it there with the black thread. "Ok William, your move."

William was at the corner for lunch where no one could tell what he was looking at. He opened the folder, started reading and learned that Marvin had an accident ten years ago and one person died. The two cars were into the intersection at the same time. The investigators stated that they were unsure who was at fault. Mr. Malloy's car hit the other car on the driver's door and the driver did not survive. The investigators suspect the deceased entered the intersection illegally, but actual proof was lacking. Mr. Malloy did however pay to the family of the diseased $250,00.00 for a college fund for the children. The case was called Accidental.

The investigators also discovered that Mr. Malloy's monthly income exceeded $50,00.00 due to royalties on his artwork. Additionally, Mr. Malloy has set up a trust fund for his children, two daughters and two sons, consisting of eight million dollars. He has a second trust set up for his grandchildren of which there are eight, in the amount of four million dollars. A third trust is for his great grandchildren of which there are now sixteen in the amount of four million dollars. He also has one great, great grandchild but yet, no trust has been set up. His total assets are in the range of one hundred million dollars. William could not believe Malloy was so wealthy, but he could not see anything he might try and blackmail him for. He decided to concentrate on Amanda. He checked his watch and thought it would be better if he got back a little early.

Marvin walked into the studio and saw that Jeremy was busy working on the portrait. He came over to check the work and asked, "How is it going?"

Jeremy had already sketched the image on the canvas, so he asked Marvin, "Did I place it correctly?"

Marvin stepped back, took a long look, "I think you might tilt the head just slightly more to the right. She is right-handed. Also the left elbow needs to be a little higher. The rest looks good, how do you feel about it?"

Jeremy studied the proposed changes and concluded; Marv was right. So took his pencil, made them, and stepped back five paces turned and looked, yes Marv was right. He turned and said, "Marv I am sure glad you noticed those placements."

Marv responded, "You should always have someone else look before you start placing the paint on the canvas. It will save you many headaches. I see you have mixed paints, are you happy with them?"

Jeremy said, "Oh yes, yesterday I spent more the 6 hours trying to get just the right colors."

Marvin spoke, "Well son, I do believe you are ready to start. Down in the cupboard by the sink I have placed my covering cloths so when you are done for the day you can cover it to keep the dust and dirt and spying eyes messing it up."

Jeremy got the paints in place and the painting began. As he started he said a silent prayer, "God guide my hands and eyes to make this my best portrait I have ever done. Amen."

Marvin was walking away knowing that this portrait was going to be talked about for years to come. He went to his workstation, uncovered the painting he was working on in secret from Jeremy, it was of his daughter. Jeremy thought it was just of an English girl on a swing in her Sunday best dress. He would love to place it next to Samantha's portrait, but he knew he would not.

Marvin was a fast painter so it would be ready in about a week. This was going to be the only new painting in the show, the others are ones he painted over two years ago. He was done with her face and was now doing her pale blue dress. The color of the dress made her blond hair just shine. He knew that this one was going to be a good one.

Chapter 16

H is phone rang, Amanda spoke, "Pick me up and let's take a ride in that beautiful car of yours in the countryside. Security will follow. There is a castle I want you to see and the people who live there want to meet you."

Marv said, "Yes Madam!" He was waiting outside of her office when she came out and he could tell she had that tired look. He stopped and got her favorite tea in a thermos, so when she got in, she leaned over and kissed him, he then poured the tea and handed it to her.

Surprised, she looked at him lovingly, "Marv you are so special." She sipped the tea; "Oh this is so good." Off they went, one car in front of them and one behind.

He looked around saying, "Did you ever wish you did not have to have the security people going everywhere you go?"

She looked at him, "Everyday Marvin, every day. They can be a pain in the you know where." The drive in the countryside was beautiful and then the castle came into view. It looked familiar to Marvin, so he asked, "Who lives here?"

Amanda had a big smile, "Why the Queen and her family Marvin." He almost choked, "The Queen".

"Yes dear, she called me today and she said, I want to meet this man who has stolen your heart. When the Queen calls you answer, so here we are." They came to a stop and even before they could move someone was opening the doors for them. They looked up at the porch and the Queens family was there. Marvin felt nervous, he whispered to Amanda, "How do I do this."

"Just be yourself Marv, look no camera's around." They went up the steps and went down the row and shook hands and then the Queen was in front of them.

She spoke, "Amanda my dear, are you feeling ok today?" She replied, "Yes your Highness."

She looked at Marvin, "You must be the man that has captured Amanda's heart, I am Elizabeth."

Marvin took her hand, "It is an honor to meet such a lovely Queen," the queen laughed, turned to Amanda, "Oh he's a good one."

They entered the castle and went to the sitting room while others dispersed throughout the castle. The Queen turned to Marvin, "Tell me Mr. Malloy, when you painted the painting that Amanda has hanging in her hall, just what were you thinking at the time."

Surprised at her question, Marv told her, "They had run out of money, his wife was sitting on the porch so he began thinking if I can get enough money for the winter they would be all right. Well it did sell for enough money, and we made it through the winter. It turned out to be my painting of necessity."

The Queen declared, "I love that story, yes we do many things out of necessity. I know I have. I understand you and young Jeremy are going to have a show in a few weeks. My good friend James told me, and I promise you, that we will be there."

Marvin was feeling so good so he announced to the Queen, "Jeremy and I have not told anyone yet but all the proceeds from the show will go to Breast Cancer research."

Both Amanda and the Queen were surprised, and both were incredibly happy. The Queen spoke up, "Marvin I need to make you an honorary citizen of England. What a beautiful gestor."

He thanked the Queen for her kind words. The Queen turned to Amanda, "How are the treatments coming along?" She told the Queen that they were hoping for a remission. The Queen assured her that they would pray for her, "Now you will have to excuse me, I get tired quicker than I used to." She looked to Marvin, "Take loving care of her," and walked away.

Marvin and Amanda made their way back to his car, he could not hold his excitement in, "I do not believe I just met the Queen. She is a lovely lady." Amanda smiled; "I knew you would like her. She is a lot more concerned about the country than people realized. She has been a great person to me. Can I change the subject now? I want to talk about how I should manage the Samantha thing. Do I go and tell Jeremy, or should I work something out with Samantha?"

Marvin gave it some thought, then answered. "I believe you should sit down with Samantha, which would be best."

Amanda agreed, "I will contact her tomorrow and arrange a time, could you go with me?"

Marvin had hoped she would ask him, replied, "Yes I would be honored." He knew she was tired, so he dropped her off and then went on home. As he was driving home he saw Molly and Stan walking hand in hand. Well, I wonder when this started. Good for you Molly. He was hungry so he stopped at the pub close to Delores's for a bite.

When he walked in Delores and a nice-looking gentleman were there together, enjoying each other. He gave her a nod and found a table, ordered a pint and some fish n' chips. As he was enjoying his food a couple of locals came and asked if they could sit with him. He said, sure be my guests. The told him they wanted to welcome him to the neighborhood and have enjoyed seeing him and the PM there. As the evening wore on they became more friendly and asked if he played poker. He said he did, and they gave him an invite to their next game next Friday night. They assured him it was only a friendly game. He accepted, got directions and time of the game, and asked what he should bring? Just your money friend, just your money. They all laughed, and Marvin left to go home.

When he got there he saw a note from Jeremy, picked it up and it read, Grandma had to go the Hospital, call me and I will give directions. He ran out to his car, called Jeremy and left for Mercy Hospital. He knew where it was, so he rushed there.

Stan Michaels saw him coming and told security to pass him through. Stan stopped him and told him, "The Doctor said it was just exhaustion and she would be staying there till morning."

Marvin was relieved and asked Stan if he had seen Jeremy? "Yes, he is with her now, just one visitor at a time. You are next in line." He sat down to wait when Molly came in looking very worried. She sat next to Marvin, he took her hand and told her, "She was going to be all right, she is just over tired. She will be going home in the morning. I saw you and Stan walking hand in hand. When did that come about?"

Molly blushed, "Just the other day and I must say I am excited about it. Did you know that Stanley is going to retire when Amanda retires? He told me that he has become lonely, and he wants companionship. That made me happy, and he wants to know me better. Stan and I are exploring each other."

Marvin was smiling, took Molly's hand saying, "You deserve to be happy, good luck." Just then Jeremy came out and told Marvin, "She wants to see you."

Marv excused himself and walked into her room. She looked up saw Marv and broke down saying, "I am sorry that I caused so much worry."

He held up his hand and said, "Stop, you never have to say you are sorry to me, I love you and that means that when you hurt, I hurt. I am so glad it was only exhaustion and not cancer related. You are my everything darling, so let me do the worrying, you take care of you."

She saw that this man was serious, and she loved him for that. She told him, "Maybe I should retire now and concentrate on the breast cancer."

He answered, "If that is what you need to do, then do it. Make the decision and follow through with it. Now I will leave you to rest but first Molly is here, and I think she needs to see you to know for sure you are alright, oh and ask her about Stan Michaels". He leaned over and gave her a passionate kiss. "Now rest," and he left.

He motioned for Molly to go in. After he got in his car he called his daughter because talking to her always eased his mind. When the ringing stopped he heard, "Hello dad," and tears started to roll down in buckets.

She asked, "What's wrong?" The whole story poured out of him and how worried he was of losing Amanda and when he realized how he felt he knew that was because of love for Amanda.

His daughter knew he was in love, but she did not know just how much. Now she knew and was happy for him and she told him so. She told him, "She was going to call her sister and brothers and let them know also because they were asking her what was going on with Dad."

He thanked her and he said goodbye, and then he dropped a hint, "I think the three of you should come over here and see for yourselves. I am going to have a show in less than 3 weeks. Let me know and I will arrange the tickets and I know a beautiful B&B you can stay in. Call me." Tired he returned home, checked the studio, and saw Jeremy's painting and could not believe how far along it was and how great it looked. Thinking, my boy, you are better than I ever was. That portrait is going to turn a lot of heads, it will leave the lookers speechless and the critics falling over each other with their compliments. Bravo Jeremy, bravo! Time to sleep.

Chapter 17

WILLIAM CAME INTO THE OFFICE early so he could form a plan. He checked Amanda's office, saw the folder tucked into the corner and retrieved it, what he did not know, the black thread moved. As he opened it, he could not believe what he was reading. I must copy this quickly before the PM comes in. He was careful to put the pages back in order. When he was through, he opened the cabinet and placed the copies in there and closed it up and locked it not knowing that the other thread moved.

He sat down and Jennifer walked in and told him that the PM was going to be discharged from the hospital. He did not even know she was there. He was thankful he did not get caught with the copies. Close call, I must be extra careful. This latest information will be the best, should be a handsome payoff.

Jennifer mentioned that the PM should be in by Ten O'clock, so I better check the schedule and make sure all is set. Amanda called and asked, "Could you have the leaders of parliament to be in her office at eleven, if that wasn't possible, ask if one was better?

William knew something important was going on, he would have to listen in to find out, only this time he needed to be extra careful. He made the call, and the meeting was set for eleven.

Amanda came in at 8:45 and went right to work. William came in and asked, "Can I be of help with your meeting." She said, "No thank you, I just have some things to work out."

After William went back to his desk, Amanda checked for the black thread. It was gone, so she knew he was snooping around. She sent a text to Chief Michaels letting him know that William found the folders. She thought, "William I have the upper hand now. Make your move and I will bury you."

Her thoughts turned to the upcoming meeting. Retiring is going to be hard. The excitement of leadership will be hard to replace. I am going to miss it, but I am going to love being with Marvin. My life has sure changed since I read that letter. I never knew a simple letter could change everything. Marvin is so filled with joy, love, understanding, compassion, I love him so.

I still do not know how this happened so fast; we were both ready for this. Whatever this is, I love it. Well, I better get ready for my meeting.

While at her desk she made some notes, then just sat and remembered the very first day as Prime Minister. She could not believe it was all over. If only she didn't have this breast cancer. The treatments were wearing her down, taking all her energy, making her feel so helpless. I hope these last treatments do the job. William buzzed her saying the parliament leaders were here. "Send them in."

Amanda took charge, "I called this meeting to announce my retirement beginning tomorrow." She paused and their reaction was by one side relieved and the other sadness. She started laughing, looking at her political opponents, "You did not think it was going to be this easy to get rid of me. When I inform the public this afternoon I am going to tell them all the dirty things you have done to undermine my actions, so don't celebrate too soon. Our government should be working on compromise, but you seem to want to try and denounce things if they do not agree with your thinking. Gentleman, time to clean things up and start thinking of the people first. That will be my farewell speech so go and prepare. If I live, I will be watching. Your only hope is that the breast cancer gets me soon because I will be speaking up as a citizen."

She hit #3 and William answered, "William, call a press conference for noon today. That's all gentleman you may go." As they left, they did not know what was going to happen. She knew as soon as they left the news of her resignation would be all over the nation. She started laughing, I don't think I'm going to miss politics as much as I thought.

Chief Michaels came in and handed her his resignation effective tomorrow. She looked at it and asked, "What are you going to do Stan?"

Well he said, "Molly and I are going to travel the world for a while then settle down. Molly was going to talk to you and let you know about us, but we were surprised at your resignation. Are you sure you want to leave? The country is going to miss you."

Amanda paused, then said, "Stan the cancer has worn me out and I need all my energy to fight it and I cannot do it and still be in office. It's time Stan, it's time. Let's go Stan, it's time to tell the world."

After her announcement you could have heard a pin drop, then the press started shouting questions. She raised her hand to quiet them down, once quiet she told them, "If you would be more courteous you just might get more information. I am going to be busy trying to live a full life, trying to rid my body of cancer. Report on that.

Back in her office she called Marvin. "Hi handsome, let's go and see Samantha." Marvin said he will be there in twenty minutes, and they would go and then have lunch. She had Jennifer come in and asked if she would work for her because she was going to need a lot of help with everything. Jennifer replied that she would be honored.

Amanda said, "Start Monday, take the weekend off, then come to my home and not the Downing Street address." She gave Jennifer the address, "we can talk money Monday."

She called in William and told him his services were no longer required. William had a look of panic but then Amanda said she was leaving the office for good, and she would pick up her things next Monday so the new PM could move in once one was appointed.

William was relieved, now he could recover his folders in the cabinet. Amanda could tell what he was thinking, now we are going to catch you. "Goodbye William, I am not coming back. Good luck," and out the door she went, a common citizen again.

Chapter 18

WILLIAM WAS FURIOUS, WELL MADAM high and mighty, I am going to make you pay big time. He thought of his father and decided to pay him a visit. His father taught William all he knew about fleecing people. He was a past master. He became involved with Amanda's husband Charles about fourteen years ago. William and his father had different last names, Jones for William, and Abercrombie for his father. Dads first name is Rudolph. He thought Abercrombie sounded more regal.

After 4 years working with Charles, he was falsely accused of a crime and was convicted. Rudolph received ten years in prison, and he was going to be released at Christmas time.

Rudolph was a tall man who looked a little like Cary Grant and just as smooth. It would not surprise William that he might have had something to do with the plane crash. He will go and see him day after tomorrow.

Amanda met Marv outside and got in his car and said, "We need to go Downing Street to pick up a few things first. Tomorrow the workers will be there to pack up her things and move them to the farm." Marv asked, "Are you looking forward to leaving office." She replied, "Well, yes and no. Yes because I am getting tired and no because I did not get everything done that I wanted to do, but I suppose you are never done. Yes, I will miss it, but it is time, I need a vacation."

Marv's ears perked up when he heard the word vacation. He's had an idea of taking her to his place in New York City, show her the town, maybe some shows and Central Park which is just across street from his apartment. "Amanda would you be up to a trip to New York City? I have a place there and it might be relaxing for you."

"Well Marv, I do believe you are right. When do you think we should go?"

Marv, "Just as soon as we can and then be back here for the show." Amanda thought, "Let's go the day after tomorrow. I didn't know you had a place there."

He told her; "I also have a studio there. Have you been there before?"

She shook her head, "Only for political things. The UN and other meetings and stayed at the British Embassy.

Marv remarked, "You are going to love being with the people. Central Park is good for walking and relaxing. Did you call and ask Samantha if it was alright we come?"

"Yes, she was thrilled we wanted to. We need to convince her to contact Jeremy somehow and maybe renew their romance." As they pulled up in front of the house they saw Alli on the porch. They walked up and Alli said, "My mommy says that you are my grandma, is that right?" She answers, "Yes but my daughter Maureen was your grandma, and I am your great grandma." Alli got excited, "My other name is Maureen.

Amanda became excited to learn Samantha had given her the name Maureen. Just then Samantha came out and asked, "Is Alli talking your heads off?"

They laughed, "She told us her middle name was Maureen." Samantha told them, "I gave her that name because of Jeremy's Mother."

Amanda thanked her and said, "We need to talk about you and Jeremy." Sammie said, "Let's go inside."

They went to the living room, sat down and Amanda started the conversation, "Sammie, how do you feel about Jeremy now that you know that he had nothing to do with my husband's dealings with you and please, call me Amanda or even Grandma."

"Well grandma, I have never stopped loving Jeremy, do you know how he feels?"

Marvin told her; "I can answer that because he told me himself that he still loves you. He said when he had dates with others he always compared them to you, but none came up to that level. Sammie, do you want to try again?"

"Yes, yes I do, very much."

Marvin continued, "Well Amanda and I have talked about this, and we think that you and Alli should come to the show and let Jeremy discover you there, that way he won't feel like we tried to set him up. May I ask, do you still have the dress that you wore for the portrait?"

Sammie looked surprised but said, "Yes I do, and I even have the shoes and jewelry I wore".

Amanda remarked, "Marv that's a fine idea, what do you think Sammie?"

"That will work out fine, should I bring Alli?"

Both Amanda and Marvin said "yes" at the same time. "Now that I retired, you and Alli should come out to the farm, we have horses, chickens, and lambs. Do you ride?"

Sammie said, "Yes when I was back in Texas, it's been so long since I have been home, my mother has been after me to come back and live but now I think I will stay here. She and my father will be sad but happy too, although I need to take Alli over there so she can learn about her grandparents."

Marv spoke up, "Maybe you and Jeremy can make the trip together."

Sammie smiled, "That has been my dream."

Amanda gave Sammie her cell number, "Call if you need anything. Marv and I will be going to New York in 2 days, but we will be back before the show, don't hesitate to contact me for anything, your family now."

As they were leaving, Alli yelled, "Bye grandma, I love you." Tears came to Amanda, "Sammie she looks just like my daughter, her grandma. I am so glad we found you."

As they drove away she looked back, and both were waving to her. "Marv, I have got to fix this breast cancer, I have too much to live for."

At the very same time Jeremy was putting touches on the portrait before covering it up to dry. Drying time should be a least a week because Marv had drying equipment. He looked around the room and stopped at Sammie's portrait. Oh Sammie I miss you, please come back to me because I need you. Just then Edward came in and saw where Jeremy was looking and commented, "I saw a woman about two weeks ago that looked just like her."

Jeremy turned, "What, where?"

"Well let me think, it was either at the airport or at the grocery store. I am not sure but if I think of it I will call you."

Chapter 19

J EREMY ASKED, "HOW ARE YOU doing?"
He told him, "Since working with Marvin, I have learned much about the art world. I did not know how much there was to learn. I figure by the time the next show is, I will have been taught much so I will be a useful helper in setting it all up, I should be able to set it up by himself. I sure love it."

Jeremy told him, "Learn it all and then you and I can become a team."

Edward could not be happier and promised him that he would absorb as much as possible. Edward asked him, "Are you ready for the show?"

Jeremy started shaking his head, "As each day gets closer, I get more nervous. This being my first, I did not know what to expect but I am surprised it's this intense. Marvin walks around like it's nothing. He's in and out of here, stays casual, looks like he not even working but I come in here every morning and there sits a new painting. It's amazing. Look at these, they were not here three days ago and now they are a finished product. His talent is amazing."

Edward told Jeremy, "Last week he sat down with me, gave me a brush, and asked what I liked in a painting. I told him I enjoyed looking at real old barns with paint peeling and had that worn out look. So he sketched a barn and told me to fill in the colors. I tried to refuse but you know Marvin, no is not acceptable, so I began, and you know after a brief time the only thing in my mind was how this painting was going to look. I really got involved and if you want to see it, he hung it up in the kitchen."

They went to the kitchen and when Jeremy looked at the painting he studied the colors Ed chose and remarked, "We should put that in the show. I see you signed it."

"Yes, Marvin insisted that I do that. Doing this gave me a new appreciation for artists. What you go through just to make a painting, the public just does not know how hard it is."

Jeremy told him; "I can guarantee that it will bring a fair price for Breast Cancer Research. Let's make sure it gets displayed."

Samantha was sitting down with Alli having supper, "Darling I have some pictures to show you. These are pictures of your father. I have kept them from you until you were ready, and I think you are now ready. As you know, Mrs. Watkins is your great grandmother. Well her daughter was your father's mother. She is where your name Maureen came from. Here is a picture of her when she was a little girl your age."

"Mommie, that looks like me."

"Yes I know, she was your daddy's mother. Her mother is Grandma Watkins. Your father is Grandma's grandson. I know this is confusing, but I will try to straighten it all out. Let's lay all these pictures out together so it will be easier to figure this all out. Let's start with Grandma Watkins. Here you lay them out. Ok next we have Grandma Maureen. Now for the one of your fathers, Jeremy O'Dell and lastly, your picture. Now that is your daddy's family and your family. What do you think?"

"Well mommy, why do we never see them?"

"Well that's hard to explain, before you were born, mommy was confused and ran away because she thought that your daddy did not want mommy, but it turns out I was wrong. Now soon, you and I are going to see daddy. I have never told him about you, so it is going to be a major surprise when he sees you so don't be afraid. I know that he will love you and I truly hope that he will love me.

Daddy is an Artist, and he is having a show of his paintings soon and that is where we will be so he can meet you." Alli felt happy but a little confused, "Mommy I think I will pray for you and daddy." Samantha began to cry happy tears and gave Alli a big hug.

Amanda and Marv returned to the farm, as they drove up he remarked about the picnic they had. Fond memories. Before the seasons change let's do it again and she said OK, "After we get back from New York. I forgot to tell you that we can take a government plane, retired PM's perk, so we don't have to bother with commercial air. Do you need to go back to your place to pack?"

Marvin thought then said, "I only need a few things and I can pick them up in the morning, my place in New York is fully furnished with everything I need including clothes. I already called to stock the fridge. We don't need wine because you cannot drink any, so we are good to go. I ordered a car for us, we are all set, oh I informed my children, and they are coming so they can meet you."

She said, "Oh my, I need to have you meet my two sons. They are busy but when we get back we will all have a dinner together. They have been asking questions."

Her cell rang and the ID showed a number she did not recognize but she answered it anyway. She motioned to Marv and put it on speaker. Marvin knew why, it could be William. She said, "Hello is this Amanda Watkins?"

"Yes it is."

"I know your secret about the child you had with another man and if you don't want it to go public I want 75,000 pounds by one week from today. Place the money in a case and deliver it to postal box sixteen in Liverpool. Failure to comply I will release all details, understood?"

Amanda replied in a shaky voice, "Yes one week from today." She heard him hang up. Marvin asked her, "Was that William." She said, "I knew he had the folder copied but I am surprised he acted so soon. I must call Stan to let him know."

She pulled out his number and punched it out, "Stan, William just called asking for 75,000 pounds one week from today, to be brought to post box sixteen in Liverpool."

Stan reacted by saying, "He must need the money badly. Let's hope he makes mistakes, and we catch him. We will put one of our agents in the post office to be on the lookout when it gets picked up. We can put a tracking device in with the money. Then when it leaves we can follow. I don't believe he would pick it up himself. We will follow the money. We can also mark the money so he can't tell. Are you ok with this?"

She listened to Stan in amazement. She had no idea they could do all that. "Yes let's do it. Marvin and I will be in New York then."

Stan said, "Yes Marvin has already talked to me about your plans. I will keep you informed of all the proceedings."

"Stanley, I trust you completely, do what needs to be done." She turned to Marv, "So you already talked to Stan. When did you do this?"

Marv says, "Well three days ago."

She was puzzled, "How did you know we would be going?"

"Well my darling, I'm a psychic." He looked at her then started laughing, "No I was certain you would go. Do you think you can capture William? I think he might be capable of doing some awfully bad things, such as hurting you."

Amanda sighed; "I still have security assigned to me even though I am retired. I think he would worry about them so I believe I will be ok, but he needs me alive to collect the money. Enough of that, let's go in and fix supper."

Marv laughs, "Oh, you mean you can cook." Once again he gets the famous elbow. Marvin looked at her, grabbed her hand, pulled her to him, "Amanda I love you" and kissed her softly pulled back whispered, "I really do," then kiss her with passion and she responded with her own passion, then saying, "let's eat later." Marv did not have to respond as she led him to the bedroom. These two love birds took their time because they could and enjoyed exploring each other knowing that both were in love.

When the morning came they woke up smiling and were anxious to go to New York. Her bags were packed, and he was stopping at his place to pick up a few things and they would be off. If you didn't know better you would think they were newlyweds. Look out New York here they come.

Marv came back out and began the drive to the Airport. Amanda was looking out the window and turned, "Marv I had the strangest dream last night, I was rushed to the ER and while there, I died. I left my body and rose and was standing with God who spoke, "Amanda it is not your time yet but before I send you back down I want you to watch."

We were back at the hospital, and I had passed, they were trying everything they knew to revive me. I got the paddles numerous times and shots directly into the heart. Nothing worked so the head doctor decided to call time of death. A young Doctor yelled "Not yet," and he raised his arm and struck me on the chest as hard as he could. The main doctor spoke to him, "What do think you are doing?" The young man spoke up, "She's not gone, she is standing with God, and he is making her whole again." Then the heart monitor started beeping, I was back. They started doing all sorts of tests and finally said I was OK. One doctor said, "I don't believe it; her cancer is gone. We have just witnessed a miracle." The next thing I knew, I was walking out of the hospital into your arms.

By this time they were going through the gate and drove right up to the plane. As they got out the security man told Marv that his car would be stored in the hanger until they returned. Boarding the plane, out of habit Amanda turned and started to wave then remembered she was no longer the PM. Her laugh could be heard over the noise of the engines. The door shut and so the trip began. The time difference between London and New York was five hours.

Chapter 20

WILLIAM WAS DRIVING TO VISIT his father thinking, not working is nice. Come and go as I please, be my own boss. If the money comes through from Amanda and I combined it with the other monies I received, I should be able to lead a leisurely life and Dad and I could work some great schemes. Dad is the expert; I still have a lot to learn. Dad is due to get out at Christmas time, no parole so we can go anywhere in the world we want to. I will have to get some fake passports but that's no problem.

He pulled into the prison's parking lot, took out all unnecessary things out of his pockets and left them in the car, and went inside. They asked him who he was visiting, and he told them, Rudolph Abercrombie. They notified the prison guard at that station, unlocked the door and William entered. He was searched, ok'd, and went to the visitor's room. Five minutes later his dad walked in. William stood, shook hands with him, sat down. Before Will could even say anything, Dad told him exciting news. "They are letting me out early. I will be a free man in two weeks from today. Time served in full. Can you pick me up?"

William smiled, "Yes I can, it will be good to have you home and I've got so much to tell you and ask you. I have a new program running and I think you will like it." Program is what to two of them called their schemes.

Dad said, "I always like innovative programs. Do you?"

"Oh yes Dad, this one is especially good."

Dad asked Will, "How come you are not at work?"

"Oh the PM retired, and they let me go. All PM's pick their own secretaries. I am liking not having to go in."

Dad laughed, "just like your old man. Have you made any plans?"

"Well dad, we need to talk about that when you come home. I do have a deal in the works now, it should be rewarding. I will know next week. Wish me luck."

"Son, you don't need any luck, you will do just fine. How's your nest egg, growing?"

"Dad, I will have it all down for you when you get home."

Dad told him, "I will get in touch about the time and date I get out," he stood and began to leave, "See you then son."

"Bye Dad!" William walked out of the prison and began to whistle, he was happy. Dad and I working together was going to be what he has wanted for a long time.

Back at the prison, Chief Stan Michaels put the earphones down and said, that was an interesting conversation. Sounds like William and Rudolph have plans. "I want to thank you warden for arranging the advance release of Rudolph, I think it will work out nicely. You've heard, catching two birds with one stone haven't you. Well I must run, thanks again."

Stan called Amanda as soon as he got in the car, she was over the Atlantic somewhere. He told her what had transpired and that he felt that everything was going as planned.

Back at Marvin's studio, Jeremy and Edward were talking when Ed turned to Jeremy and said, "I saw this artist on the TV this morning taking some paint and placing it in some cup and then placing another color on top and adding three more colors in but never stirring it. Then she had a large canvas. She placed the canvas on something to raise it up and then she started to tip the cup and pour the paint on the canvas in small circles and if formed an interesting pattern. I thought she was done but then she picked up the canvas and started to tilt it so the paint would move around, and the pattern spread. It turned out fantastic."

Jeremy saw he was excited, "that is called an acrylic pour, want to try it?"

Edward thought that would be fun, "let's do it."

Jeremy said, "You pick the colors you want. I will go get a canvas for you." He came back with a large one, 1.5-meter x 3.5 meter. "Now Ed, the secret is knowing how much paint to mix, but first we need to lay down a base coat. Now that will serve as background color and the other paint will be allowed to move around easier. What colors did you pick?"

He had red, light blue, dark blue, light green, white.

"How about the background color?" He chose a light grey. Jeremy said, "I will place one color and you can do the rest. Because this is a large canvas we will need a lot of paint. First the base coat, lets mix three oz of paint to one oz of water. For the other colors let's mix two oz to one oz water. Now after you mix the colors we will put them in a larger cup that we can pour all the rest of paints on top of each other. One thing to remember is that the last paint in will be the first one out of the cup."

After all was mixed Jeremy poured down the base coat and evened it out with a spatula. Edward put the colors in a cup and then he pinched the cup together and began to pour round and around. It made a circular design. After the cup was emptied there was a circular design.

Jeremy told him, "Pick it up and tilt it." The design went into different shapes. When he was done the designs formed looked beautiful. Jeremy told Ed, "We need to let it dry then we can seal it and it will be ready to sell."

Edward felt like an artist full of pride. He said, "I must show this to Marvin."

Chapter 21

AMANDA'S AND MARVIN'S PLANE WAS touching down, both were excited to be in New York. As they left the terminal Marvin's driver was there to pick them up. On their way to Marvin's apartment Amanda was impressed.

She told Marvin; "I have never bothered to see this city as it really is. I was always too busy with government problems to notice. I didn't even know that so many people lived here."

They pulled up in front of Marvin's apartment building and the doorman opened the door and said, "Hello Mr. Malloy good to see you again and this must be the lovely Ms. Watkins, welcome to New York. We all saw you press conference the other day and I must say we admired it when you removed your scarf. We will pray for you madam."

Amanda was overwhelmed with such greetings. It took all her strength just to say thank you. Just then a couple came walking down the walk, "Welcome home Marvin and you too Ms. Watkins." They went inside and waited for the elevator, two people got off, said hi Marv, welcome home.

Amanda was just amazed. So many people who knew him. They got in and Amanda asked, "Where are the bags?"

"They are being unloaded and they will be brought up." He punched in the sixteenth floor and up they went to the top level. He unlocked the door and when they went in, and Amanda's eyes got large. She could not believe how much room he had. It was a big suite, three bedrooms, three baths, a very large living room overlooking Central Park, the view was gorgeous. "Marvin, why didn't you ever tell me about this place?"

Marvin laughed, "This little ole place. I need it for when the children come to visit. My son Harold is an engineer, my son Thomas is a doctor doing his residency hear in the city, my daughter Emily who is a designer, and Suzzanne who is a homemaker in Arizona. Between the four of them I have five grandchildren. Love them all. I am having supper brought in tonight so we can rest, tomorrow we can walk through the park, there is something I want to show you. Then we will be free to do whatever you would like. Have you seen Phantom of the Opera yet? "NO," then we will have to see it, you will love it. I will arrange for the tickets. Let's see, today is Friday, how about Sunday?"

All Amanda could do is shake her head yes. She was tired, so Marv showed her to their bedroom with the king-sized bed and all the comforts. She needed a nap, the cancer tired her quickly. Marv showed her the bath, she saw the huge tub with jets and said, "I will love that." He offered to fill it, but she said, "Later maybe you could join me, but right now I need sleep."

Marv said, "I will leave you; I have some arrangements to make. Sweet dreams darling," and kissed her softly and left. Marv went to his study and made calls to his children. They would all be there by next Tuesday. He was anxious to see them, it had been quite a while since he had seen them.

As he sat there he began to think about their relationship. He started to visualize how he and Amanda would be in various situations. He saw picnics, dancing, relaxing together, reading books together, just being together. He thought, everyone should be in love with such a person as Amanda. He told himself, I was in love all those years and I couldn't save her and now he was with another, and he felt helpless again. He said a silent prayer, "God, please be with Amanda through this illness, keep her safe. Amen." As an after though the said, did you hear me God?

His phone rang and it was his son Thomas the doctor. "Tom my boy, how are you doing?"

Tom answered, "I am very busy Dad, being a second-year resident, they keep me on my toes. Learning to be a Heart Doctor is much tougher than I thought. You must be aware of so much. So Dad, you are in the papers every day. How are you handling it?"

Marv began laughing, "I never gave it a thought, but Amanda warned me they would become a nuisance. Are you free for supper?"

"Yes, I am off today."

"Good, we are having dinner in, so you can meet Amanda and it will be quiet and no one interrupting us."

Tom became quiet but then asked, "Do you mind if I bring my girlfriend with me?"

Marv smiled; "You mean you found a girl to put up with you? Please bring her, I need to meet this girl."

Tom began laughing, "Dad I love you, be happy, see you around six."

"Goodbye son, I look forward to seeing you, it's been too long."

Back in London things were happening. Molly and Stan were making plans for their world tour. William was plotting schemes that he and his dad could work together. Edward was thinking of Jennifer and wondering if she might go on a date with him.

Jeremy was looking at Sammie's painting and wondering if she might still be in London after Edward said he saw her. Delores was enjoying her newfound popularity, thinking why I didn't do this sooner. She was also smiling because Marv had reserved the whole house for his family when they are coming over for the art show. She was so glad that she had meet him. He and Amanda are meant for each other.

Samantha was showing her daughter Alli, some recent pictures of Jeremy that Amanda gave her.

Alli said, "When can I meet him?"

"At the art show dear, at the show."

The parliament was debating who the next Prime Minister might be. They were leaning toward the same group that Amanda Watkins recommended, the conservatives.

Yes, things in London were moving along. Nightlife was coming alive, and Londoners were in a festive mood. The world thought that the English were stuffy but when you got the privilege to know them, they were the same as the rest of the world. They loved, they hurt, their blood was just as red as the rest. Their compassion was strong, their fortitude made them strong. They were good and bad, but like the rest, good.

Amanda, when she was Prime Minister, tried to let the world know, the English cared. They worried, they loved, they fought but in the end, they stood, faced the flag, and said, God Bless England. Yes, things in London were moving along.

Chapter 22

Back in New York, Amanda awoke and heard the bath running, she arose and walked to the bathroom and there was Marv, naked stepping in and she said, "Do you want company?"

He turned, "I would love company, do you have someone in mind?" If she had been closer he would have received her famous elbow. She undressed and stepped in with him and said, "Darling, I never thought love could feel this way. Charles and I had a stiff union, but you and I have a romantic existence. I get excited just sitting next to you. I want to be with you forever."

Marvin leaned into her, kissed her, and then said, "Amanda you are the love of my life. I feel we are complete together." He turned on the jets and she sighed, that felt so good. His smile was large, his laughter was loud, his was enjoying himself. He looked at her, "Let me wash you," and she said, "Only if I can return the favor."

They had love in their eyes. Later as they were dressing he told her about dinner and that his son and girlfriend would be there. She told him that she looked forward to meeting his son. What did you order for dinner? Well my son's favorite is Chinese so that is what I ordered. She remarked, "I love it too. Tonight will be fun and I hope I pass inspection."

He told her, "Darling you cannot miss. I have never met his girlfriend, so I am curious. He has never brought a girl home before. So my dear, we both will be having firsts tonight. Now what should I wear?"

Amanda laughed, "Oh now you are a comedian. I love you Mr. Malloy. Let's go get ready."

They buzzed him from the lobby, "Your son is here with a lovely young lady. They are the way up."

Marvin went to the door and when he heard them he opened it and hugged his son and then he looked at his date and thought, wow she looks good.

Tom introduced her, her name was Cindy, and she is a surgical nurse. "Dad, it's been too long." He turned to Amanda, "It's a pleasure to finally meet you. Welcome to New York."

She looked at him, he is so handsome like his father, "I must say, I am excited to meet you. Your father and I have become as one in such a brief time. From the very beginning we both knew that we belonged together, and I hope you will approve."

Thomas smiled, "I now know why they made you Prime Minister, you are very convincing. Should I say, welcome to the family?"

Amanda grinned, "Well Thomas, I sure hope that soon you will be saying that."

Marvin asked, "did you just accept my proposal?" Well here it comes, the famous elbow.

Cindy was watching all the banter going on thinking this family is full of love. She spoke up, "Folks, I love the fact you can talk to each other this way, my family does the same thing. I feel at home already and Thomas, I accept."

Thomas said, "in case you are wondering, on the way over here I asked Cindy to marry me." He pulled her to him and kissed her.

Marvin was as happy as Thomas. Amanda said, "I think we should celebrate."

Marvin got the wine, poured three glasses, and gave Amanda grape juice. He explained that Amanda could not have wine due to her medication. They toasted to a successful union. They sat down, ate their dinner, and enjoyed getting to know each other.

After Thomas and Cindy left Amanda told Marv, "You remember that dream I had about the doctor who hit me on the chest?"

Marvin nodded yes, "Well that doctor looked exactly like your son. What do you suppose that means? Do you think it is going to come true?"

Marvin said, "No it was just a dream." They walked arm and arm toward the bedroom, Marvin looked at her, "I am so happy, looks like a wedding soon."

Amanda looked at him, "Are you talking about ours?" Amanda's two sons traveled the world, both were working for the British Government, as good will ambassadors. Charles Jr was in India and Deacon happened to be arriving in New York and Charles Jr was now on his way. They stayed in touch with each other, and both had to be at the UN in 2 days, something to do with the Russians. It was all hush, hush.

Deacon was at the embassy and Charles Jr would be there shortly. Deacon was thinking of his mother and wondering how her treatments were going. The last he had heard about her; she was at her press conference when she pulled off her scarf. He was surprised when she retired as PM. He knew she had her reasons but usually she would discuss it with both. Since their sister died the three of them became very close. When he saw pictures of her and this Malloy fellow he wondered why she hasn't talked to either of them about it.

He tried calling her but found out that she was in New York. Well when Charles Jr arrived the two of them would find her, confront her, and ask just what is going on. He went down to the main office in the embassy and asked if they knew where she was. They told him yes even though she had retired they would still know where she was because she still had a security detail. She is at the apartment of Mr. Marvin Malloy. The gave him Marvin's private number. He decided to wait for his brother to arrive. He looked at his watch, he should be here within the hour.

Also arriving in New York were Marvin's three other children. There is Harold from Wichita, Emily from Chicago, and Suzzanne from Phoenix. Daddy always kept a three-bedroom apartment available for them, so they were meeting up there. They had already talked among themselves about Dad's romance with Amanda. Turns out three for it and one against it. Suzzanne was the one against it because she felt that someone that old didn't need to be with anyone, they had the children to be with. The other three just knew she would object, and they also knew that dad would tell her, it's my life not yours and I will live it my way. They hoped she wouldn't put up an argument. They all agreed that they would talk to dad in the morning.

Amanda and Marv decided to take an evening walk in Central Park. As they got down to the sidewalk Amanda was surprised to see a beautiful horse and buggy waiting for them. The driver, Mr. James greeted Marv saying, "Hello Mr. Malloy so good to see back, we missed you."

"Thank you James, let's go through the park, you know where to stop." Amanda was thrilled with the ride, she put her arm around Marv's and snuggled closer and commented, "If only my children could see me now."

Marv asked, "Where are your son's now?" "One is in India, and I do not know where the other one is."

Marv then informed her that his three other children just arrived in New York, and she would be meeting them tomorrow morning. They didn't know it yet, but he was planning a brunch for 10:00 AM. He had left them a note at the apartment they were at.

Amanda became amused, "I wish my boys were here then we could have a, the gangs all here party." Just then her cell rang, and it was her boys calling. "You're where, I don't believe it. Well tomorrow morning at 10:00 you need to be here for a brunch, see you then, love you, goodbye. Would you believe that my boys are in New York? Looks like we are going to have, the gangs all here party."

Marv was smiling, "I think God is trying his best to bring you and I together."

As they were going through the park she was amazed at the number of people enjoying themselves. The coach stopped, they got out and Marv walked her to an exhibit. She looked and saw 12 paintings and the artist was Marvin Malloy. She was so impressed and while standing there six people came up and asked Marv for his autograph. What impressed her the most is that all those people knew who he was, and it seemed everywhere they went the people knew him. She was used to people knowing her but here in New York Marv was the star. She squeezed his arm, "Mr. Malloy the celebrity." She whispered to him; "All these people probably wonder who is the floozie on your arm." Marv got a big laugh, "Yes but you are a pretty floozie." Here comes the elbow again.

Chapter 23

I T WAS EVENING IN LONDON and William was going to make a call, but he read that Amanda was in New York and decided to call around 10:30 NY time which meant that he would have to call at half past three in the AM London time. Good that will give me more time to write down what is needed to make her agree to pay the 75,000 pounds. Dad is going to be proud of me.

The truth be known, William always wanted his dad to be proud, even as a child. Dad had a way of ignoring him but when he was bullied at school and he stood up and fought for himself, dad was so proud.

When they called Dad to the school he stood up to the headmaster and told him, no one was going to bully his boy, if they did he would come back and punish the headmaster. Even though William was removed from the school, he was proud of his father. He learned that if you let them push you around you will never get ahead. Well Ms. Amanda you are not going to get ahead of me, I'll show you. Your secret is not so secret. Maybe after you pay I will release the contents to the press. Yes, that is what I will do.

Well Monday is the day for payment, so I better arrange for someone to pick it up. I will check to see if they have delivery pickups. Dad is going to like having use of this money. He will be proud.

When morning came Marv got up thinking wow, brunch has turned into a feast. My four kids and Amanda's two. It should be interesting to watch how they will interact with each other. The one thing I am positive about is my love for Amanda. I had no idea this would happen, but it has, and I am so happy.

I just hope that Stan's plan works. I will feel better when William is in jail. He has become trouble for us. Monday will tell.

Amanda walked in, "I woke up and you were gone, everything OK?"

Marv said, "I was just thinking about the brunch and how it would go with my four and your two children and about William."

She spoke up, "Our children will be OK, but William is another problem that will soon be over. Stan assures me that we will catch him. He needs to be put away. Stan let me know that Williams father is being released soon, that might be a problem, I just don't know. Seems like everything comes at one time. You don't suppose it is because I fell for you so quickly?"

Marv laughed, "My lady, I am the least of your problems," and he reached out and gave her a hug. The doorman called and said, "The caterers are here, I will send them up." They arrived with the food and all the dishes and silver and even the table for serving. They set it all up and the guests started to arrive.

First Amanda's two sons were there. Amanda introduced both to Marvin and they looked him up and down. Charles Jr. spoke first, "Mr. Malloy," Marv interrupted, "Please call me Marvin and before you ask me questions let me say, I love your mother very much and I would never hurt her, and I am going to stand by her side as she deals with this cancer."

Charles Jr smiled, "Well Marvin, what I was going to say is that I have enjoyed your paintings so much, and I have the Mountain Sunset hanging on my wall."

Deacon then spoke up and said, "Well I do not have any of your paintings, but I did investigate you and I was deeply impressed with what you have accomplished in your lifetime. I am pleased that you and mother are now together. She has been lonely these past few years but one look at her tells me she is happy. I thank you sir."

About that time Marv's children showed up. After introductions were made Harold the oldest spoke up to Amanda, "He complimented her on her stance she took with the Russians and then the removal of her scarf. When you did that it showed me what kind of woman you are."

Emily then spoke, "I must say, welcome to the family although I never dreamed that I would have two more brothers."

All laughed but Suzzanne. She was doubtful about the whole thing. She kept quiet but her body language told a different story and both Amanda and Marvin could tell how she felt. Marvin squeezed Amanda's hand and she knew what Marvin was saying to her. They all looked at the food and started to go around the serving table and fill their plates. When they sat down Thomas stood and offered a prayer. "Dear God, bringing these two families together was your work and we promise to see it through, and we ask that you be with Amanda and touch her with your healing hand and rid her of this breast cancer. Amen."

Amanda had a few tears and said, "Thank you Thomas and thank you to all of you for being here today. Marvin and I fell in love the first time we saw each other, and we promise that we will be true to each other and to you."

You could hear Amanda's sons say here, here. Just then Amanda's phone rang, the ID showed unlisted, she motioned to Marv, and they left the room. She turned on the speaker and then heard the garbled voice and knew it was William. He warned her about not paying the bribe and what would happen if the money was not in the postal box next Monday. He said, do you understand? She replied yes, and he hung up.

She was shaking but she called Stan and reported what was said. Stan assured he that they would take William down Monday. She composed herself and returned to the guests, and they never knew how shook up she really was.

Brunch went smoothly but she had concerns with Suzzanne. She was going to take her aside and talk to her without her father being present. She hoped to do that before they left. After the meal was over they talked together and started to become more at ease with each other.

Thomas told them of his engagement, and they toasted to him. Amanda and Marv could see that Suzzanne was being a little more at ease, so Amanda asked her to follow her, and they went into Marv's study. When the two of them got there Amanda could see that Suzzanne was puzzled so she went right to the point. "Suzzanne I could see that you did not approve of your father and me and I want you to tell me what is on your mind."

"Well, I get the feeling that my father is replacing my mother with you and that bothers me."

Amanda saw she was hurt so Amanda said, "Let me tell you something Marvin told me. I too was concerned, so when he told me I felt better. He said this, "I am not replacing my wife with you, I will always love my wife, you are an addition to my wife, and I love you."

Suzzanne heard this and Amanda could see her fears disappear and she hugged Amanda and when they came out of the study Marvin could see them smiling and holding hands. He felt so good and everyone in the room understood what had taken place.

Marvin yelled, "Group hug" and they all gathered around laughing and had a joyous hug. Amanda remarked, "It's been a great morning." You then could hear Emily say," love wins again!" All were happy, especially Amanda's sons because they were worried about the cancer, and they now had others to turn to if they needed to.

Just then Marvin's phone rang, and the ID said Richard Mackenzie. He went to his study and said, "Mr. President old friend what do you want. He responded, Marvin I know you are in New York, so I have put together a thank you party, honoring Amanda for her service to the world and it will be tomorrow night in New York with about 100 of her friends. Do you think you can get her to attend without telling her the real reason?"

Marvin said, "Wow you don't ask for much do you. I suppose it is going to be formal. We will have to go shopping and I will tell her that you are being honored to keep the surprise. Will that work?"

Richard laughed; "I knew I could count on you. Hey, do want a job, I need a man like you."

Marv smiled, "And ruin our friendship, no thank you, but I would like you to be my best man."

The President was flattered and accepted. "Talk to you tomorrow night, I will have my people give you all the details today. Bye Marv and thanks."

He came back into the room and told Amanda, "They had to go shopping for a dress for her because tomorrow they were going to a party honoring the President and he asked if they could come."

Amanda said, "Of course we will." Her sons already knew that the honoree was going to be their mother, because the President already called them this morning. Intrigue carries on. Marv looked at them and could tell that they already knew. All said their goodbyes and the two of them were alone.

The caterers cleaned up, Marvin took care of the bill, and they sat down to rest. Amanda leaned over, "Mr. Malloy, you are an amazing man, I love you so much. Since you came into my life, you made me wonder how I ever got along without someone to lean on. You know Marv, I bet if we went back to bed we might rest or we might-----," Marv grabbed her hand, bent over, kissed it saying, "My lady the bedroom awaits, follow me." Two people were smiling, and he asked, is everything alright?"

She said, "Yes and it's getting better."

He looked at her and said, "I think we will go shopping later."

"Oh yes my love, I need to rest before I go shopping."

He looked at her with an amused look and proclaimed, "You would look good in a paper sack."

Chapter 24

MEANWHILE ALL SIX OFFSPRING DECIDED to go have some expresso and talk about the situation. They saw a Starbucks, went in, ordered, sat down and the discussion began with Charles Jr. beginning. I want you to know that your father has been just what my mother has needed. With this breast cancer, things have been difficult for her and us. We didn't know what to say or how to handle things. Your father demonstrated to us how to go about it."

Harold spoke up, "Well father has had practice, our mother passed away with breast cancer, so he has had experience. I must say, I enjoyed meeting your mother, she is one brave lady and when she took off that scarf, the whole world loved her."

Deacon spoke, "When that happened I felt relieved for some reason."

Thomas told Deacon, "You felt relieved because you were probably holding it in and suddenly it came out."

Suzzanne spoke up next, "I was concerned about this union not because of your mother but because of my father."

They all spoke at once; "We know you did not approve."

Emily asked, "What did Amanda say to you to change your mind?"

She told me what father had told her, "That he was not replacing his wife with her, she was an addition to her."

Charles Jr said, "What a profound thing to say, that's brilliant, maybe your father should be a diplomat."

Harold spoke again, "No he would probably start WWIII. He speaks his mind and believe me when he does, you will know just where he stands."

The six of them shared a good laugh and somebody asked, "When is the wedding?" No one knew but they all said, "Soon!"

As they departed they agreed to meet again so their parents would know they were in support of them. Thomas then asked, "Is everybody going to the show in London?" It amazed all; they were all going. Suzzanne piped up, "Might be a good time for a wedding. Did you know that even the President was going to be there? Great time for a wedding."

Back in London Stan and Molly were having a late dinner and discussing Amanda and all she has and is going through. Molly told Stan that she was glad the Amanda had resigned because, "The pressure was not doing her health any good."

Stan spoke up, "She is dealing with other pressures as well."

Molly's ears seemed to stand up, "What do you mean?"

Stan knew he made a mistake but now he had to figure a way out. Molly being a smart woman, already knew what Stan was referring to because her and Amanda had already talked about it. Molly leaned over to Stan, he thought she was going to give him a kiss, "Do you mean the blackmail?"

Stan looked shaken; "You know."

Molly said, "Yes I know all of it. That is the same person who blackmailed me. I need you to nail him against the wall. You do know he is still asking for money don't you."

Stan had to admit he did but said, "Monday will be the day of reckoning."

Molly smiled and leaned over to him, "Stan you're my man! Let's get out of here and go to my place."

Stan said, "What about dessert?" Molly grinned, "Honey, I am dessert." With that said they left in a hurry. When they got to the parking lot they saw Jennifer and Edward walking hand in hand, Stan said, "Look at them, young love will never die."

Molly replied, "Ours never will either."

Just then Jennifer and Edward hailed a cab and were off. Stan wondered, "Where do you think they are going?"

Molly smiled, "Probably back to her place, just like us."

What they didn't see was William standing in the shadows thinking, I should have eliminated her a long time ago, she is a nuisance. I hope she won't interfere in my plans about Amanda. If she does it will be bye, bye Molly."

William's thoughts changed; he was thinking how his father would deal with this. He did not want to upset his father; he wanted him to be proud of him. His thoughts went back to Amanda, after all this is over I will have to eliminate you too. He was having thoughts that even scared him and he did not know how to handle them. Well, I will ask father. Monday is going to be a good day. The pickup person is hired and will deliver the money to the apartment I rented, then after two hours I can go pick it up. After that I can get the money into the account in Switzerland and be home free. Nothing can stop me now. "Ms. Ex-Prime Minister, you belong to me now!" With that William entered the restaurant for supper feeling on top of the world. No one in the crowd had a clue of what he was going to do, made him feel superior. His waiter asked what he would like for dinner, and he said bring me the best in the house and bring me a scotch neat.

Marvin came back into the bedroom, "Ok time to go shopping. I already called them to let them know we are coming."

She looked at him in amazement, "Do you know everyone here in New York?"

He said "No, this is the store that my wife always shopped in. They know me well there and they also know you will be with me. Our story has been in all the papers you know."

She laughed, "Marv you continue to surprise me, I love it."

He said, "Well-being a former Prime Minister, I think they know you as well. Come old girl let's go."

If he would have been closer he would have gotten the famous elbow. "Look who's calling me old, look in the mirror fella."

"Touché Amanda, touché." Off they went. His car and driver were waiting for them. They went about 20 blocks and stopped in front of this elegant women's store.

Once inside everyone said, "So good to see you again Mr. Malloy and this must be the lady you told us about. Hello Ms. Watkins, welcome to America."

Amanda was impressed with everyone. "Show me something in red and I will need everything to go with it."

The owner said, "Call me Martha," and then Amanda said, "Call me Amanda."

Martha said, "I take it, it's head to toe."

"Yes it is."

"Well I have something special you might like". She turned to her assistant, "Bring out number sixteen, it should be perfect for Amanda and bring that red scarf with it. Now Amanda, "How about shoes, hose and everything that goes with it."

Amanda was impressed, "Oh I think I am going to like it here." She saw the dress and loved it, so she went to try it on. While in the dressing area Martha brought her the scarf and styled it so it was attractive but not overpowering. She came out and modeled it for Marvin and he was speechless. She looked at him, "Well say something don't just stare."

He stammered then said one word, "Beautiful."

She turned to Martha, SOLD. She reached for her purse and Marvin said, "Oh no, this is my treat."

She knew better than to argue, so she just said, "Thank you."

Marvin told Martha, that as usual she did good. "Thank you," and out the door they went. He told the driver to take them down to times square, they would have lunch. Off they went. They pulled into a private parking garage and the three of them were on their way to lunch.

Amanda was surprised and Marvin explained that the people who worked for him all knew that when he had lunch, they had lunch and if Marvin wanted, they would eat together and today he wanted.

Amanda thought that was wonderful and she wished she would have done the same thing when she was PM. Walking in Times Square was exciting, seeing all the people. They stopped at a little diner, walking in and all the workers hollered, "Marvin, where have you been hiding? Who's the broad?" Marvin started laughing because he knew that Amanda would be surprised.

Amanda roared back; "I am the ex-Minister of England who the hell are you."

The whole crowd roared, and Amanda became one of them. She turned to Marvin; "I have been here before." They sat down and the food was on the table before they even ordered. The owner came over, "Amanda so good to see you again, who's the bum you came in with."

"Oh him, just someone I picked up on the corner."

The owner smiled, leaned down, and said, "We have all been praying for you in your battle. You hurt, we hurt.: It was then that Marvin saw Amanda's picture on the wall behind the counter and it was signed. He leaned over to Amanda, "I thought I was going to surprise you, but you got me good this time." The driver spoke up, "Boss, you been had today."

Amanda laughed so hard, it felt good. The owner came up to Marvin, "this one's on the house because you were finally smart and brought our favorite customer with you." He turned to Amanda, "if this bum gives you trouble, bring him back and we will take care of him." He hugged Amanda and gave Marvin a thumbs up. As he was leaving he turned to the driver, "See you around Roscoe." He knew all his customers. When they were back in the car his driver said, "Boss if you could have seen your face when she yelled out, it was priceless. Best day in a long time. Ms. Amanda I loved it. Anytime you are in New York, you call Roscoe, I will be your driver."

Chapter 25

THEY WERE ON THEIR WAY back to get ready for the gala for tonight. He wore his tuxedo, and she looked fabulous in her red dress and scarf along with a beautiful necklace he borrowed from the jeweler. He stood there and looked at her and said, "I want to tear it off right now, you look so beautiful."

The doorman called saying your car is here and when they got in the car she said, "I feel like Cinderella going to the ball."

He chuckled, "Don't lose your shoe." She gently nudged him with her elbow. They arrived and there were many limos' present. When they got out the onlookers began applauding them or it was just her. The security team at the door which included her team ushered them in and escorted them to the front table.

Ellen Mackenzie was waiting for them. They said their hellos, the New York Senators, the Mayor of NY were at their table. They all greeted Amanda and to her surprise they were also friends of Marvin. They talked of Marv's and Amanda's relationship and how fast it happened. Amanda told the story of Marvin's letter to her. Marvin added the part when he saw her picture on the magazine.

They all heard the music, and they knew that the president was making his entrance. He waved to the crowd and made his way to the table. He kissed his wife and greeted the others. He stopped in front of Amanda. "My dear friend, Ellen and I pray for you every day, be well, we love you."

They all sat down, and dinner was served. The conversation was brisk and centered around when Amanda scolded the Russians and how they retreated from their position.

The dinner ended and the mayor went to the podium, quieted the crowd. "Ladies and Gentlemen, this evening we are here to honor a great person who has made a difference in our world. The world has never experienced a leader for all the people as this leader is now. I will turn this over to another leader who is for all the people, ladies and gentlemen, The President of the United States." Much applause was heard lasting for four minutes. He said his thank you to all and quipped, "I hope that when you honor me you are still applauding."

Amanda turned to Marvin, "Who are they honoring?" Marvin smiled, then she heard the President say, "When I first met this woman right after I was elected I was skeptical she could lead. She soon proved to me she was very good at her job. In fact over the years I would call her and ask for advice."

Amanda knew then they were talking about her. She leaned over to Marv and said, "Oh I am going to get even with you for this." The President went on to explain a few instances that her advice put him on the correct path. He then looked straight at Amanda and said with tears in his eyes, "Madam Prime Minister, your greatest challenge lies ahead of you. I watched your press conference when you removed your scarf, Amanda that was the greatest thing I have ever seen done. The women of the world salute you."

The crowd erupted into a standing ovation that lasted for six minutes. When they sat back down the President continued, "I have the great honor in presenting the first annual Creator of Peace award to my very good friend Amanda Watkins, former Prime Minister of Great Britain." She stood and walked up to the podium, hugged the President, and stood there until the crowd sat back down. She began, "As I was coming here tonight I was told that the President was going to be honored so I am totally unprepared for a speech. But if you want to know the truth, when I was Prime Minister I used to throw out my prepared speeches and speak what I felt. I can tell you that when I spoke to the Russians I had this prepared speech and just before we went on the air I folded it up, gave it to my assistant and said I am going to speak what I feel." She had to pause because the audience were on their feet again. "Because I am now just a citizen of the world, I will say this and you must excuse my language, to the leaders of every country in the world I say this, get off your money grabbing assess and start listening to the citizens of the world, they want peace now, give it to them." Then she sat down.

The crowd went wild, the press went wild, the President smiled and hugged her. The President returned to the podium. "Ladies and gentlemen as you know I will be retired in January, and I would like to propose now that Amanda and I lead a movement to all the retired leaders of the world to work to bring about peace in this world of ours. Will it be easy, no, but if we can save lives it will be worth it? I want to thank all for coming, it has been quite a night. Good night, God Bless you all."

Back at the table Amanda looked at Richard, Ellen, and Marvin, "Let's go dancing." The three looked at each other, "Let's do it." Richard had his security chief over and whispered, "We want to go dancing, take us somewhere."

The chief said, "I know just the place," and talked into his wrist to let the other secret service people know the plans. One of them remarked, never a dull moment, and all concurred. They all piled into the Presidents car and off they went. The first thing the secret service chief said was, "lose the press."

They came to a little club that only held 100 people, but they made room for them. The President asked the Chief, "how did you know of this place?" All he said was, "I got married here." They were greeted like old friends and the band asked what do you want to hear? The party began.

After a fun night Amanda and Marvin finally got home and were amazed that they were not bothered by the press. They saw an early headline in the paper with Amanda's picture. Big letters, "Get off your assess." Amanda mused, "misquoted again."

Marvin pulled her close, wrapped his arms around her saying, "I think we should get married." Amanda looked at him, "I agree, when shall we do it?"

They both thought and both came up with how about, just before the show. "Good all settled. I suppose we should tell the children."

"Yes I think we should." It was time to retire, Amanda spoke, "Mr. Malloy I owe you one for not telling me so watch out, you will not see it coming."

Marvin smiled, "walk with me my love." As they reached the bedroom, both had that look in their eyes.

Chapter 26

SUNDAY MORNING ARRIVED IN LONDON. A cool morning, the birds singing, Samantha and Alli were dressing for church. Samantha went back to the church after Amanda found them and Sammie realized, she was an answer to her prayers. She and Alli both were much happier now and her prayers now include Jeremy. Church was wonderful and Sammie felt at peace.

Her and Alli were walking through the park when she thought she saw Jeremy. An artist had set-up an easel and was painting the children playing. She did not get to close because she and Alli were going to be at the show. She sat down and watched.

Yes that was Jeremy, busy and talking to the children as he painted. Some of them even watched him paint. They were amazed at how fast he was. He started on a tree and in less than five minutes he was done. Some of the mothers stood behind him watching and admiring what he was doing. She herself wanted to go up to him and say hello but knew she couldn't. She missed him but could not make herself do anything about it. She was a loner not a mixer. Getting close to others was the hardest thing she ever had to do until she met Jeremy. They both felt that they were the same kind of people. She hoped that when she saw Jeremy at the show, all would return to normal like before. She decided to go home before he discovered she was there. She waved at Alli and Alli walked right by Jeremy without looking at him and hand in hand they left and went home.

William had lunch and he saw a newspaper on the chair, so he picked it up and Amanda's picture was on the front page. She had a metal around her neck and the headline read, "Money grabbing assesses." He picked it up and read the article. He was amused because tomorrow was the day that she must pay. Tomorrow would be great and next Friday his father would be released from prison. A good week indeed.

Sunday was a lazy day for Marvin and Amanda. Nothing planned, just relaxing. All the children checked in, so they told them about the wedding plans. Just before the show. Be there was the order of the day. They all said they would, and Amanda's boys said they predicted that it would be before the show.

Marvin asked his children how many would come; the total was sixteen and Amanda's was eight. They would only need lodging for Marvin's sixteen. He called Delores and asked if she could put them up. She could take nine and the other seven could stay at her friends B&B around the block. He thanked her and said don't forget, "You are invited to the wedding and bring a friend."

Amanda's cancer was bothering her, and she decided to go to bed early. Marvin had a worried look, but she told him it was going to get better. "Marv I just found you, I don't want to lose you."

Marv told her, "Whatever comes, he will be by her side.

As she crawled into bed Marvin joined her. "It's too early for you Marv," he replied, "I will stay with you until you fall to sleep, I love you."

It took Amanda ten minutes to fall asleep, Marv got back up and called Stan about tomorrows payment to William. Stan answered thinking it was Amanda, but when he heard Marvin's voice he felt better. Marv asked him, "If everything was in place and about what time did he think the money would be picked up."

Stan told him, "There is not a time, they must be on watch all day. I feel positive that William will not pick it up, but a delivery person will. There are people that will follow. We have cars and even bicycles if needed. The money has secret marks that only can be seen by us. We will get him tomorrow."

Marvin was satisfied that all was being done. Amanda will be happy once William is caught. He has caused enough problems for her family.

Monday morning found William in the flat he rented in the outskirts of Liverpool. He planned for the pickup take place at 11:25 AM. He chose this time because the delivery person would remember the odd time easier. He was confident it would go smoothly. Ms. Amanda, your money will sure come in handy. Today I cannot miss, every detail is perfect.

At the postal office, Stans men were on duty. Outside there were three men dressed as street workers digging a hole. Across the street were two cars. One heading north and one heading south so whichever way the delivery person went they could follow. They placed a notice in box sixteen that there was a package too large for the box so he would have to go to the window to get it. There they could take a picture of him, and he would not know it. All was set, now they waited. At 11:24 AM, the delivery man walked in and unlocked number sixteen, saw the notice and went to the window. Everyone was on alert, they gave him the package which had a tracker in it, and out the door he went. He got into his car and headed south but turned at the next intersection and went north as ordered. Now both cars were following but they were alternating so as not to raise suspicion. They reached the outskirts of town, and the delivery man went around the block as ordered. They knew that William was checking for cars that might be following so one turned left and the other passed right by the flat.

William was satisfied and signaled the driver to stop in the rear of the building. The car that past by made a quick turn and they saw where he stopped, and they saw William come out and get the package. He paid the driver and he left.

William went back in, and Stan got out of a car and signaled his men to surround the building. Stan and two others went in and showed the manager William's picture, he told them that he was in Two C. They found 2

Two C and knocked on the door. When William opened the door his face got long, and he knew he was in trouble. Stan smiled and said, "William you are under arrest for blackmail of Amanda Watkins." They went in the apartment and William had already opened the package with the money. They took pictures of the money and of William and they had pictures of the delivery man all the way from the postal office to the drop zone. William sat there devastated. "Tell me Stan, how did you know?" Stan looked at him, "William, we just outsmarted you, that's all." They picked up all the evidence and placed handcuffs on William and took him away.

Stan called Amanda, "It's over, we caught him and he's on his way to headquarters now."

Amanda felt a great relief come over her and tears fell. She thanked Stan for the way he delt with William. When she hung up Marv gave her a hug, "Now you can relax." The excitement caused pain to run through her chest. The first thing that came to her mind was a heart attack, but the pain ceased as quickly as it came. She looked at Marvin, "Do you think this might be a warning?"

Marv said, "That's possible, you have had a lot of stress lately." She agreed, "It is time to slow down a bit. Let's go back to London, I will be able to relax there much better."

Marvin was expecting her to say that, for he could feel her discomfort. "My darling if you need to go home we will. Call your people and let them know and have them call us back and tell us when we should be there."

Amanda called, "The pilot told her that they could leave in Two hours," and she told him, "We will be there."

Marvin had already gotten out the suitcases and started packing. "Darling, call your boys in case they need a ride home." She did and they indeed needed a ride. "They are going to meet us at the plane."

Marv said good, "That will give me more time to get to know them better." As they were leaving he asked the doorman to watch his place. He gave him a key, check it once a week.

Amanda was surprised. He told her that, "Barney and I had been friends for over twenty years. Barney and his family have been here, and I have been at his place many times. We became very close, when his wife was sick I sat with him at the hospital. When my wife was there, he sat with me. That's friendship."

Amanda said, "Marvin you're a good man." When they arrived at the plane her two sons were already there. They boarded, buckled in and were about to start when the door opened again, and the UN Ambassador came on board. He apologized, saw Amanda, and said to her, "Madam Prime Minister you caused quite a stir Saturday night. It turns out you and the President will get your wish, leaders from all over the world want to join in. Madam the two of you have done more for world peace in one day than the UN has done in ages, Thank You."

Amanda was blushing but kept her composure and asked him, "Join us when you are retired." She was the person who appointed him to the UN. He agreed since he was now out of a job since she retired. Once in the air everybody settled in knowing that when they arrived they would have gained five hours.

They touched down and Amanda said, "home sweet home." Her son Deacon said, "maybe Marvin doesn't feel that way."

Marvin answered, "Wherever we will be is home. Home is not a place; it is who you are with that makes it a home."

Stan met them and filled them in with all the details. William had to go in front of the Magistrate, and he set the bail at 50,000 pounds. He had the funds and is now out. Trial date has not yet been set. Amanda was not happy, but the courts have spoken.

Chapter 27

THEIR CAR WAS IN THE hanger, so the four of them piled in and off
they went. Marvin dropped the boys off at their office building and
they drove to the farm. As they approached Amanda felt at ease. She loved
this place.

Suddenly she said, "Stop! Look over there, that would be a good place
to have a wedding." It was the barn and Marvin had been in there and
knew it was immaculate.

He said, "It's just what we need. You know we will have to call
everybody; we do not have time to send invitations. As soon as we get in
let's make a list of who to call and let's not make it too big."

Amanda thought for a moment, "I have a lot of politicians to invite and
the Queen and her family. Sorry to say, you won't have that many will you?"

Marvin gave it little thought and replied, "Well Richard and Ellen,
but are we going to have enough room?"

Amanda smiled, "the last time I had a party there we had 400 people
with room to spare, so yes we will have enough room."

Back at the studio Jeremy was checking the portrait to see if it was dry
when he noticed Marvin's piece drying also. First he checked his then he
took off the covering that is over Marvin's. It was a portrait of a young girl.

Jeremy called Ed over, look at this. Ed studied it, "My that looks so
real, it's like she could jump off the canvas."

Jeremy proclaimed, "That is Marvin's style. I am trying to make my
paintings the same way."

Ed remarked, "Jeremy you are close to being there now. It's amazing how real the girl looks."

Jeremy then said, "This girl looks so familiar I cannot place her. She looks like someone I know."

Ed looked at Jeremy, and he could see that at that instance, Jeremy knew. "That picture looks like my mother when she was a little girl. I wonder if Amanda gave him a picture and he did a painting. If we put it next to Sammie's portrait, you would think they were mother and daughter. They have the same mannerisms. It's uncanny how they go together. I think I will ask Marv if we can put them together. Amanda's portrait is done and ready."

Ed then said, "Let's gather up what we can and transport them to the gallery. I can start on arranging them with your help."

Jeremy remarked, "Well our partnership begins."

William was released from jail and was thinking of what to do. When he got to his apartment his father was there. Surprised, William asked, "Why are you here early?"

Rudolph replied, "They released me earlier than expected and my term was classified as served in full. Now tell me, why you got arrested."

William told him the whole story, all about the blackmail scheme. "I haven't quite figured out how they knew about it yet, but I will. That lady is not going to get the best of me."

Dad thought for a long time and finally said, "I think you and I need to get out of the country. I know where we can get passports and name changing documents for 1000 pounds apiece. Do you have the money?"

Will answered yes, "It's in Swiss accounts under different names so no one knows who we are."

Dad spoke up again, "Son you and I are going to make a good team and after things settle down we can come back in disguise."

William had a big smile on his face, "Let's do it father. The sooner we do the sooner we can get back at her."

Amanda and Marvin had been making calls all day and were getting tired. Molly called and said, "She would come out and help."

Then Delores called and said, "She would come out and help." Between the four of them they should get it done easily. They would start in the morning.

Then Marvin remembered that he needed to go in and begin setting up for the show. It was only one week away.

Amanda told him, "Go do what you must do. We will call Stan to see if he can help. We want a good show." She called Stan, and when he found out Molly was going to help he said count me in.

Marvin laughed; "You're going to make this a party aren't you. You can call it a pre-wedding party. Let's fix supper and relax." He had bought some steaks and cooked them on the grill and while they were cooking he made the salad. She was enjoying watching him take charge. She thought this union was going to be great. The thought went through her mind, oh Marvin where have you been all my life?

The next morning Marvin went into his studio and was surprised at all the work Ed and Jeremy had already accomplished. He was impressed with how Edward has advanced. He was going to make a wonderful person in the art field. He saw his painting standing next to Jeremys and it looked so natural. Mother and daughter, nice but he couldn't tell Jeremy yet the truth.

Jeremy spoke, "What do you think, they look so natural together, it's almost as if they were mother and daughter, and the girl looks like my mother when she was a girl. Did Amanda give you a picture of my mother to paint?"

"No, it's just a girl I saw in the park. Well, let's have the movers come today and take all the paintings down to the gallery."

Edward interrupted and told Marvin that, "He and Jeremy have already taken half of the paintings there, we just need to take the rest and I have a truck here now." Ed wanted Marvin to know that he could take charge.

Marvin looked over in the corner and saw the painting that Ed had done. The colors were just right and sitting next to it was an acrylic pour that Ed also did. He picked up the pour, saw Ed's name and commented, "Now this will be sold in minutes. Good job Ed, you need to do more of these and the colors you chose for the barn are perfect and it too will sell fast. In fact all the paintings should sell quickly, I am pleased with all of it, great job." They loaded up the rest of the paintings and headed for the gallery. When they got there and unloaded, Marvin could see the work that Edward had already done. He was pleased and told them so.

They continued to set up the paintings. What they did was mix them so the audience would have to look closely to see who the artist was.

Marvin even brought the painting of Delores. She would be surprised at seeing it. In all Jeremy had twenty-five paintings and Marvin had fifteen. Marvin did not want more; this was to be Jeremy's show. They centered Sammie's portrait and the set Alli's next to it. Together they looked so natural. The gallery advertised the show as, See Marvin Malloy's new find, London's own Jeremy O'Dell, Opening on Sunday, May 15, 2021. All proceeds will go to Breast Cancer Research.

After Jeremy read that, he felt so proud to be compared to Marvin. Marvin looked at the set-up and told Edward that he did a great job. He leaned closer and told Ed that after he and Jeremy should team up. Ed smiled and informed Marvin that they had already reached that conclusion. Marvin asked is everything in place. When Ed said yes, Marvin told him, "He was going back to the farm and don't forget the wedding, I want you and Jeremy to act as ushers. My two son's and two daughters will be standing up with me along with my best man President Mackenzie and Amanda's two sons will be standing up with her with Delores and Molly alongside. I thought it was going to be a little quiet wedding, I should have known better."

William and his dad Rudolph were in the back of a little print shop getting their passports and new identity's. This was the proprietor's main source of income. All the underworlds knew of him as did Scotland Yard. But on this day they were not watching. Somehow their efforts were needed elsewhere. Rudolph failed to tell William that he created a diversion so they would not be watching. He learned in prison where and what they were watching. He felt safe knowing they were elsewhere. As he was leaving he told the proprietor, "Scotland Yard was watching him, time to move your business." It took only fifteen minutes for him to vacate. Nothing left but a fake printing press.

Samantha called Amanda and told her, "I wish her and Alli could attend the wedding but knew that would not be possible."

Amanda thought for a moment, "I will call you back. Molly, we have a project. We need to get Samantha and Alli here for the wedding without Jeremy being the wiser, how shall we do it?"

Molly was thinking and if you saw her face, you could tell she had an idea. "Well, I know a make-up artist who could transform them, and you would not know who they are. We could have costumes also. If Jeremy was five paces away he would not be able to tell if it was Samantha or Alli. Call her back and ask if she would be willing."

Amanda commented, "I knew I asked the right person." She returned Samantha's call; she told of the plan and got a yes. "This is going to be fun, let's not tell Marvin."

Then they heard, "Tell me what?" They looked like two young schoolgirls caught in the act of mischief, "Well I guess we will have to tell him now." After hearing the story he laughed and told them, "You better not get caught."

Molly quipped, "who us?" This was turning into quite a different wedding than Marvin thought it would be and left the room shaking his head.

Amanda spoke up, "Men just don't understand." The room filled with laughter. The wedding was only two days away and lots had to be done. They already had the caterers, tables, chairs, but needed music. Just then Amanda's phone rang, and it was Delores. She asked, "Do you have music yet," and when she heard no she said, "Well I do. My nephew has a small band, and they play at weddings every week and since this is on a weekday they are available."

Amanda said, "Great and we will even have a picture with them to use as advertisement."

Delores said, "They agree, they are standing right next to me now".

Molly smiled; "I think we are all done."

Samantha was excited, knowing that she would be seeing Jeremy again and he not knowing it would be her. She called Alli in and proceeded to tell her that they were going to Grandma Amanda's wedding, but they were going to play dress up. Alli asked why and she told her, "So daddy would not recognize them before the art show. We are going to change the color of our hair and change how our faces look. Does that sound like fun?"

"Oh yes momma, can I wear lipstick?" "Oh we will put a little on just to change the color. The wedding is Thursday so tomorrow we will go have it done and grandma said she would be there."

"Momma, I love grandma and Mr. Malloy too. When is the art show momma?"

"It's Sunday dear."

"Oh goodie, then I will meet father."

Samantha turned because she didn't want Alli to see the tears rolling down her cheeks. Just then there was a knock on the door and there stood Marvin. They invited him in.

Marvin asked, "Do you have transportation for tomorrow and Thursday?" Samantha said no, so Marvin offered her his car to use. Sammie was speechless, Marvin explained "his children have the use of two limos, so his car is available." He handed her the keys, "I have a car waiting, enjoy it and I will see you at the wedding."

As he was leaving Samantha just stood there, she waved, and he drove off. She turned to Alli and spoke, "We have a car let's go and get some fish and chips," and the two of them with big smiles climbed into that Rolls and happily drove off. As they entered they saw two people enjoying their dinner and when they looked up the man had a look of concern.

Edward and Jennifer were the couple. Edward said, "I don't believe it, there is the woman Jeremy has been looking for." Jennifer looked and she knew it was Samantha and Alli. She grabbed Edward's arm and said "Do not tell Jeremy. Amanda has planned for them to meet Jeremy at the art show. She is going to bring them back together."

Ed asked how "Do you know?"

She gave Edward a funny look, "Do you know who I work for? I'm the one who started the search for her. Jeremy does not know he has a daughter yet."

Edward shook his head, "I want to see the look on his face when he sees her, it will be priceless. I think I will stand ready so I can take a video of it, what do you think?" She looked at him with love, "It would be wonderful. They are going to set it up so she and Alli will be by their portraits."

Back at the farm everyone was busy making sure the barn was clean and all the tables and chairs were set up. Amanda had lots of help. All the neighbors around came to help for they were all invited to the wedding. Amanda had announced that no gifts would be allowed and if anyone chose they could give to Breast Cancer Research. Her two sons with their families and all of Marv's family came around to inspect everything and were amazed how it was going. They had gathered for a pre-wedding dinner. Marv's family was amazed how smoothly things were moving.

Marv told them that as PM she knew how to give orders and boy could she ever. That brought about a big laugh just as Amanda walked in.

She looked at Marv, "Are you telling stories about me again?"

He gave that, ah honey you know I love you look. Everybody was laughing at that, and Harold looked at his dad, "I think you met your match dad."

Over at the stables Amanda decided to have two carriages hitched up so if anyone wanted to, they could go around the farm see for themselves how lovely it really was. Marv's grandchildren loved it; you could hear them from a long way away.

Amanda announced that dinner would be served in one hour. There was going to be twenty-seven for dinner and Marv had the grill already to start cooking.

Amanda's cooking staff was amused, they were taking bets that he would burn some of it. He was cooking steak, hamburgers, hot dogs, all American food. He had to give the staff the recipes for macaroni salad, potato salad, Waldorf salad, and assorted pickles, olives, cheeses, and of course buns for the sandwiches.

Marvin excused himself, grabbed his sons and off they went to cook. Marvin did the steaks; Harold did the hamburgers and Thomas did the hot dogs. It was just like old times when they lived together as a family. Soon they were hollering Dinner is served. As everyone sat down Amanda stood and offered a prayer. "Almighty God, thank you for bringing these two families together. Guide us to do your will. Amen."

Then all the talking began, and the jokes were coming fast. Everyone had a great time, both families learned just because they were from two different countries, they were the same. All the grandchildren had a wonderful time together.

Amanda and Marvin stood back and watched holding hands, Amanda said, "We are so blessed."

Marvin became a little emotional, a few tears fell, and he turned to her, "I love you," and then recited, "Roses are Red, Violets are blue, we became us, that's me plus you."

Amanda smiled, "Oh my, a poet. I am going to love being Mrs. Malloy."

Marv grinned, "I thought I was going to have to be Mr. Watkins." Of course he got the famous elbow. They gave each other a hug and watched the grandchildren.

Chapter 28

WILLIAM AND RUDOLPH HAD THEIR new passports and now they had to learn their new names. William became James Dunn, a citizen of Canada. Rudolph became Alistair McDougall a citizen of Scotland. Both had addresses and all the pertinent information available.

Rudolph now Alistair said, "Well James we must decide where we want to disappear to."

William now James hesitated to answer, and his father scolded him, "You must forget William and start using James. It is not going to be easy, but it must be done. It will not be hard for me because I have used several names in my lifetime. Now James, where shall we go?"

James was shaken but he tried to think and after a short time he suggested Denmark. From there they could travel around Europe to work their schemes. Alistair thought that was a good idea and while there they could get new passports with different information. He told James, "Good thinking."

James took over and called for tickets to travel, leaving on Thursday at noon. Alistair reminded him that they could not take anything with them. They would buy all knew clothing in Denmark. That way the police would think they were still in the country. Their delay would be an advantage to James and Alistair. They decided that they should leave the house at different times in case they were being watched. Plans all done, they broke out the scotch and enjoyed having a drink together. Father and son, now working as a team.

Chapter 29

THAT EVENING BACK AT THE Stafford House Delores was talking to Marvin's children. "Well now, how are you liking London? Is it everything you thought it would be?"

Thomas spoke up, "I find it beautiful and the people from all over the world mixed and becoming a true world city just as Toronto is. New York is too."

Delores commented, "I have been to New York, but she prefers London, but this is home."

Harold spoke, "I enjoy the Royal Family and all they do and must put up with. They are living in a glass bubble; I don't know how they do it."

Emily and Suzzanne told her they enjoyed the Arts and Museums. "The history is rich going back many hundreds of years."

Delores then told them how their father helped her and got Amanda to help also. She was so grateful and happy now how her life has made a turn for the better. "I believe God sent your father to us and I am blessed to have met him. Amanda told me to tell you that tomorrow she has arranged for you to see the matinee of Phantom of the Opera."

They all looked at each other and were happy. All were thinking this lady has power. Delores planned for someone to watch the children and they all walked to the pub for the evening and when they went through the door they were greeted with a big hello, welcome, let's party.

Everyone was in a happy mood and having fun when who walked in,

Marvin and Amanda. They had set this up and without anyone knowing, paid for the whole thing.

Delores said, "The neighbors will be talking about this party for a long time." It lasted until the wee hours. No one went home early. The mayor of the community stood up as best he could and made a speech. "Marvin since you came to us, we have become more aware of each other and how much we depend on one another and Amanda, you have been our Prime Minister but more important you have been our friend. We will miss you as the PM, but we will be by your side in your fight with cancer. Our prayers will be there for you to use when you need them."

Both Marvin and Amanda had tears, but they were tears of friendship. Amanda hugged everyone in the pub they all began hugging each other. The bell rang for last call and a quiet came over them and Amanda spoke, "I became PM because of people like you, God Bless England."

Chapter 30

Well the big day is finally here. Things were busy around the farm. Caterers, florists, security, and guests starting to arrive. All the cars were going to be placed in the meadow by valets. All total there would be over 400 people there. The President of the United States and all the secret service people were now there. The press was being kept to the outside edges. When they showed up, Amanda went out among them and gave an interview and when finished asked politely to respect her guests. If they did not she told them they will be removed, and security would make those decisions.

When Amanda returned to her dressing room Molly and Delores were there to assist her. She had her dress hanging up and it was full length with a v neckline. The color was a light pink rose. When she put it on the ladies said it was just right. She was going to wear a white wrist corsage. She wore a string of pearls with matching earrings that had belonged to her mother. Delores gave her a light pink handkerchief that she could tuck in her sleeve. Her shoes were low heels of white. Molly said, "we got to have something blue?" Amanda laughed and showed her a blue garter. She chose not to wear gloves. She would only wear a wedding ring that will match the one Marvin would wear.

Suddenly her nerves kicked in and her hands began to shake. She thought of her cancer and some tears began. Molly and Delores hugged her told her she was going to beat the cancer so her and Marv could have a long life. She thanked them and then heard a knock on the door.

Jeremy came in to wish grandma well. Amanda asked if he was ready for Sunday's show. Then Charles and Deacon came in, they would be escorting her down the aisle, one on each arm. They kissed her and told her she was making the right choice.

During this time, Marvin was acting nervous. He was in what they call an afternoon coat. It looked very formal but not quite tails. Along his side was his friend Richard, and his children were with him. His two daughters were going to escort him down the aisle and his two sons and Richard were going to stand up with him.

Molly and Delores were standing with Amanda. Marvin looked out the window and saw a woman and child going to their seats. He said softly, wow what a makeup job. If he didn't know he would never have known they were Samantha and Allison. Sammie's natural hair was brown with reddish highlights and Allison is the same. Sammie had on a dirty blond wig and Alli's was tucked under a flame red wig. Their facial make up was outstanding. You could not tell who they were. He was going to tell Amanda when they were at the alter that they were here and give her a brief description. She was going to be shocked.

Thomas spoke up and said, "Ten minutes gang, time to get into position." Marv could feel some nerves kicking in. Harold asked him, "Where is the honeymoon Dad?" Marv said it would start after the show Sunday. "We are going to drive around Scotland for a week and then come back here." They all started to go get in place.

The music began and Marv's sons and Richard were in place and his daughters were on his arms and they started walking down the aisle. As they passed Samantha, Alli he gave them a wink, and Sammi knew that Marv knew. When they reached the alter the girl's kissed dad and went to their seats to be with their families. They turned and could see Amanda and her sons waiting, the boys on each arm began the walk. She did not see Sammie siting there. When they reached the end of the aisle her sons kissed her cheeks and joined their families.

William and Rudolph now known as James and Alistair were standing in line to board the plane. They went through, showed their passports, got the ok and went down to way and entered the plane. James was nervous but Alistair was cool. He had done these many times. He leaned over to James and told him it will get easier. James was sure the police would come on board and take them off. They were pushed back and then the plane started to taxi toward the runway. They turned and the plane roared down the runway and then they were in the air. James let out a big sigh and Alistair patted him on the knee and whispered, "Relax we made it."

Meanwhile back at the wedding, the Reverend was saying that both Amanda and Marvin wanted to say their own vows.

They faced each other, held hands and Amanda began. "Marvin when I think back, it was because of your letter that we stand here today. When I read it I could tell you were a man who was caring but I didn't know you were so handsome." The audience chuckled at that. "I believe that God made that letter reach me because God knew that I needed you. I read that letter about three or four times before I decided to find you and that was probably my best decision as Prime Minister. When you came through my office door I looked, and I knew that I needed to know you better. I could feel it and we spent the entire afternoon and evening talking about ourselves, leaving nothing out. When we started to dance I could tell by the way you were holding me you were for me. Yes I knew that quick. So my darling, I love you and I promise to you that we will be together always."

Marvin smiled when she finished, and he began. "Amanda when I went to that mailbox in Arizona the first thing I saw was this magazine with your picture on the cover. When I got back to the house I studied it, and I could see the hurt in your eyes. As I looked further I could see rays of happiness in them also. I looked you up on the internet and discovered the loss you endured so I knew your pain. We both lost spouses and I wanted to sit down and ask how you were dealing with the pain. I wrote you that letter as one person to another who could feel the pain. I too believe that God played a hand in bringing us together. My darling, I too promise to be by your side, I will always love you and whatever happens, know that I will be right there."

Both turned toward the Reverend, he went through the service and at the end, "I present to you, Marvin and Amanda Malloy, husband and wife," the audience stood and clapped as Marvin kissed her for a long time. When he finished he whispered in her ear where Sammie and Alli were.

She looked and thought, what a beautiful disguise. They started down the aisle and when she came to Alli she took off her corsage and gave it to her then continued walking. Alli was so happy. As they stood in back in a receiving line the staff rearranged the chairs and placed them with tables in record time. They made a space for the dance floor and the band set up and started to play. The party began.

Everyone was enjoying themselves. The mix included politicians, dignitaries, and so-called commoners. You could not tell one from the other. Their friends from the pub started singing and soon all joined in. Well known English drinking songs. The American friends joined in as best they could and leading the singing were Delores and Amanda.

Soon Molly joined them and the three of them were performing for the whole crowd. Marv and his Klan sat back and took it all in. Everyone was in a happy mood. The band started to play upbeat dance tunes and all the men were in line to dance with Amanda and all the women were in line to dance with Marvin.

They went round and round when suddenly Marvin grabbed Amanda and whirled her around and all were shouting kiss, kiss. Well Marvin could not resist so he kissed her like the honeymoon had begun. The crowd roared, more, more. The party lasted until late into the evening.

Marvin went to the microphone with a sign and thanked them for being there with them to celebrate and when he showed them the sign he told them that from now on this would be their trademark. He held it up and what they saw was large letters, M&A.

Soon after, the party broke up and those who stayed got a chance to sit and relax. The two families sat there and talked and laughed about the evening. Most everyone was tired. Marv looked over at Amanda and he could see the pain in her eyes.

Worried, he went to her side, held her, and asked, how do you feel? "Oh, I just have a little indigestion, I will be all right." Somehow Marv did not quite believe her, and worry entered his mind. So he stood and proclaimed, time for the party to end, my lovely bride and I must be somewhere else. That brought a few laughs, but they understood and prepared to leave.

Molly and Delores both said they would see her tomorrow and Edward and Jeremy said they would meet at the gallery tomorrow. Everybody climbed into the cars and off they went. As the last car was leaving, Marv and Amanda turned down the lights and went up the steps to the bedroom.

Marv looked at her, Amanda you became the center of my life the first day I met you. I want to call you, my sunshine, my inspiration, my reason, I love you. She pulled him to her and gently kissed him and ignited a fire in him. He whispered are you ok? She smiled when I am in your arms everything is ok. She reached up and undid his tie, then moved to his shirt. He looked into her eyes, Oh I like where this is going, please do not stop. She continued, she removed his shoes and socks, took his belt off, undid the button on his pants and let them fall to the floor.

There he stood with just his shorts on, and she took a step back as if she were going to leave him there. He spoke, aren't you going to finish? She came back to him and removed the shorts.

She backed up a bit and looked at him from top to bottom and back up again, she paused, well I think we are ready to go to bed now and get a good night's sleep.

He looks at her, that's not fair. With a serious look on her face she says, gotcha! She told him, "If you could have seen the look on your face when I walked away, priceless." She stood before him, "Well Mr. Malloy, don't just stand there, undress me."

It did not take Marv long and when he was done he picked her up and carried her to the bed, laid her down, crawled in and pretended to go to sleep. Yes he got the famous elbow. Sleep was the last thing they were thinking about.

Chapter 31

FRIDAY MORNING ARRIVED AND THE Malloy's slept in. Around 10:00 they dragged out of bed, Marv asked, "what you are going to do today."

She told him, "Her and Molly and Delores were going to see Samantha and Alli and set things up for Sunday. What are you going to do?"

He told her he had to go to the gallery to make sure that everything was as it should be. He also told her; "I have been very impressed with Edwards's work. He is a fast learner. I am sure glad that I stole him from you. He is going to make a good art dealer as he grows older. I will get something to eat later with the boys. Tell Sammie and Alli hello for me."

He kissed her and left. As he got to the gallery he worried about Amanda. She had some pain last night in bed, but she would not give in to it. She complained this morning of indigestion. He decided to talk to Thomas before he went back to New York and get his opinion of the situation. Thomas was a second-year resident as a cardiologist. His family was going back to the states on Monday. Then he remembered that he neglected to tell them that he bought the ranch in Montana that he and his wife were at when he painted the picture hanging in Ten Downing Street. The ranch was only 200 acres, but the house was large enough for all to stay in. Right now he had caretakers watching over it. Well he would tell them tonight. He walked in the door and the first thing he saw was Samantha's portrait along with Alli's. They fit together nicely.

He looked to his left and there was Delores's portrait. Hers were surrounded by smaller paintings of Marvin's. The set-up was perfect. He looked at Jeremy's set-up and it too was perfect, centered by Sammie's portrait. Then there was Amanda's portrait, currently covered in a position of importance. This was going to be a good charity show. He saw Edward and called him over.

Edward asked if anything was wrong, "No I just wanted to tell you that the job you did was outstanding. You young man, will go a long way."

Amanda, Molly, and Delores were in Amanda's car heading for Samantha's place. They were talking about the party and teasing Amanda about the late night. If you did not see them you would have thought they were teenagers. They stopped in front of Sammie's house and Alli was on the porch still wearing the corsage. Her hair was still colored from yesterday. She saw them coming up the walk, she went to the door, "Mommy grandma's here." Sammie let them in with hugs all around.

Amanda asked, "Is Sunday's plan all set?"

Sammie said, "Yes and I am excited. Are you sure he still wants me?"

"Oh yes, you are all he talks about. Alli is going to be a big surprise for Jeremy." Amanda went on to say, "You are going to be a great addition to the family, I only wish Jeremy's folks could be here to see you."

Molly turned to Alli, "Tell me, are you excited."

Alli started to jump up and down, "Yes, yes, I want to hug Daddy and I want him to hug Mommy." It seems Alli was wise for her age. It was going to be wonderful to see this family reunited. When Amanda told Charley and Deacon about Samantha they worried that it might not work out, but Amanda was sure it would. They promised to be there for support. Sunday was going to be magic. Amanda suggested they go to lunch, so they all piled into the limo and away they went. Molly suggested that they go to the farm, so they do not run into reporters and pictures get into the papers. Amanda said good, I did not think of that.

Chapter 32

James and Alistair found their mark. She is a widow who lost her husband Three years ago and he was an executive in a German power Company. Her name is Kathleen Mueller, 62 years old. Alistair met her at a senior gathering that included dinner and dancing. He asked if he could join her table and she said yes. She was tired of eating alone. He asked a lot of questions and he answered hers, only his answers were false.

James came walking by he stopped and said, "Alistair so good to see you, is our appointment at the bank still on for tomorrow?" "Why yes it is Mr. Dunn. Be there at Ten, I have set two hours to conduct our business. Let me introduce Mrs. Kathleen Mueller, this is James Dunn a leading industrialist. Mrs. Mueller's husband was Egon Mueller with the power company. Maybe you have heard of him?" "No I haven't but I have had dealings with his company."

"Mr. McDougall here is with the bank that my company is dealing with. It's been a pleasure Mrs. Mueller and if you need a reliable banker you can't go wrong with Alistair."

Well James has planted the seeds now Alistair has to get them to grow so they can reap a large harvest.

Down at the pub, Delores and gang was talking about the wedding and how much fun they all had. Most of them were still amazed that Amanda invited them. Delores stood up, clinked her glass until all were quiet. She raised her glass and said, "Let us pray for Amanda and her battle against Breast Cancer." All said here, here.

Delores told them, "I was with her today and she could see that she was not feeling good. She needs our support."

Marv was looking out the window. One more day and it would all come together. Great show, Jeremy getting together with Samantha, he and Amanda leaving on a trip to Scotland. He heard the doorbell, so he went to the door and Stan was standing there. Inviting him in he asked what brought him out there?

Well he said, "William and his father were missing. We think they might possibly have left the country. We raided a print shop and found trace evidence with William's name on it. We cannot prove it but it's possible."

Marv said that he would tell Amanda. Stan said thanks and left. Amanda came down, who was at the door? Marvin told her what Stan had said and he could see the look of disappointment in her eyes. She said, "Will I never be done with this man?"

She walked with her head down and her shoulders slumped. She looked like a defeated woman. He put his arm around her, then they walked into the kitchen where the cook had prepared breakfast. They sat down and Amanda looked at him, "I'm ok now. What would you like to do now?"

He thought for a moment, "Let's just relax, how about a picnic? We could take a book along for you and I will paint the picnic scene with you sitting there looking beautiful."

She smiled, "That sounds perfect. The cook overheard this and immediately started preparing the food, the wine was already chilled, the cheeses were ready, and the bread needed to be sliced. She told them, "You go get ready, I will take care of everything." Amanda thanked her "When you are done take the rest of the day off. Fix some lunch and go home and take your husband on a picnic." Her eyes lit up saying, "Now that would be a wonderful surprise. I will do it."

Amanda and Marv went upstairs to change into relaxing clothes and Marv got his painting kit along with an easel and canvas. They went out the door with a happy look and headed for the meadow. The birds were singing, it was a gorgeous day. Marv set up his paints and Amanda got out her book. He asked her what the book was about, and she said it was called, "The Lovers" she said, "It was fiction, but she suspected it was more about the writer than fiction. It felt like our story, it seemed to be parallel to you and I."

Marv commented, "I will have to read it." It was peaceful and quiet but every once in a while they would stop and talk about their future and then go back to what they were doing. Marv told her about the house he bought in Montana and would like to stop there in May on their way to Richard's and Ellen's place. He also told her that his family would be leaving on Monday to go home. He would like to have them, along with her family, for a get together Sunday afternoon.

She said, "I have watched them, and I believe that everyone gets along fine. Should be fun. Marv, we are so blessed, can you believe how fast we came together? At times I sit there and cannot believe it has happened. You my dear are my everything, I love you."

He stopped his painting, set down his brush, went to her side and kissed her and began making love right there in the meadow. The two of them were hungry for each other. It was like they were in a different world together. They both reached the peak together and were filled with love and happiness. They looked toward the sky, and they saw rain clouds and thought they should go back to the house before they got soaked. It was a wonderful afternoon.

Chapter 33

LATER THAT DAY THOMAS CAME by for a visit and he and his dad went into the study to talk. Marv was concerned about Amanda and asked him to spend the night and escort her to the show tomorrow. She was complaining about heart burn and indigestion. Thomas was thinking that it might not be what she thought it might, it might be heart problems. He said he would stay. Marv felt relieved and thanked him.

As they sat around talking, Thomas remarked, I have never seen two people so happy together. Can you explain it to me? I just hope my lady and I will be that happy."

Amanda answered him by saying, "Happy yes, but you must realize that both of us where married before with people we loved, so we could recognize feelings. When we met for the first time I knew this man was of interest to me. When your father saw my picture, he knew that he was going to try and meet me. Instant attraction came into play. Now let me ask you, how did you feel when you first saw Cindy?,

Thomas did not have to think, he said, "Immediately, she rocked my world. That first look was all I needed. I believe I loved her then."

"Well my boy, you just answered your own question, instant attraction. You are your father's son." While she was talking Thomas noticed her winching with pain. He made a mental note of that. Amanda was tired from the day's activities and retired early.

Marvin said he would be up in a few minutes. He turned to Thomas; "Did you see it?"

Thomas said, "Yes dad, I did. I believe that it might very well be a heart problem. I will keep a close watch tomorrow for anything."

Marv thanked him and went up to their bedroom. Amanda was already in bed when he came in, she asked, "What were you two talking about?"

Marv could not tell her a lie, so he said, "Your health."

She nodded her head, "I thought so, I will be all right Marv."

He told her, "Just making sure my love." He undressed and she started to tease him, "My, my, Mr. Wolf, what big -------- toes you have." He laughed, "Oh just my toes huh." He crawled in and she whispered, "Oh my mistake."

"Miss Amanda, I love you, now time to sleep." All he heard was, REALLY. Before they both knew it, morning had arrived. Show day was finally here.

Jeremy woke up tired because he could only get about two hours sleep. Edward was just as nervous. Marvin was relaxed because this was going to be Jeremy's day not his. Samantha and Alli were both nervous because Sammie was going to reunite with her lover and Alli was going to meet her Daddy. This was going to be a day of surprises.

Marv had to leave early so he would be at the gallery along with Jeremy and Edward. He asked Thomas to care for Amanda. She said, "Go I will be all right worry wart." So Marv left them.

Over at Samantha's house she was a bundle of nerves and her daughter said, "Mommy relax, it's going to be a fun day." For one so young she was a wise girl. Sammie said, "Thank you, I will relax", but she knew she couldn't. They got dressed into the same dresses they wore for their portraits. When they were ready they looked beautiful.

Over at the Stafford House, Delores was ready, but Marv's family was behind as always. The limos were lined up and ready. The drivers were taking bets as to which limo would be the first to go. The winner would get Twenty pounds. There were four limos.

Soon the first set of people came out and it was Suzzanne's family that would be in the Third limo. Winner! Shortly all the limos were filled and off they went like a parade through the neighborhood. Most of the neighbors would be there because they had become friends with Amanda and Marvin.

Molly and Stan arrived at Amanda's to ride with her. As they walked in Amanda was coming down the steps. She got almost to the bottom when she collapsed clutching her chest. Thomas was there to catch her and laid her down. He recognized immediately she was having a heart attack and hollered to call an ambulance. He stayed with her and monitored her. She managed to tell Stan to call Marvin and tell him to go on with the show, she would be all right.

Thomas looked worried but he said OK to Stan. Molly told Stan, "Do not call, go in person it would be better, so he left but he asked Molly to call if any changes occurred." She nodded yes and he left.

The ambulance arrived, checked her vitals, gave her a Nitro glycerin tablet, and place her on a gurney and loaded her into the ambulance. Thomas told them he was a Heart Doctor, so they let him ride along. Things were fine until they reached the hospital then everything went wrong.

Meanwhile over at the show, Stan came in looking for Marvin. He saw him down by the portrait that was covered so he went to him. Marv looked at him and knew something was wrong. He told him about Amanda and what she said. He wanted to rush out but then thought of her and knew he should stay. He motioned for Jeremy to come over and told him what happened. He too wanted to go but knew she would be upset if he did. So both stayed. People were coming into the show, so they mingled.

Thomas was calling periodically to update them. So far all was ok. Marv saw the friends from the neighborhood, saw his family then saw Amanda's family. He pulled them aside and told them what was going on, so they left for the hospital. The show was packed with people, it was turning out to be a big success. Sold signs were going up at a fast pace. He called Jeremy over; it was time to unveil the portrait. He and Jeremy went to the portrait.

Chapter 34

B ACK AT THE HOSPITAL THINGS were not going well. Amanda's heart stopped twice and was on the edge of stopping again. Thomas watched the British doctors looking for differences. He could see none which surprised him. Then suddenly her heart stopped again. They tried paddles, shots directly into the heart, compressions, nothing was working. She had already been down longer than patients usually were, so they decided to call time of death.

As they were calling it Thomas hollered, "No she is not gone, she is standing with God can't you see her." He reared up and hit her chest as hard as he could without breaking her ribs and within Thirty seconds her heart began to beat.

The doctor asked, "Who are you?

"I am an American heart doctor, and she is my mother-in-law." She opened her eyes, looked around and saw Thomas and everyone was surprised to hear her say, "Thank you Thomas for bringing me back, just like in my dream."

They started to run all sorts of tests and they all came back negative. They checked for breast cancer, and they could find none.

The cancer Doctor then said, "Ladies and gentlemen we have just witnessed a medical miracle." Amens could be heard around the room.

Over at the show Stan pulled Marv aside and told him Amanda was ok. He went and told Jeremy, "Let's do this."

Jeremy spoke to the crowd; "This portrait will be hanging with the rest of the Prime Minister's portraits. It is our gift to England."

Marvin and Jeremy stood on each side and began pulling down the covering. Samantha and Alli were now in the front watching. As the covering was coming down Jeremy heard a young voice saying, "Look mommy it's grandma."

He turned and saw Samantha standing with a young girl. It was the first time ever he saw his daughter.

He looked at the girl and he could see his mother. He walked over to them, looked into Samantha's eyes, "Where have you been and why did you leave me?"

"I have been in London all this time and your grandfather convinced me that you wanted me gone. Did you?"

"How could you think that? Let's talk after the show."

She nodded and said OK. Jeremy then hugged her and whispered, "I love you."

When he stepped back, he saw tears coming down her face. Just then he felt a pain in his left kidney area. It went away quickly but it reminded him of the time he lost his right kidney ten years ago. He told himself it was going to be all right, move on. The show was a complete success.

Marvin walked over, "I see you saw Samantha and Allison, is everything all right?"

Jeremy was shaking as he looked at Marvin. "Did you know she was going to be here? Does grandma know?"

Marvin explained that "Amanda and He found out about her a few weeks ago and searched for her and when Amanda saw Allison she knew she was yours. We made some hard decisions and thought that with her coming to the show it would be a perfect way for you to see her and Allison. We know you love her, now you have a daughter that needs you and her mother also needs you. Go to them, your new life awaits you."

Marvin was watching Jeremy when suddenly Amanda shows up along with Thomas. Puzzled he asks Thomas what they are doing there.

He told his father, "I could not keep her away. When she awoke she was fine, nothing wrong and even her breast cancer was gone. The Doctors called it a miracle."

Amanda stood in front of her portrait and said, "Marvin you did a splendid job."

He pointed to the artist's name, and it read Jeremy O'Dell. Amanda felt proud and happy, she walked over to Jeremy, hugged him, and said, "I love you."

Just then Allison saw her and with a loud voice, "Hi grandma." Amanda reached down and gave Allison a kiss, stood up and looked at the two of them and remarked," are you two back together?"

They looked flustered but both said "yes" at the same time. She grabbed Allison, "show me around the show" and off they went. You would swear that both were the same age.

Edward and Jennifer came up to them and Jeremy introduced Samantha to them. Samantha felt at ease with Jeremy's friends and then Jennifer spoke up, "Didn't I see you performing at the karaoke last month?"

"Yes and it was so much fun. I really enjoyed it. I didn't realize I could entertain so many people."

Jennifer smiled, "You should do that for a living, you are so good."

Samantha shook her head, "I don't know about that, I only sing for fun. You should hear our daughter; she is the singer in the family."

Jennifer asked, "Samantha are you three a family now?"

"No but we will be soon. Next week we are going to get married. Will you stand up with me and Edward will you stand up with Jeremy?" The couple was surprised, and they accepted.

"We must tell Amanda and Marvin. They are going to go on their honeymoon next week to Scotland. We will give you the details later."

Amanda and Marvin were going around the gallery talking to the patrons, thanking them for their support and looking at the paintings on display when they saw Delores looking at her portrait. She stood there in disbelief; she did not know Marvin had painted her likeness and he even had her new look.

On her arm was her new beau. They walked over then Amanda said, "Hello Delores and Jefferson how nice to see you again."

Delores turned, "Amanda I thought you were in the hospital, how are you feeling, and I did not know you knew Jefferson."

"Oh we have known each other for a long time. Darling let me introduce you to Jefferson Smythe, Barrister whom I have known for many years, long before I got into politics."

"Mr. Malloy, I have enjoyed your work for many years, and I have one of your pieces in my home, so nice to finally meet you and congratulations on your marriage to Amanda. This portrait you did of Delores is quite marvelous."

Marvin was impressed with Jefferson and happy for Delores, she finally had someone new in her life. He shook hands with Jefferson and then reached for Delores and gave her a hug. "Were you surprised when you saw your portrait?"

"Oh my goodness, you cannot imagine when you see yourself in a portrait how you feel. I could not believe what I was seeing. When did you do all this? You never seemed to be working and yet here it is."

Marvin smiled at her, told her she was a very good subject and he wanted to thank her for all she did for him. "Delores I want to give this portrait to you and your family, enjoy."

"Oh Marvin you are so kind, I thank you so much. You and Amanda enjoy your trip and when you get back we will get together for some dinner."

As they were speaking the crowd grew larger and they could hear them saying how beautiful the lady is, not realizing she was standing there with her back to them. When Delores turned you could hear the buzz as they realized she was here.

Marvin smiled, said his goodbye's, and went to find Amanda. Jefferson leaned down and whispered, "you certainly have some important friends."

She looked at him, whispered back, "Yes, but you are the most important." The crowd was thinning out as Amanda was watching Jeremy and Samantha holding hands, looking at each other, both smiling and Allison looking up at Jeremy with a loving look.

She tugged his arm, he looked down and then she said, "I love you daddy." This brought tears to Amanda's eyes, tears of joy. They all heard the announcement that the gallery was closing, the crowd was leaving. The only ones left were both families, along with Molly and Stan, Edward and Jennifer, and Delores and Jefferson. Marvin told them that they were all going to Editors for dinner to celebrate Jeremy's success. The gallery people gave Marvin an envelope with the results. He looked it over, put it in his pocket and said let's go. Thirty happy people were on their way.

Chapter 35

WHEN THEY GOT THERE STAN pulled Amanda and Marvin aside and told them that they had a lead on the where abouts of William and Rudolph. Looks like they went to Denmark. We saw them on the surveillance cameras at the airport. We contacted Denmark to be on the lookout for them. Even though they are traveling together only William is a fugitive. Rudolph is clear of anything so far. Stan then told them that he opened a Private Investigation Agency, and you are my first clients. They agreed to work with Stan as long as it took.

Dinner was served and Amanda stood and offered a toast. "To my wonderful family, new and old, we celebrate Jeremy's success today and celebrate the reuniting of Samantha and Jeremy along with our newest member Allison. God Bless all."

The room was filled with clinking glasses and much joy. You could hear some saying "Here, here!" Happiness filled the room.

The meal was served, Marvin's favorite, pot roast and new potatoes. He was in his glory. While eating he pulled out the envelope and re-read the results. He showed it to Amanda, and she was impressed.

Marvin stood, "I want to let everyone know how the show went. First, every painting was sold, and the total for Breast Cancer Research is over 150,000 pounds. Everyone did a good job, but I would like to thank my assistant Edward. This was his first show and without him we couldn't have done it. Thank you Edward."

Jeremy stood, "let me say thank you to everyone but most of all, to

Marvin who taught me so much these past weeks. His expert guidance meant so much. Next I want to thank my grandmother, she knew my feelings and she went forward to search for Samantha and bring us back together. Next I want to thank Samantha and Allison, I love you and will you marry me?"

Samantha cried and Allison shouted "Yes!" Everybody laughed as the two of them hugged and kissed. Jeremy picked up Allison and gave her a big hug and kissed her on the cheek. It was a good party, and everyone left happy.

Over in Denmark Rudolph was reading about Amanda and Marvin's wedding. He turned to William, "You know son, I always liked that woman, she had a terrible husband, I hope this one is the one she needs."

William looked surprised, "Are you kidding me dad, I thought you hated her?"

"No, it was her husband I hated. He is the one who got me put in prison. Someday I will tell you the whole story, but not now. I know I said I wanted to put her in her place, but it's the company I want to harm not her personally, and there is a story about Jeremy you will need to know, but we can discuss it later before we return to England."

Delores and Jefferson returned to her house, "Why didn't you tell me you knew Amanda?"

"Well I never gave it a thought.

"Years ago I worked with her husband Charles at his company. I was his company's at large attorney. I also did personal work for them as well, then later I worked with Amanda's people to help her get to parliament. It was an exciting time in her life and as you know she became a very good Prime Minister. How did you become good friends with her?"

"Well, when Marvin came to this country, he stayed at my B&B. That's where it all began. He had a meeting with Amanda, and it grew from there. They are both my newest best friends. No wait, you are my newest best friend. May I kiss you?"

Now Jefferson scoped her into his arms and proceeded to give her the kiss of her life. "Why Mr. Smythe, where have you been all my life?" she pulled him into her, and the dance began. Both were smiling and holding each other tight so the other couldn't get away. Jefferson spent the night.

Jeremy followed Samantha and Allison to her house, and they all went inside. Allison sat on her daddy's lap and Sammie told him how his grandfather said that Jeremy did not want her, and he gave her money to leave. She thought Jeremy was done with her, so she took the money, $250,000 but decided to stay in London. She soon found out she was pregnant and then Allison was born. She followed Jeremy's activities but felt lost.

When your grandfather died I received an insurance payment of one million dollars. Your grandfather just did not want me in the picture, but I am so glad your grandmother found me, and now I have found you. Your daughter is also glad you're here. She loves your grandmother also. "Jeremy, my life these past 5 years has been hollow but now that we are together, it is becoming full, I love you."

Tears started down his cheeks, and he stood and had a group hug with Sammie and Alli. He looked at them, "let's get married next week."

The smile on Sammie's face was large and Alli hugged them both. Allison was finally going to have a daddy. Jeremy grabbed his back in the left kidney area. Years ago he had lost the right kidney due to kidney disease and now the left one was acting up. He hoped it was just a pulled muscle. He knew if it was his left kidney he was in trouble, but he was not going to tell Sammie at this time.

His grandmother knew about his kidneys, but he didn't know if he would tell her. His thoughts went back to Sammie and Alli, what a day. Successful showing, seeing Sammie again and then learning he had a beautiful daughter. I am blessed.

Sammie's thoughts were on Jeremy, he is so handsome, he seems to still love me and now that he knows about Alli, I think he is happy. Life is going to be as it should be. Next week we will be husband and wife, a family. She noticed he grabbed his kidney area but decided to wait to see if he would say anything. Today, life became good.

She spoke, "Jeremy, after we get married, do you think we could go and see my parents in Texas? They have never seen Alli, and I know they will love you. I told them about you before Alli was born. I know you will win them over. Don't worry about money, I have plenty for us. When we marry, it will become our money. Do you have a passport? Alli and I have ours. Since she was born she has dual citizenship."

Jeremy replied, "I would love to go to Texas for our honeymoon and meet your parents. Let's leave next Thursday."

Chapter 36

A MANDA AND MARVIN RETURNED TO the farm; both were tired needing rest. Amanda's ordeal at the hospital was tiresome, she had all she could do to stay awake.

Marvin looked at her and knew, "Darling you need to rest. I think you should go to bed. In the morning we can decide when to leave for our trip."

"You're right Marv, I am tired. Why don't you lie down with me and hold me until I go to sleep?"

So they undressed, got into bed and it did not take long, and they were in dream land. They slept through the long night, arose rested and began a new day.

Amanda looked over at Marv, smiled and said, "Darling I know how we can start the day, she slipped out of her nightgown, held her arms wide, inviting him into them. He stepped into her and began kissing her all over her. He could hear her gasp and moan; he was loving it, she pulled him closer. She suddenly pushed him over and she began kissing him all over, she rose and told him she loved him and quickly continued kissing him and was in heaven. She said to him, now my love, now! One hour later, they both headed to the shower, still feeling charged up, and enjoyed each other again before finally washing up, dressing, and heading for the kitchen to make breakfast.

After they made his coffee and her tea, Marvin looked at her and said, "Darling I sure do like the way you start your day, I love you."

Amanda responded, "You know, for an American, you're not half bad." When she saw his look she broke down and laughed and couldn't stop until he grabbed her and kissed her.

After they had breakfast Amanda called Jeremy to find out their plans. He told her that Sammie and he were going to marry on Wednesday and then on Thursday they were going to go to Texas to visit her parents. Amanda told him that her and Marvin would be there to see them get married and officially welcome Sammie and Alli into the family. That made Jeremy very happy, said goodbye and hung up.

Amanda turned to Marv and said, "looks like our trip won't start until Thursday.

Marv grinned saying, "Well, maybe we should jump back into bed." He got the famous elbow to the ribs.

She got out the maps for Scotland to decide where to go and what to see. He bent over her, "My ribs feel like they are broken." He almost got another shot to the ribs.

Amanda got a call from the PM office asking her when she was going to clean out her office so the new PM could move in. She thought about it and then said today. She hung up, looked at Marvin, "I need a ride into town so I can clean out the office. I don't have too much, so it shouldn't take too long. We could call Delores to see if she might be free to have lunch."

"Sounds good darling, you get ready, and I will call Delores." When he called her he found out that Jefferson was with her, and both would join them for lunch. As they left he told Amanda what the plans were.

Amanda was amused, "My, since Delores had her makeover she sure has been active. Now she is with my friend Jefferson. How intriguing." They reached the office and found Jennifer was already there. Amanda called her to meet them. They went up and began removing her belongings. On the desk was some mail that was addressed to Amanda.

Most were from well-wishers, but one was from the Royal Bank. Curious, she opened that one first, it read: Madam Watkins: Your daughter, Maureen O'Dell left instructions for us to notify you in the event of her death, that we send this letter to you after five years to inform you that she has a safety deposit box with you as her next of kin. Her instructions will allow you access to said box. Please call us when you can come in and deal with these instructions. Sincerely, Gordon James, President, Royal Bank.

Amanda just stood there not saying a word, she handed the letter to Marvin, he read it, handed it back. She said, "I have no idea what to make of this. I did not know she had a deposit box. I wonder why all the mystery. I will call Mr. James and maybe we can go after lunch or first thing tomorrow."

"Why don't you wait until first thing tomorrow morning, in case we need a longer time to deal with whatever it pertains to?" Amanda called and made an appointment for in the morning. She knew she would be wondering all night, but she did not think it could be anything major. If it was, she would already have known.

They finished and asked Jennifer to join them for lunch and went off to Editors. When they got there Delores and Jefferson were already there. Amanda asked Jefferson if he knew about Maureen's bank box. He answered no, he really did not have any dealings with her. I do remember that she always had this mysteriousness about her, at the time I dismissed it.

"Well I will just have to wait until tomorrow. Maybe having some mystery will be fun." They all had a good laugh and proceeded to have lunch. The topics of discussion were many and Amanda broke the news that Jeremy and Samantha were to be married on Wednesday. Then her and Marvin would be leaving on Thursday. She turned to Delores with a smile and asked with a grin, "What's going on with you?"

Even Jefferson was smiling knowing Amanda was having fun trying to trap her. Delores caught on so she decided to play along. "Oh Amanda I have been having so much fun with my knitting group, you know, knit one, pearl two. Then I go on to my reading group and we discuss everything but the books, but we never talked about you."

Amanda laughed and Marvin declared, "she got you!"

Jefferson spoke up and told Amanda, "It was always a pleasure working with her through the years and now you deserve to relax and do things you had to put off all these years."

She thanked them and then told them that the doctors ran many tests and discovered that the cancer was in remission. "I look forward to doing the many things I couldn't do before. I am going to deal with abused women and children plus women with Breast Cancer. Marvin has decided to work with the women and children and create a series of books of art all done by them to help support the centers.

Jennifer spoke up, "I would be happy to help either of you if you need me." They both said, "Deal."

Chapter 37

RUDOLPH RECEIVED A MESSAGE FROM Mrs. Mueller that she was called home for an emergency and was sorry they could not meet. "You know William, this could be an ok thing to happen, let's think of going back to London, you can keep your disguise and I have many things I need to take care of, things from my past that need to be addressed."

William was puzzled, "Dad, what from the past do you need to take care of?"

Rudolph hesitated, "William, once I deal with the people involved, I will tell you the whole story, it gets very involved. Have faith son, I do believe it will work out and if it does, things will change."

William was perplexed, what was going on. What was father hiding? How am I going to find out? I think it's from the past but how far back. When I get back to London I will have to do some investigating, I believe it must be something from long ago. Well I won't push him; he will come around. Well I will work on my disguise so I won't have any trouble getting back in the country then I think I will set something up to destroy that woman.

He took out his false passport and thought he should change it with his new disguise and new name. Dad said we could do that here; he knew where it could be done. He contacted the Swiss bank to draw out more funds he would need. He still had plenty of money in the account to last for a long time. No need to tell father how much, he would want a big share of it, and I am not going to share that much. Let him get his own.

Trouble seemed to be in the air. Little did he know, his world was going to fall with a big bang.

Jennifer went home to Edward, "did you know that Jeremy and Samantha were going to get married Wednesday?"

"Yes he called about an hour ago and wants me to stand up with him. I told him, yes I would. Are you free to go? Samantha is going to have Alli stand with her."

She was smiling, "Yes I can, Amanda and Marvin will be there also, I had lunch with them at Editors, Jefferson and Delores were there also. Edward, I think I am falling in love with you, how do you feel?"

To answer her, he took her into his arms and kissed her first tenderly, then with more passion, "Yes my love, I do love you. The first time I saw you, I knew." They stood there in each other's arms, she was shaking with joy, and he was holding on for fear of losing her, they both leaned back looking, and both could see the love, their love for the other, When Edward whispered, "My darling, let me be the one you desire and need for all time, I love you so much."

He heard her voice crack when she said "Yes." She held him so tight she took his breath away. She wouldn't let go; she found her love. Edward felt like he was in heaven, he was so happy. She finally relaxed her hold on him, he looked at her, "Darling when you are ready, I want to marry you, please say yes!"

He felt her shiver a little then she tilted her head, her eyes seemed to be looking through him, she smiled, "Your sweet soul now belongs to me, I say yes."

He wanted to pick her up and carry her to the bedroom but told her, we will wait until the honeymoon. She said thank you but hopefully that will be soon. Both were happy but decided to wait until tomorrow to make any decisions, they just wanted to enjoy this day.

During the evening there was a warm rain, but the morning sun arose and promised them that the day was going to be a good one. The birds were happy, singing like a grand chorus, their harmonies blending in, God was the director, the sound was sweet, the day was going to bring surprises to everyone. The day began and all who looked, could feel goodness and joy, but those who did not look did not know what was instore for them.

Amanda awoke feeling nervous wondering just what could be in that safety deposit box and why would Maureen wait five years to have it exposed. She reached over to her phone and saw that she had a message from Jeremy that came at 4:32 AM.

She had a bad feeling, so she called him immediately. It rang four times then the voicemail recording came on, so she left a message, call me as soon as you here this, Grandma.

She got up, headed to the shower, this day was going to be full of surprises. She hoped that they would be good ones not bad ones.

Marvin came in and asked if she needed help, she said always, he joined her. When they were finished they both looked happy. They decided to go into town for breakfast then go on to the bank. Amanda looked at Marvin, "Darling, I do not think I could do any of this without you, you have become, my Mr. Everything."

Marvin answered, "Amanda, you are my love and together we are a team, a team that's called M&A, we have become US, instead of you and I. They checked their watches and knew that they must go to the bank. They walked into the bank and waiting for them was the bank President.

"Madam so good to see you again, I hope that your retirement is going to be everything you want it to be." He escorted them to the box and opened it for her. "I will leave you, just call when you are finished.

Amanda was nervous, she opened the box and the first thing she saw was a letter addressed to her, from Maureen. She picked it up, her hand was shaking, Marvin took it and opened it up and placed the letter in her hands and asked her, "Do you want me to leave?" She shook her head and told him she needed him here. She opened it up and she recognized Maureen's handwriting.

Mother I know you are surprised reading this letter, but I need to tell you about my life after marriage that you had no idea of what I had to go through. My marriage to Keith started out to be wonderful but in a short time turned into a nightmare.

I went through many abuses from verbal and violence. Most of the time he would tell me no man would ever want me, and no man would think I was pretty, so I should be thankful to him for rescuing me. I began to believe him more and more. I came to believe that Daddy knew but choose to overlook things, because he wanted Keith to remain in the company. The company always came first with daddy, and you knew that even though you never called him out on it. You too were being manipulated as I was. As you look back you will realize you were.

One night at one of the company Christmas dinners, a beautiful man introduced himself to me after watching Keith degrade me verbally to dance. We were dancing and when it was over he just left me standing there in the middle of the floor. He never even said anything to me, and I walked away fuming. I stood over in the corner and this man walked up to me and introduced himself to me explaining that he was new to the company, telling me that a beautiful woman should not be so sad and asked me to dance.

I was so mad that I accepted. We were dancing and I felt so at ease with him, I really enjoyed it. He escorted me back to my corner, thanked me and walked away. Keith came up to me and loudly scolded me for dancing with a nothing man, how dare I. I was so mad and crying I left the room and went out of site down the hall. A few minutes later this man came up to me and said don't cry. He held me in his arms, and it felt so right. He kissed me and I became so excited. I started to return to the hall, I heard him ask if he could see me and when. I turned, went back to him, kissed him, and said soon. That mother was the beginning of the most beautiful affair. I really loved this man.

Amanda just sat there and could not believe what she just read. Even though there were more pages to read she was overwhelmed with this news. She had no idea Maureen was abused and she couldn't remember any tell-tale clues something was wrong. She knew there had to be many, but she just didn't see them, or she didn't want to see them. As she thought about the statement that Charles may have known, she had a hard time believing it. She asked herself, how could have I missed it, how could have I not known. It makes me feel like a bad mother.

She talked to Marvin, and he held her, consoling her. She looked at Marv and said, "I need to go on, there is more." She opened the remaining pages and began. I know you are wondering who this man is, but I will reveal his name soon to you.

Amanda stopped reading, tears were falling, she turned to Marv and said, "How could I have not seen any of this, how could I have not been aware of what my husband thought?" She asked Marv to get a bag so she could put everything in it and take it all home. There she could take her time and sort through everything in her own time.

Marv came back in with a bank bag, and they loaded it up and left. When they got home she decided to look at the contents tomorrow because she needed time to digest what she has already read. So to get her mind off all that information, she said, "let's go pack for our trip, it will help me to clear my mind."

They went upstairs and began to pack and soon they had all things ready. They sat down and talked about the letter. Marv asked, "How do you feel?"

She thought and then told him, "Well I read things I never expected and things I could not believe. I had no idea my daughter was being abused and I have a hard time believing my husband was so cold toward Maureen."

Marvin and she sat down on the bed and said to her, "Maybe you should start writing all this down and then you could put it order so it might be better to understand."

Amanda looked at him for quite a long time then spoke, "You know, maybe there is book there. I have been wanting to write a book about things that I have experienced." Sadness crept in and she told Marv, "I can't remember what Maureen's voice sounded like, it's gone."

"I know darling, I can't remember my wife's voice either. Somedays when I try it just is not there." Marv knew she was depressed but he vowed to help her any way he could. She looked over the letter addressed to her again, checking if she missed anything.

The other letters had a ribbon tied around them and were addressed to Maureen. Up in the left-hand corner was the initial, "R." She opened the first one.

My darling Maureen, it gave me great joy to spend the afternoon with you today. Getting to know you was exciting and I look forward to seeing you again. "R."

It was just a short note, but it did say a lot. As she continued to read she could see a pattern. They were getting more explicit. They showed that they were getting closer and closer. About four notes later, "R" talked of how lovely it was making love to Maureen. He claimed that she gave him a part of heaven. He told her that she made him feel so in love with her.

Amanda began to wish she could read the return letters from Maureen. She knew in her heart that they would have said that she loved him too. She decided to go to the last letter out of curiosity. My darling Maureen, how excited I was when you told me you were pregnant. I know that this child will be wonderful because he or she came from love.

She did not have to read anymore to know that "R" was the father and not Keith. She turned to Marvin, "I need to find this "R" because he is Jeremy's father. Let's call Stan and get him started in the search."

At the bottom of the bag she found an envelope with pictures in it and opened it up. They were pictures of Maureen with this man who Amanda assumed it was "R" they looked very happy together. As she looked at "R" she could see features of Jeremy in his face. She thought that she may have seen him in the past but could not recall where.

She began to tell Marvin about Jeremy's past medical troubles. "Jeremy had lost his right kidney to disease about eight years ago. Now we worry about the kidney disease coming back. If it does he would have to go on dialysis until a replacement could be found."

After telling Marv about this she called Stan and asked him to come over because she had a job for him and his new agency. Stan told her he would be there in one hour. She asked Marvin, "Do you think he was the father?"

"Well, bring me pictures of Keith and we can compare." She had some right there in the office, so she laid them down, side by side and began to look. They studied them together and finally Marv commented, "I do not see any factors from the pictures of Keith, but I do see some from "R" what do you see?"

She studied some more, "Well, I see the eyes are similar and the chin is shaped the same, so I would have to believe that "R" is the father."

"We will give all of this to Stan when he gets here and let him go to work. Now let's set it aside and start to think of our trip." They pulled out the maps and laid out a plan of things to see and places to spend the evenings. Amanda would certainly be recognized, so they had to adjust the plans.

Chapter 38

BEING A RETIRED PRIME MINISTER was a joy and a curse. Privacy was a thing you lose, so you adjust. Stan arrived and they explained what they wanted him to do, and he told them it would be difficult job, but he was sure it could be done. What he didn't tell them at the time was that he recognized "R" right away. As he left he knew where he needed to start looking.

Over at Samantha's house everyone was busy preparing for the wedding. Alli was trying on her new dress and Sammie was trying to make a wedding cake. Jeremy was talking on the phone to Edward about tomorrow's plan. "Do you think we should have a dinner? We could do it in Editor's banquet room."

"Yes we need to have a dinner, I will call Editor's and set it up for you. How many are coming?" They both counted, came up with fifteen people. Jeremy then planned for tickets for their trip to Texas to see her family. Samantha had called home and told them they were coming. She could hear their excitement in their voice's.

Jeremy grabbed his left kidney area again and Sammie saw it again. "Jeremy what's wrong? I have seen you grabbing you back three different times, are you not feeling well?"

Jeremy knew that he had to tell her what could possibly be wrong. "Eight years ago I lost my right kidney to disease, now I am worried that my left kidney may be going through the same thing. If that happens, I

152

will need a transplant to take care of the problem. It's only a slight ache right now, but it does worry me."

Sammie gave him a hug, "If you need anything, tell me, no more holding back. We have done that to each other for too long." Jeremy knew then that she really did love him and was going to be his partner in whatever came their way. Alli watched both and knew something was not quite right, she could feel it. She went to daddy and gave him a big hug and he leaned over and kissed her forehead.

You could feel the happiness in the house. Jeremy bent down to Alli, "Tomorrow I will become your daddy and that will make me the happiest man. How are you going to feel?"

Alli smiled, "I have been waiting for you daddy, welcome home." They had a group hug and the two grownups had tears in their eyes. Tomorrow was indeed going to be a big day after over five years of separation.

Stan was in his new office and was having a meeting with his employee's. He was telling them about Amanda's case and what they needed to discover. Birth records, any traces of pictures, etc. He withheld R's name for now because he wanted to inquire with the police in Denmark. He had a feeling he would be seeing Rudolph soon.

So he got his people searching for any records they could find. He did tell them that they would be looking for the real father of Jeremy O'Dell. The meeting broke up, Stan stayed at his desk and called Molly. When she answered he asked about William and Rudolph?

Of course she knew about William because of the blackmail and him being Amanda's secretary, but she did not know much about Rudolph. She remembered him working at the Watkin's company when her and Charles were having an affair, but she omitted that piece of information. She did tell Stan that he was a nice-looking man, very pleasant to her when she came around. She offered that Charles told her that he was doing a good job. Stan thanked her; told could not wait to be back in her arms. After the I Yu's, they hung up.

William and Rudolph were gathering their things after William got a new passport with the name, Thomas Gladstone, British Citizen. Rudolph did not need a new one because he was not a fugitive. They purchased the tickets to return to London for later that evening. The customs offices were usually not busy in the evenings so it should be easier to slip into the country.

William did change the color of his hair to blonde with a mix of grey. It made him look somewhat older and he liked it. Of course Rudolph reminded him that the key to fooling the custom agents was to ack normal. A little nervous because calmness was a red flag, and we don't need that.

William was a little upset with his father, he did not have to be told all the time how to act. He wanted to say to him, "Give me a break, I know what I am doing." But he didn't, he let it slide. They decided to have lunch and then head off to the airport. Rudolph was somewhat excited to be returning. He had plans of which he never told William about, but he knew he would have to tell William that he was not his real father, he was adopted when he was three years old. He knew he should have told him long ago, but you can't go back.

Chapter 39

MARVIN WAS IN HIS STUDIO when his phone rang, and he was surprised when he saw the ID. Richard, President of the United States. He answered with, "Hey you old fart, then he heard, please hold for the President." Richard heard that and began to laugh loudly. "Boy you just got caught. Marvin I am planning an anniversary party do you think you and Amanda can come? It's going to Saturday June 18th in New York City." Marvin thought for a short minute and said, "Yes we can. We will stay at my apartment and enjoy the city and your party." They continued to talk about everything but politics although Marvin did ask him if he was looking forward to retiring and got a positive answer. Richard told him to enjoy their trip to Scotland and relax. "Why don't we plan a trip together after I'm out of office? We can let the ladies pick our destination."

Marvin scratched his head, "Do you think that would be a good Idea, no telling where we would end up. I know Amanda's always wanted to go to New Zeeland. I will run it past Amanda and you can run it by Ellen, then they will be on the phone working it out and we can go along for the ride." They laughed as they hung up.

Rudolph and William got to the airport and went through customs with no trouble. William's disguise was perfect, but Rudy didn't need one.

Little did they know, Stan had asked the British customs to be on the lookout for Rudolph. He knew that William wouldn't be far behind. He was feeling lucky. This investigation could prove to be easier than he thought. As the evening approached the wind calmed down and folks came out for walks someone was knocking on Delores's door.

A well-dressed man about in his mid-forties. Delores answered, "YES!"

"Hello Mrs. Stafford, my name is Todd Evans, and I am a producer for the local TV station, and I would like to talk to you about doing a new talk show for our station. I have watched you since becoming good friends with our former Prime Minister, I have been impressed with how you react to different people and your look photographs well."

Delores was surprised, "Why in the world would you want me?"

"We are not looking for a celebrity, we would like someone who represents the people. Someone who does not compete with the guests but is interested in them as people and we believe you are that person. We have interviewed your neighbors, and all seem to think you are the woman for the job."

She invited him in and wondering why me? He continued telling her that this program would concentrate on the everyday aspects of the guests lives. The more he talked the more she became interested. He would like her to come down to the station for a test run to see how the cameras would see her. She was still puzzled but did want to explore it and see where it would lead, so she accepted. Excited she called Jefferson to tell him the news. Oddly enough, he already knew, they had gone to him first because he was on their board. He told her; he did not want her to find out from someone else.

Surprised, she remained excited, her thoughts were new beginnings. Jefferson asked her to dinner to celebrate and to just be with her. He was growing very fond of her. His thoughts of Delores were becoming serious, and he wanted to see where it might lead, hopefully, more romance.

Jeremy awoke, excited and nervous, wedding day. Amanda had arranged for her minister to perform the ceremony at 1:00 PM and then they would all go to Editors which Grandma was more than happy to provide. He felt a slight pain in the left kidney area and thought not today please. Go away until later.

Alli was already up and was super excited. She thought of Jeremy and was happy he was going to be her father. It is going to be so much fun. She heard her mother call, breakfast is ready, she and Jeremy met in the hall and down they went. They looked at the table and said what kind of breakfast is this. Samantha laughed and told them that this is a Texas breakfast, so you better get used to it, Bacon, eggs, fried potatoes, ham, sausages, Texas toast, jellies, hot sauce, OJ, the works. They started eating and commented how they loved it, which made Sammie very happy. The day started off with all in a happy mood. Afterword's they got ready for the day Jeremy and Sammie had been dreaming of for about for five years.

Amanda had sent a car to them, and they were on their way. Arriving at the church everybody was there, and the short ceremony took place. Alli was standing up for her mother, Edward was standing up for Jeremy and the Minister's words spoke directly to them, "Be with God." These three words made Jeremy choke up because he felt that his kidney was once again going to be a problem. He silently asked God to watch over him. The Minister announced that they were, husband and wife, heard the applause, kissed each other, and kissed Alli, and down the aisle they went. Happiness filled the room. The stood around a short time and off they went to Editors for a party.

Once there Marvin stood and offered a toast. "I have only known these three for a short time, but in that time I have become very close to them, Samantha, your beauty, and intellect are your treasure, Jeremy your talent as an artist will take you far, and Alli what can I say, since knowing you my days have become much brighter. Happiness to this family always."

The clinking of glasses could be heard, they all said, "Hear, Hear." The party lasted for three hours, The newlyweds went home to pack for Texas, the Malloy's went home to make final preparations for their trip to Scotland, Jefferson and Delores went to the TV station to meet with them, Edward and Jennifer began talking about their relationship and Stan got a ping on his phone letting him know that Rudolph and William were back in England. He alerted his crew, and they were on the lookout for them.

They did spot Rudolph, but William's disguise got past them. When the two-meet outside they took pictures and followed them. Stan called the Scotland Yard to inform them, and they moved into action. They located them and stepped in to arrest William for fleeing the country. They didn't have any charges on Rodolph, so they released them. Stan's men kept a watch on him so Stan would know where he could be reached. Turned out to be a good day's work. As they were taking William away he had a look of, help me father, but he was not saying a word. He knew he would no longer be able leave the jail, so he had to accept his predicament. He did give his father the information about withdrawing his money from the foreign accounts so he knew he would be taken care of.

The next morning everybody was on the move. Jeremy's family heading for Texas, Amanda, and Marvin for Scotland. Everybody had their own wants and needs, things returning to normal, whatever normal is. Delores and Jefferson were back at the TV station doing test runs with the camera and things looked good. They brought in fake guests for Delores to talk to, and she turned out to be a natural. Everybody was happy and they took her into the offices and offered a contract. Alas the Delores talk show was born. They projected about two months to organize before the first airtime. Delores told Jefferson, "It is amazing how fast your life can turn around. This new adventure is going to change a lot of things for me."

After William was arrested, Rudolph went back to his apartment to do some soul searching. He thought of Jeremy and wished that he could have known him growing up, but Maureen would not divorce Keith for some reason. He suspected that her father was the bad guy. He knew that Charles was a crook in his business dealings but proving things was the hard part. He had tried but got framed by him and sent to prison for eight years.

The plane crash went through his mind, he was not sorry for Charles and Keith but was devastated because his one true love also perished. He got out some old pictures of Maureen, looked them over and in his solitude, cried and sobbed. After he settled down his thoughts went back to Jeremy and his new family. He felt positive that they would be okay, so he felt it better that he does not interfere.

Hungry, he went to the pub, grabbed a newspaper to read, ordered his food and then saw Jeremy's and Samantha's picture along with Allison in the just married column. Looking at Allison he saw Maureen. That was his granddaughter, he felt a sense of pride, sat up straight, yes he had pride for the first time since he left prison. He read that they would be going to Texas to visit her people for the honeymoon. He felt a sudden loneliness, he could not be involved with their lives. Lucky Amanda.

As Jeremy was boarding the plane he felt a sudden pain and knew then that his kidney was the problem. He decided that when he returned he would go to see his doctor and get it fixed. He was not going to ruin this trip, just tough it out. When the plane took off he heard Alli go Wheeee, up we go. When they land, they would be in Dallas, Texas. All Jeremy could think of, "Howdy Pardner!"

Samantha leaned over, "What's so funny?" He told and she broke out in a big laugh. "You are going to make a funny sounding Texan with that accent." The three of them relaxed, turned on a children's movie and their adventure began.

Chapter 40

S TAN WENT TO THE JAIL to talk with William. William was so depressed they had a suicide watch on him, but Stan did not think that was necessary. William has been an actor all his life, fooling people. Stan was trying to determine if William knew anything about Jeremy. After their conversation he reached the conclusion that William knew nothing.

What Stan did not know was that William was adopted and not Rudolph's real son. From there Stan went to the records office to try and determine proof of fatherhood of Jeremy. Going through the records he did find one that said Keith was the father, but as he looked at it, something was wrong. It just did not have the look of the rest of them. He held it up to the light and could not see the water spots that the rest of them had, so he knew it was false. He did not say anything to the clerk, because he knew she could not do anything about it. He did write down the numbers of the certificate.

He then went to the head of the department to talk of possible fraud. He suspected that Maneen's father had something to do with it. At that time Charles had a lot of influence, he could demand and receive what he needed. He presented his case to the director, "Do you think that this could have happened?"

"Most assuredly, it has happened many times before. Sad to say but if enough money passes, it will be done. We have discovered many cases like this taking place during that time. Documents of all kinds were forged by the previous directors, but I do think that we have made the necessary changes to prevent it from happening again."

Stan was impressed with his friend, "Could you look into it for me, I do need the information for my client?" They shook hands, Stan left to join Molly for a late lunch. These two people seemed to be a mismatch but were so happy together it was working. Love wins again.

As Amanda and Marvin were driving to their first destination they were discussing the newlywed couple. "OH they looked so happy! I feel that they have a bright future and that Alli is precious, smart for a girl of five going on six, but Marv, I have something I need to tell you.

As you know, Jeremy lost the right kidney but now his left side is bothering him, so now if the left goes bad he would have to go on dialysis and get a transplant. I have noticed him grabbing the area of the left one but hope that it is not the kidney. He does not need that now."

Marv drove on, "Darling, that news is sort of shocking, but now they have been very successful with these transplants. Finding a donor can be difficult at times, but they check all family members first. It should work out. You know that when I was younger, I signed up to be an organ donor but now I believe that I have past the age of donation."

They drove on for a little longer, came around a corner and there stood a broken-down house, no windows, wood bleached by the sun, shutters blown by the wind, chimney in pieces, shingles, mainly missing and Marvin says, "Do you suppose that is the cottage we are going to stay in?"

While he was laughing he felt the famous elbow once again. Even though they had just started out they were having fun, enjoying themselves, learning each other's likes and dislikes, they were in love! They found the B&B they were going to stay in for two days, walking hand in hand inside, the honeymoon joy began.

Jeremy and Sammie along with Alli landed in Dallas and waiting for them were Martha and Bradley Bernard, Sammie's parents. After Sammie was done hugging them she introduced Jeremy and Alli to them and they had a big group hug. Sammie had not been home for over five years, and she vowed she would never stay away that long again. They had about a two-hour drive to their homestead.

Bradley was an electrician during the day and a small rancher by night. He scooped up Alli and said, "Let's go see the horses." He and Alli went off, laughing, hand in hand. Jeremy was as excited as Alli, he never had seen a ranch before. All he could visualize was cowboys with six shooters. As he looked around he soon discovered it was not anything like that. He was already enjoying this trip when just then the pain came back. He was determined to hide it, but Sammie saw it. She could tell by his look if it was severe. So far, it was mild, but it was there.

They gathered up the luggage and started in when they heard Alli yell, Bradley had saddled the horse and had Alli riding already. She was a natural, looking like she belonged there. Samantha was happy they decided to come. She gave Jeremy a kiss, whispered, "I am so glad we came; I have missed my folks so much."

It was evening back in Scotland, Amanda and Marvin were sitting outside around the fire pit talking to the other guests of the B&B., when one of them said, "I feel like I should know you and I am trying to figure out where from. Who are you?"

Amanda was amused, "Why I am the new Mrs. Malloy. We just got married and I am just getting used to being the new Mrs. Malloy."

"Well I know you from somewhere. Wait a minute, are you Amanda Watkins, former Prime Minister?"

"Guilty as charged." Everyone got acquainted with each other and talked about just being relaxed. The stars were out, and the wind lessened, a romantic evening. As Amanda and Marvin went back to their room they felt a sense of relaxation. This trip is turning out to be just what they needed.

Marvin remarked, "I think we should take our time in returning, we both need to rest. How is your chest where Thomas hit you?"

"Oh it is still sore but getting better. For whatever reason, I am glad that the Breast Cancer is gone. It may be back, but we can deal with that when we need to."

As they went into their room Marvin could see the friskiness in Amanda's eyes, so he started to yawn as if he was tired. He loved teasing her; he poured it on some more. Finally she took hold of him, "Hey fellow, no play acting tonight, tonight you are mine!"

Rudolph was in his room reading the paper. He learns the success Jeremy had at his showing and of his marriage. He wished he could have been there with his son but, not meant to be. While in prison he followed him as best he could. He knew he worked for Amanda in her office and hoped that someday he could present himself as his father. He read the reviews of the Art Show and was quite pleased. He laughed; he must have gotten his talent from his mother because he didn't have any. A tear came to him as he thought about his beloved Maureen and recalled how she died. It had to be terrible.

As he thought of her, he tried to understand why she stayed with Keith. The man was a tyrant, even to Charles. He could not figure out what hold he had over Charles. It must have been something major. He did know Charles was shady, but he could not put it all together and he gave up trying. He served his time but resented that Charles framed him. He saw that all of Jeremy's paintings were still on display, so tomorrow he would go look at them.

Samantha and her dad were walking around the barns looking at the livestock. She commented that she missed this place, but she was happy in London. Dad asked her about money, she laughed, "Dad I have plenty, don't worry, we are comfortable. I would like to have you and mom come over to see us, you would love it. It's not Texas but it will be fun. He smiled but said what she expected, cannot leave the ranch. She knew then that she would have to work on her mother to get him there. Her father got a serious look on his face, "Does Jeremy have something wrong; I saw him holding his back like he was in pain?"

"Well dad, something is wrong, but he has not told me yet just what it is. I have made up my mind that tonight I would ask him." As they walked into the house they heard a loud sound coming from Sammie's bedroom. She rushed in and saw Jeremy doubled over in pain, holding his back. The pain was intense, so they called 911. He told her, "It's my left kidney, it feels like it is blowing up. I have been feeling it for quite a few days now, hoping it would go away. I lost my right kidney about eight years ago, so I know what it is."

When the ambulance arrived they did his vitals and gave him some pain medication so he could calm down and then transported him to the hospital. Once there, they confirmed that his left kidney had enlarged and was the cause. They eased the pain with treatments and advised him to see a urologist soon once he returned to London.

After three hours they released him, and they returned to the ranch.

He went to bed to rest and fell to sleep right away. Sammie and her parents talked of Jeremy's problem. The talk of a transplant came up knowing that would be problem. Finding a match could take a long time. Alli was upset and worried about her father. She knew that something was wrong, "Mommie, is he going to be alright?"

"Yes dear, he is going to be ok." After supper, Jeremy came out of the bedroom still tired but looking better.

"Sorry folks, I did not mean to cause trouble. About 8 years ago I had an attack and lost my right kidney. When the pains started on the left side I was afraid that it was my left kidney. I have worried that something like this would happen. If it gets worse, I will have to go on dialysis so my blood can be cleaned. From what I have read that can take up to three hours or more three times a week. I think they now have at home machines to do the job. Just know that whatever I need to do, I will. The Doctor told me I should be able to be here with comfort until we get back to London. Now, what have we got to eat; I am hungry."

Alli listened, took daddy's arm, "Sit here daddy, I will take care of you. Grandma showed me how to make a sandwich. Do you like ham or should I make peanut butter?"

The kitchen was filled with laughter and the tensions eased. Bradley spoke up, "I have decided to take the time off while you are here so we can enjoy ourselves and I talked to your mother, and we decided to come to London for next Christmas."

Sammie jumped out of her chair and gave them both a hug. The feeling in the kitchen was of extreme joy. Bradley picked up Alli, "Young lady, tomorrow you and I are going to ride the horses. If you are going to be my granddaughter, you must learn. By the time you return to London I will make you a true Texan." Oh, this trip was going to turn out to be wonderful. A family bonding together.

Chapter 41

THAT AFTERNOON IN SCOTLAND, MARVIN was taking research photos for future painting and Amanda was admiring how he worked. "Marv I have been thinking about the book I need to write. Everybody will expect me to write about my time as Prime Minister, but I think I need to write about my family and you and I coming together so quickly.

Here we are, a widower and a widow, joining together. I believe our story is the one that needs to be done. I could even put your letter in it. When I read that letter, something touched me, I cannot explain it I just knew I had to meet you. Did you feel the same way?"

"Amanda, when I saw your picture on that magazine I knew we had something. How can I explain it, I do not know? There was something in your eyes that drew me in. I saw the sadness there and then saw the happiness. I never really expected my letter to get to you, but God had reasons for it to reach you.

That very first day when we went to Editors I knew, I knew you were meant for me, and I was not going to let anything come between us. I loved you from the first time I saw you."

As Amanda was digesting what Marvin said, she told him, "When you came into my office I felt tremors in my body and my first thought was, yes, a real man. I must say Marv, you have proved to be all that I needed." She stood, hugged him, kissed him. "My darling, I do not ever want to be apart from you, I Love You."

Back in London Stan continued looking for the real birth certificate of Jeremy. He knew that somehow it was placed somewhere it might never be found. He called the director to see if he had come up with any ideas as where to look. "Hi George, how is the search going? Any luck?"

"Funny you should say that Stan, I hold in my hands what seems to be the real certificate. It passed all the parameters of authenticity; we have a winner. It does say that the father is Rudolph Abercrombie."

"Well that is who I thought it would be. I will stop by this afternoon and pick it up for my client. Thanks George, you saved me much time."

Amanda is going to be surprised, now maybe she can learn the whole truth about Keith and Maureen's marriage. She also needs to learn about her husband's activities. Charles was dealing with the criminal element selling his goods on the black market to whatever group came up with the money. His armory division sold under the table to many rebel groups. I just need to uncover the documents of proof. I will have to take Amanda with me to gain access to the records, seeing as she is the head of the company now. This will cause trouble at the company, but she holds all the cards, they cannot refuse.

Delores and Jefferson were looking over notes for her first interview. It is going to be with the acting Prime Minister, Gregory Mullins, leader of the conservatives. There will be a good chance that he will get the position. Instead of political questions they focused on more personal questions.

When Delores began, she let the audience know that she was nervous. It did not take long for Delores to relax, and you would have thought she was an old friend talking to another old friend. Afterword's the producers loved it; they knew they made the right decision with Delores. This show was going to be the teaser for the regular show.

Back in her dressing room, Delores told Jefferson how much fun it was. She looked at him, "Let's go celebrate." She took his arm; "I am going to take you to the pub by my house so we can be with my neighbors and friends, you will love them." When they entered the pub, all the gents stood and hollered Delores, she waved and introduced Jefferson to them all and the party began. Singing, dancing, darts, and much drinking. They were happy for Delores and her newfound friend. She leaned over to Jefferson, "I think we should film a show from here with these folks, what do you think?"

"Delores, you need to do what you think is right and as your new manager, I agree." She stood up, placed her arms around him and gave him a warm and deep kiss that had the people applauding, yelling "Go Girl." Delores's new life was fuller than it ever was. When they were leaving, they were arm and arm.

Jefferson smiled, "Darling you sure do make life exciting. How about you and I move in together?" Delores stopped in her tracks, "Jeff you surprise me, I never would have thought you would ask me that. I am not ready for anything like that." They walked into the next block when Delores stopped, turned to Jeff and said, "I think this show is just what I need." Delores thought about Jefferson, is he really the man I want. He's fun but is that enough? I just don't know.

Amanda was checking her emails when she came to the one from Stan. She opened it and read, "Amanda, I have found the correct birth certificate and it does show who the real father is, and it is not Keith. I will fill you in as soon as you return. I also have more news to share."

Marv stopped the car, got out quickly grabbed his camera and started taking pictures. She turned and saw this old broken-down older barn and she knew it would soon be a painting. She loved watching Marv work; he would get that serious look and she knew that the painting would be outstanding. It was like the artist could jump inside the painting and arrange how it would look when finished. His work was a new fascination to her. She did not realize how much work went into creating a thing of beauty. They would be getting back home tomorrow so tonight she had a surprise for Marv. His favorite dinner and a special desert. Tonight was going to be fun.

Back in Texas Alli was riding a horse like she was born to it. Samantha was watching, remembering when her daddy taught her how to ride and she could see the look in his eye, one filled with love for this little girl who in just three days stole his heart. She thanked God for bringing them all together. She looked over toward her mother standing with Jeremy, he had his arm around her, she saw happiness, her family was complete. Whatever Jeremy needed they would all support him.

She thought of Amanda, the woman who had the courage to bring them all together. She told her folks about her and would bring them together when they came to London. She showed them a picture of Maureen, Alli's grandmother, how much her and Alli looked alike. Next week they would all be back in London and just maybe, everything would be normal. She laughed, what is normal?

So many things to think about. Family came to mind. These past few months have been so fulfilling and now Jeremy was with her, we are so blessed. She thanked God for the blessings she received and prayed that God look after Jeremy and make him whole again. Amen.

As the sun rose, the sky turned orange with red blending in, the clouds taking on many colors, a new day was here. The blues came along with the reds. The beauty in the sky was marvelous and it was the best that could be.

Morning arrived in Scotland, Amanda and Marvin were up and preparing to depart and return to London. She checked her messages and found one from Samantha. She learned that Jeremy had an episode with his left kidney but was better. She passed the information on to Marvin. He was most concerned about Jeremy's condition.

"Darling, is Jeremy going to need a transplant?"

"Well I am not sure, but we need to get the best Doctors for his case."

"Darling, I believe that we need to let Jeremy and Samantha take charge. I do know you mean well, but this is their life now and we need to stay in the background and just support them. They will do fine."

Amanda looked at Marvin, "I understand what you are saying, it's just that I am used to taking charge. Maybe it is because I have this need to be the one who is the fixer of things."

"Amanda, your life has just gone through a drastic change, it is going to take time to return to a more normal life. You must remember that you need to let others step up and learn to take charge. Relax darling, things will work out. You must see that there is more than one way to solve a problem."

They loaded their things in the boot when Marvin took Amanda's hand, pulled her close, "Mrs. Malloy, you are my love, I promise to be by your side always, so you will remember, I give you this necklace to remind you that my love is never ending. Look on the back and you will see what you mean to me." She turned it over and saw the engraving, M&A. As she looked up into Marvin's eyes, a tear rolled down her cheek. "Marvin, I have never been loved like you are loving me. I feel so free with you, knowing you will be there for me."

Chapter 42

RUDOLPH WAS IN HIS APARTMENT when there was a knock on the door. He went to the door and looked through the peep hole and saw Stan. He opened the door and Stan said "I bet you never thought you would be seeing me. May I come in?"

Rudolph opened the door and let him in. He offered Stan a seat, "So what do you want?"

"I have a client who hired me to search for a document to prove fatherhood."

"Let me interrupt you, are you talking of me being Jeremy's father?"

"Yes I am. Are you his father?"

"Yes I am, and I have known since before he was born. Maureen and I were lovers and I tried very hard to convince her to leave her husband, but she wouldn't. Keith had something over her, but I could never figure what it was. Maureen never knew this, but I went to Keith and tried to convince him to set her free. He never did. I can tell you this, I do not want everyone to know that I am his father, I don't want Jeremy to know either. After I die you can tell him but right now I do not think it will do him any good. Selfish, yes but that is the way I want it and you can tell Amanda if you choose, let Jeremy go on thinking Keith is his father."

Stan was surprised at this revelation. He had gained a new respect for Rudolph. "Rudolph, I want you to know that I am working to find proof that Charles framed you and caused you to go to prison. If I find it I will bring it to you." Stan got up to leave, offered his hand to Rudolph. He took it and even said "Thank you."

After Stan left, Rudolph could not believe what Stan told him about finding proof of his innocence, he always knew he was framed but to have someone else believe it was promising. Where he might look for proof was puzzling, but he knew it was out there somewhere.

Stan left Rudolph and decided to talk to Molly, because she was Charles's mistress during that time. She just might have some information that could lead him to the proof. He would like to find it so everything could be cleared up. After calling Molly they decided to meet for supper at the pub. The traffic was light, so he made it there in record time. When he entered she was already there?

"Stan, you look delicious, I ordered you a drink."

"Darling, my day has been busy but tonight I am yours."

"Oh, that's sounds yummy, kiss me for starters." Stan gave her a kiss that told her that he was anxious, "Dear you look ravishing."

Stan decided not to bring up Charles tonight but would wait until tomorrow. They ordered their dinner and talked about their day. Molly told him that Amanda would be back tomorrow. He told her, "I need to talk to her, and I want you to be with me when I do." Molly smiled, "Of course I will, whatever you need I will be there for you."

While Stan and Molly were enjoying dinner, Edward and Jennifer walked in looking like two young lovers. You could see the joy on their faces. They spotted Molly and Stan, waved, and were led to their table. Jennifer went to their table and told Stan that Amanda said she could see him at three o'clock. He thanked her and she went back to her table. Molly remarked, "Were we ever that young?"

Stan said, "It was so long ago, I don't think so." Outside it began to rain, washing away all the day's troubles, so a new day would bring new hopes and dreams.

During the night, Jeremy got out of bed and stood on the porch gazing at the stars. He could see so many more here in Texas than he could in London, because there were no city lights. His father-law joined him, "Son I heard you get up, are you okay?"

"Yes, I am a little sore, but I am feeling better."

"Well Son, the one thing I have learned in life, is to never hold anything in because it will hurt more if you do. Asking for help is a difficult thing to do but you need to trust in others. It took me a long, long, time to seek help but once I did things changed. They will for you too. I do not know what kept you and Sammie apart, but I can see the love you have for her, so treasure it, enjoy it and things will work out."

He left Jeremy standing there looking at the stars again. He already loved his in-laws, he felt happier now than before. His mother came to his thoughts, and he could see her plainly watching over him and he told her, "I love you mom!" He looked around and she was gone.

In the morning, Alli told her father that she saw grandma last night, she kissed me and then she was gone. He looked at Alli and said, "I saw her too and then she was gone."

Samantha heard them, "Who did you see?"

"Oh nothing dear, just a dream." He leaned over to Alli, "Our secret." Alli giggled, "OK."

After breakfast Alli, Sammie, and grandpa were going riding to check on the cattle. Alli was turning out to be a natural at riding. Grandpa was loving it. When Sammie was Alli's age she too was a natural. He thought hopefully, they would move back to Texas to take over the ranch for him. They had plenty of space to build a house. He wasn't getting any younger, and he would like to take trips with his wife while still in good shape. He thought about going to Alaska for a summer. He already investigated renting a place in the bush. His wife was all for it.

She has been there before and telling him what it was like sparked his interest. They both would like to go to Australia and New Zeeland also. But first they needed to convince Jeremy and Samantha. At the same time both said, "Let's talk about it at supper." The plan was put into place.

Amanda and Marvin got back around noon, refreshed from the trip, unpacked, went through the mail, found nothing unusual, saw that the fridge was stocked, made lunch, and sat down and Amanda started to talk about the book she wanted to write. Their story.

She asked Marv, "tell me about when you first saw my picture." He told her before, but this time he added more details. As he was telling her, she could see how excited he got. Just listening, she knew it would be vital to the story to tell it like he lived it.

Marv, I have a question? "Should I make it fiction, and should I make up different names?"

"Yes different names and you might want to make up different occupations to protect yourself."

She did not even think of these things. "You have given me plenty to think about. I would never have thought of this." She went off to her study to jot down some notes and consider doing a rough draft. "Let me know when Stan gets here."

Marvin got out his camera to begin working on his plans for a next painting. He had an idea what he wanted to paint, and he saw that he needed to combine three photos into one so he could paint all aspects he needed into one. He would take it to the studio and begin sketching. He could already envision the angles he wanted and where to place them.

He thought of Edward, this would be a good painting for him to help and learn. Ed had a good eye; he just needs to develop it more.

Stan arrived a little early, but he was anxious to tell Amanda how much he discovered. He wondered how she would take the news that Rudolph was Jeremy's father. After talking to Rudolph, he gained a new respect for him. Amanda answered the door, gave Stan a hug, and was surprised to see Molly with him. Marvin came from the study, greeted them, and escorted them to the study.

Stan began, "I have found the original birth certificate, I also have discovered some evidence of wrongdoing from Keith and Charles. I asked Molly to join us because she was as you already know, Charles's mistress and might have knowledge of what was taking place at the time."

Amanda said, "Molly and I have talked about this time, and you may be right, there just might be something she knows but doesn't realize how important it might be."

"Since Stan asked me to be here, I have tried to look back and recall our many conversations, and to figure out just what Charles was saying to me."

As Stan opened his briefcase, he got the certificate out along with the phony one. "If you look at this one you will see the watermarks are different from the real one is. Hold them up to the light and it is easy to detect. Now the phony one says that Keith is the father. We know this to be false because of what Maureen's letter tells us. Now we look at the real one and it says, Rudolph Abercrombie is the father." He let that sink in for a moment. He could tell Amanda was surprised but Molly did not look surprised at all.

"I remember him, he was tall and handsome, but Charles did not like him at all. I remember he was talking to Keith and telling him he was going to get even with him. He was very angry at him." Stan then told them, "Rudolph does not want Jeremy to learn that he is his father. I also learned that William is not his son, he adopted him when he was three years old from the orphanage that he came from. When you gave me this assignment, I was already knowing who the father was but did not know about William. I had a talk with Rudolph yesterday and he has known all this time he was the father. Maureen asked him to remain silent about it but has never figured out why."

"Amanda, he sent you a message, he thanks you for being who you are, and he wishes that you do not reveal his identity to Jeremy. He feels that to tell him might be bad for him. All he asks is that you send him pictures to see Alli's progress. She looks so much like Maureen."

"I also uncovered some proof that Charles framed Rudolph so he would be sent to prison. I do not have all of it yet, but I will find it. Amanda, Charles sold guns and ammo to rebels and the underworld. Amanda, your husband was a crook, a big-time crook, and Keith was his partner. Because of this I believe that Maureen knew and that is the reason she would not divorce Keith. She was protecting Rudolph. I told Rudolph that when I gathered enough evidence I would turn it over to the right people so he can be pardoned of his supposed crimes. I am going to leave it all here, I have copies to work with. I hope I haven't upset you."

Amanda took the papers, "No, I am not upset, I think I knew most of it but didn't want to face it. Later I will contact Rudolph and have a long talk. I need to set things right." She placed the papers in her safe and thanked Stan for his hard work and hugged Molly, suggesting they talk and try to piece things together.

Molly agreed, "I will come by tomorrow and bring my papers and see if there is anything of use." Marvin stayed quiet and observed. He formed opinions but would tell Amanda when everyone was gone. Stan and Molly said their goodbye's and left.

"Marv, what do you make of all this?"

"I think Molly knows more than she is saying. I watched her closely; something was troubling her, and I am not sure she is willing to tell you. I believe she and Charles were a lot closer than she's telling you. Her body language was giving her away."

"Do you really think that? I thought she had been open with me, but I will dig a little deeper and see what happens."

"If you need help, I will be around."

Amanda went to her study and looked over the papers Stan left, and she saw Rudolph's address, she wrote it down and placed it in her briefcase. If she could, she was going to contact him with the hope of talking about his time with Maureen. She needed to know more. She felt lost, so she pulled Maureen's letter out and reread it again while thinking of the new information she had. It all started to make more sense to her. She set it aside, knowing that she would come back to it later. She opened her computer and brought up the notes for her book. The preliminary title was "The Widower." She wrote down chapter one and began.

Marvin came in about three hours later and he saw chapter four written on her computer. "Wow, you have been a busy lady today. Are you happy with what you have written so far?"

"After I have written ten chapters I will let you read them and be my first critic, okay?"

"That sounds good to me, darling. Tomorrow I will be going to the studio to start on my new painting, so you will have the whole day to test Molly. Good luck with that."

Allison was turning into a very good rider. She loved the horses and the cattle. Last night at supper she asked, "Daddy can we move to Texas? I could have my very own horse." Of course everybody laughed but Allison did not know but she had just planted a seed. Whether it would grow, nobody knew, but the idea was there.

Jeremy's kidney was acting up again and he was thinking about returning to London to see his doctor. He was sure that he needed a transplant. They told him years ago it could happen. He made up his mind to talk with Samantha. He knew she and Alli would be disappointed but getting better was his priority. Just becoming a family was exciting and he wanted to keep on being a family. He decided to talk to his father-law first. He found Bradley in the horse barn, "Dad can I talk with for a minute? I am still having trouble with my kidney, and I think we should return to London and have the doctors look at it. I know that Sammie and Alli will be disappointed, but I need to take care of this before something happens."

"Well son, I have been watching you and I saw this coming. Martha and I talked about this last night and then we spoke to Sammie, and she has seen it too. We expected this to happen, so go and talk to Sammie and make arrangements. Your health comes first."

He went back inside the house and found Samantha and Alli, sat them down, "I think I need to go back to London and go see my doctor about this kidney. I do not want to delay because it could turn out to be very serious."

"Jeremy, I agree with you, let's make the arrangements and after you are fine we can come back and spend more time here. Alli loves it, so let's take care of you first."

"Darling, I love you." They had a group hug, then Jeremy got on the phone to make the arrangements. After, he called Amanda and asked her to make an appointment to see the doctor. That taken care of he started to pack their things. He felt sad but knew he had to go home. He called Edward to meet them at the airport, so they had a way to get home. That done, he went downstairs to the kitchen to talk to Martha and Bradley.

In the short time he had known them, he felt like he was their son. He looked around and thought we could live here and love it. They all sat down in the kitchen and Jeremy told them, "Since I have been here I have come to love it here and I want to thank you for accepting me as your son. It means the world to me that Alli also loves it here and as soon as my kidney problem is taken care of, we will come back and think of moving here. I can do my artwork anywhere in the world. My mentor Marvin has shown me, they will come to me. We have seats on the morning plane, but we will return as soon as possible." There were hugs all around and a few tears to go with them.

Chapter 43

Edward put the phone down, "That was Jeremy, he's coming home tomorrow and asked me to pick them up at the airport. He told me all about his problems with his kidney years ago and now the left one is causing trouble. He is worried about needing a transplant."

"You know darling, we never know when trouble will grab us, so let's live for today and not tomorrow. I would be lost if anything happened to you.

"Edward, I think instead of waiting, we should get married now." Edward looked surprised, but as he thought of it, she could see his expression change to a smile. She knew then he would say yes.

"Darling, I agree, let's do right after Jeremy and Samantha get back." She almost knocked him over, she gave a squeeze and said "YESSSSSSSSS!"

To say she was excited would be an understatement. She immediately sat down and started to make planes for the wedding. "Now let's see, Jeremy as best man, Samantha as maid of honor, Alli as flower girl, oh we need a ring bearer. Who do we know? How about Marvin?"

"Don't you think he's a little too tall?"

Both laughed, "We will find someone."

Edward looked at her, "Let's go and find a ring. I know, let's call Delores and see if she can help."

Delores answered the phone while in her new office. "Find some rings, yes we can do that, if you let me bring a camera crew to film it for my new show."

Edward agreed, especially when she said the TV station would pay for them for doing a show on young love. They got to the Jewelers and the crew was already there following Delores's instructions. She told them how it was going to be done and what questions she would ask.

They entered and the show began. They spent three hours there getting everything perfect and came out a happy couple. Delores spoke up, "We will probably air this next month. I'll be sure you get a copy of the show. Have you selected a date yet?"

"No we are waiting to talk to Jeremy and Sammie to get home tomorrow to figure it out, but it will be soon."

"Keep me informed, I would like to film it and show parts of it on the show." Delores said her goodbye's, thanked them for thinking of her and left with her crew.

Jennifer looked down at her ring, put her arms around Edward. "I love you Ed, now and forever." Ed was moved to tears and just held her close, never wanting to let go. He had this thought if he let go she would be gone. Love wins again.

This day in London was a day of joy, sun shining brightly and everyone in a happy mood.

At the jail though William was looking out the window wondering where his father was. He had not been there since he was arrested. William worried, did his father feel ashamed of him, did he feel disappointment because of him? As he wondered he got notified that he had a visitor. His dad, Rudolph was here. They escorted him to the visiting room and locked his wrist in a handcuff, then his father came in. "Dad it is so good to see you, are you doing alright?"

"Well son, I came today to give you some advice and I hope you will listen. I have talked to your Barrister and the prosecutor is willing to make a deal if you plead guilty to one count of blackmail. They are willing to drop the other counts. I highly recommend that you take the deal because your sentence will be much less. I know this will seem harsh, but it is the best deal you are going to get. What do you think?"

"Yes he told me about the deal, and I have been thinking about it, but I wanted to hear what you thought about it. Did he tell you how long I might have to be in prison?"

"Well, they are willing to agree on five years. If you decide not to take it, you could get fifteen to twenty years. It makes sense to take the deal. Your thirty-two now and when you get out you will be thirty-seven. You might get out early with good behavior, possible in three years. Take the deal son."

"Ok dad, now tell me about prison and what I can expect."

Rudolph told him about his experiences and how to get along in prison so they would not bother him. They talked for another thirty minutes and when Rudolph left he felt certain that William would take the deal.

When Rudolph left the jail he realized it was time for supper and thought he would go to his favorite pub, so he made his way to it. He walked in and saw a beautiful lady sitting all alone. He passed her and gave her a smile and she returned the smile. He sat down just a few tables away and while he read the menu he could not keep his eyes off her. The waiter went to her table, and he spoke like he knew her.

He called her Mrs. Stafford; she ordered her meal and saw him looking at her. She smiled again and he nodded to her. He raised his wine glass as if to toast her and she raised hers. She asked the waiter to ask him if he would care to join her. He walked over to Rudolph and asked him, Rudolph looked at her smiled, and got up and moved to her table.

"Hello, my name is Rudolph Abercrombie, I am pleased that you asked me to join you and you are?"

"Well hello, my name is Delores Stafford, and it my pleasure, believe me."

The two of them had that get acquainted talk and both became comfortable with each other. He stated he was single, and she stated that she was dating someone, but it was not serious. You could hear them laughing and getting along great. Rudolph asked, "Do you like dancing?"

"Oh yes, my late husband and I used to enter dance contests."

"Well there is a dance hall in the next block, would you like to go?"

Delores hesitated then answered, "Oh yes, I would love too. I haven't been since my husband passed and I feel comfortable with you, so let's do it."

They got up to leave and everyone could see that they were a happy couple. It was only in the next block, so they walked, and Rudolph offered his arm and Delores took it. The entered the dance hall and there were quite a few couples there, they had live music, so they checked their coats and proceeded to head for the dance floor. The band was playing a waltz and away they went. They were having a good time and when the slow dance came on the got close and moved to music, they looked at each other and both could feel a connection.

Delores leaned in, whispered, "Do you want to go to my place? I will not have any guests until this weekend."

Rudolph was excited, "I would love to go to your place, but I do not have a car."

"NO problem, we will use mine." So they danced one more dance and got their coats and left. When they got to Delores's, she put on some music and danced, Rudolph leaned down and gave her a kiss.

He pulled back and she moved in closer, kissed him hard and then asked, "Shall we go to the bedroom?" She took his hand and led him to her room and clung to him tightly, kissed him and began removing his shirt. They wasted no time getting undressed and began the dance. They were so good with each other that Rudolph stayed until after breakfast the next morning.

Chapter 44

AMANDA AND MARVIN WERE HAVING breakfast, talking about their day and what they would be doing.

"Well I am going to go to my studio and start working on my latest painting and sit down with Edward and discuss his future."

"Delores and Molly are coming over to talk about the past and I hope she will tell us more about Charles and her time when they were together. I did ask Delores over for support. If she can come up with something substantial, I will contact Stan and have him listen. Right now I am going to go in the study and write another chapter in the book."

Marvin kissed her goodbye, and she sat down and began Chapter five. She had written up to point where she was telling about finding the granddaughter. She had to stop and think things through, she wanted to get it right. This book was turning out to be about hers and Marvin's lives. It was hard writing about this and trying to hide the fact that a lot of it was true. She has already inserted fiction in it, but the reality is most of it would be true.

She had just finished the chapter when the doorbell rang, and she knew it would be Delores and Molly. The went to the kitchen where she had coffee or tea along with scones.

Delores opened the conversation and told them about last night. "I met this gorgeous man last night in the restaurant, asked him to join me and we had a marvelous dinner together. I have never done anything like this in my entire life. He asked me if I liked dancing, I told him yes and we went down the street to a dance hall. Oh could he dance; he swept me off my feet. We were both so excited, that I asked if he would like to come home with me. I know that sounds foolish, but you just had to be there. We got in the door, and I played more music, and we dance again to the slow stuff."

"Every move made me more excited, and he was just as excited, and I asked him if he wanted to go to the bedroom with me?"

"My goodness Delores, I never would have believed that of you, Amanda would you have believed it?"

"No I would not but I want to hear the rest of the story. Come on Delores, details."

"Well in my whole life I have never experienced love making like that. This man was the very best. He was concerned about my feelings and not his own. He did not leave until after I fed him breakfast. That was the best night in my entire life, and he asked me if he could see me tomorrow night. What do you think?"

"My goodness Delores, finding a man this considerate is special. When Charles and I were together, I never once had a night like that, but the very first night with Marvin I did, and let me tell you that all those years with Charles turned out to be wasted. I am so happy with Marvin."

Molly hesitated but began, "When Charles and I were having the affair I must confess, he was a lousy lover, and he did not know, at that time, I was also seeing two other men. I used Charles as much as he used me. I guess you could have called me a money grabber."

"Molly, the reason I asked you over I think you are holding information back. We have settled our differences, so feel free to say what you know because I am searching for answers that will help me understand the feelings that Maureen was having."

"Yes Amanda, I have been holding back." As she was telling the story Of Charles's dealings, Amanda began to understand things that he had done. It started to make sense now.

She picked up the phone and called Stan and told him that Molly was telling about Charles's dirty dealings and of Keith's involvement. Stan said he would be right over, and he was going to bring over two investigators and a secretary to make notes.

Chapter 45

MARVIN'S NEW PAINTING WAS ALREADY sold to a wealthy art lover. He made sketches and placed them to find out the best arrangement. As he worked, Edward came to talk with him. Marvin looked up, "Congratulations Edward, you surprised me, why so soon?"

"Well, when we learned about Jeremy's problem, we both thought, we do not know the future, so let's not wait. We are both excited and anxious. You will be there, won't you?"

"Amanda and I wouldn't miss it." Then they talked about Edward's future. Edward was thinking about working with Jeremy as his lead man. Marvin offered him the position of director of his New York Gallery. "You are ready Edward, after seeing the job you did with the show here, I know that you could handle it. Also you would be spending time between here and New York. I will start you out at $100,000 per year and if everything works, then we will talk about some serious money.

Go and talk it over with Jennifer. By the way we can find a position for her at the gallery. After the first year if all goes well, I want you to move back to London and open a gallery here."

"I am so surprised by your offer sir, you have caught me completely off guard, I don't know what to say. Jennifer is going to be completely surprised."

"Why don't you do this, go to New York for your honeymoon and stay in my apartment and then visit the gallery and see if it is what you might like to do and bring back your answer to me here. Call her and let's go to the pub for lunch and fill her in on the details."

They got to the pub before Jennifer did and ordered drinks. About ten minutes she came in and sat down with them. The waitress took her order and the lunch orders. Edward began to tell her of Marvin's offer, and you see excitement in her eyes. She asked Marvin, "Are you serious about this?"

"Yes I am, everything Edward has told you is true. Do not decide today, talk about it tonight and let me know tomorrow. I have already decided for you to use my apartment while you look around New York and as my wedding gift to you, I will pay for an apartment to live in while you are there that first year. Now let's enjoy lunch and talk wedding."

Marvin's phone rang, it was Amanda. "Marvin, you were exactly right, Molly was holding back much more information than we thought. Stan got it all and is going to use it to further the investigation. He said if he finds enough it will prove that Rudolph was innocent of all allegations. He thinks he can do it. When you get home I have a juicy story from Delores to tell you. You will love it."

"You alright?" Marvin nodded yes and went back to eating his lunch, "By the way Jennifer, I have an offer for you at the gallery, organizing all transactions. You are very good at that, and I am sure Edward would enjoy working together with you." They talked for at least an hour before they went back to the studio.

Chapter 46

JEREMY AND SAMANTHA WERE BACK in town and Jeremy's kidney was not doing good. He called the Doctor and could not see him for at least three weeks. Upset, he called Amanda, and she said I will take care of that, we will have you there tomorrow. He knew that when Amanda wanted something, she got it. She learned how to be tough as Prime Minister. He turned to Sammie and said, "Nice to know the right people."

Sammie hugged him, "Is it bad darling?"

"Yes it is, I honestly think I may need a transplant. Now that might take quite a long time. The match must be close to mine and finding one will be tedious. I think we will need a lot of prayers. Let's pray that they find one quickly."

Just at that time he was doubled over with pain, and it lasted for over ten minutes. Alli saw it and she started crying, "Daddy be ok, we need you now."

Sammie comforted her and she stopped crying. "What can I do Daddy to help you?"

Daddy looked at her and started to cry himself and said "let's pray Alli. Dear God, you brought us back together, now we ask that you help us through this so we can be a happy loving family. Amen."

Samantha felt sick to her stomach and rushed into the bathroom. When she came out she looked at Jeremy, "I think I may be pregnant. I do not think that was illness, I think that was morning sickness. I am going to the store and get a pregnancy test to find out. If I am I will be very happy, will you?"

"Oh yes!" Just then the phone rang, and it was Amanda. "You have an appointment at 8:00 AM tomorrow morning, I will meet you there."

"Thanks grandma, but there is no reason you need to be there."

"Sonny boy, I need to be there as much as you do. You may be my grandson, but you feel like a son to me."

Jeremy felt relieved that Amanda was in his corner, and he knew that she would be there whenever he needed her. Now he thought of Sammie and wondered if she was indeed pregnant. If she is I will be happy and I know that Alli will be thrilled having a sister or brother around. We will see tonight when Sammie takes the test.

Sammie went to the pharmacy and bought a test, brought it home. She went into the bathroom and did the test. She then waited because she did not know if she wanted to be pregnant. She saw herself in the mirror and decided that she indeed wanted it to show positive. She looked, stared for a minute, placed it down and entered the kitchen. Alli and Jeremy looked at her and he said Well? She had a hard time Keeping a straight face, but she did. Well the test was ---------- positive, I am pregnant.

Alli yelled hooray and Jeremy hugged her, kissed her, I am so happy.

Sammie spoke, "let's wait to tell everybody, I will take another test in a few days to make sure that it is positive. They do read wrong sometimes." It was a sad and now happy household now.

Marvin arrived home, "What's new?"

"Oh, it's been a big day here. First Delores told us about her meeting a new beau and what a great lover he is. He was with her all night and left after breakfast. She said she has never had a lover like him before. I told her that Charles was not a good lover and that the first time with you was the best for me. Then Molly spoke up and told us that when she was Charles's mistress, she was seeing two other men and Charles never knew. Crazy beginning. Then Molly told us all she could remember. Charles was selling guns to who ever wanted them.

He was also smuggling dope and contraband of any kind. She told us of things that could prove that Rudolph was innocent of any charges. If we find it then he would be a free man. Stan has two of his men on it. Molly was worn out when she got through. I told her that we were ok. Finally,

I got Jeremy an appointment with his kidney Doctor at 8:00 AM in the morning and I am going to be with him."

"Now, how was your day?"

"Well, as you know, I spoke to Edward about the New York position, then I thought about my opening a gallery here in London in a year and I would transfer him back to London as director of the gallery. I also offered Jennifer a job overseeing all transactions. She would be just right for it."

"There you go again, stealing my people. First Edward and now Jennifer. Maybe I should call Scotland Yard and have you arrested."

"Now Amanda, you know Jennifer would be going to New York, how would she work for you?"

"Ha-ha, got you going didn't I."

Marvin couldn't believe he fell for it. "You got me good Amanda." Then she gave him the first five chapters so he could read and critic it. She was going to wait until she had ten chapters but needed input now to keep her on track.

"Now Mr. Malloy, I do believe supper will be ready in about ½ hour so you have time to shower and freshen up, then I think we should have a date tonight, go to the pub and visit our new friends before we have a romantic interlude back here. Do You approve?"

"My-my, you have it all planned out, what would you have done if I said, not tonight dear, I have a headache?"

"Ha-ha, I guess I would have made you take a bottle of aspirin." "Oh my, you are going to get it tonight."

"I sure hope so!"

Chapter 47

STAN AND MOLLY WERE AT home talking about today's events. Molly looked at Stan and asked, "Do you think bad of me for my past? As I was talking about Charles, I was watching you and I could not tell how you were feeling. Are we ok?"

"I will say this, yes I was bothered some, but then I thought of us now, and I realized that you are a different person now and you are the one I love."

"Stan you are my true love, the one I have been searching for all these years and I am yours forever until death do us part." They hugged and the food they ordered arrived and they sat down for supper and discussed the facts Molly presented.

Stan had opened a bottle of wine; he held up his glass and offered a toast. "Molly, tonight I want you to know that my love for you has filled my heart to capacity, I want to be with you until the end of time. May our life be filled with happiness."

They clicked glasses and Stan saw tears flowing from Molly's eyes. He wiped them away, kissed her, I love you Molly." They had their supper while Stan asked her questions about Charles and Keith, and did she know how they went about everything.

She did tell him, "I remember them dealing with the Mulligan family and I think they dealt with drugs and prostitution. They were always arranging trips for their ship that really did not have anything to do with the company."

Stan was intrigued by this news and phoned Amanda. "Amanda, what is your status with the Watkins Company?"

"I am the owner of 75% of it and Jeremy owns the other 25%, although I am not involved with the day-to-day actions because of my former political involvements."

"Would you object if we had a surprise inspection of the records? We could go in there the day after tomorrow at opening time with accountants and security people, close it down for the day, send everybody home from the top on down to the lowest person. Let them know that they would still be paid for the day. I want to catch them, so they do not have a chance to destroy anything of importance to us. I must believe that there are still people doing illegal things."

"Stan, thank you for thinking of this, I need to step up and begin running the company. I know of a man that might be able to do it for me. So, the day-after-tomorrow is a go, and I will lead the charge through the door.

"Amanda, I like your style, see you there."

Amanda called Jeremy immediately, "Jeremy we are going to have a surprise inspection the day-after-tomorrow and you hold 25% ownership and I want you with me. We will be looking for documents concerning illegal activities. In the past there have been many, and we need to protect ourselves, so we do not lose the company. So can you be there?"

"Yes grandma, I will be there."

She looked at Marvin, shook her head, "It's going to be a surprise day at the plant, want to tag along?"

"No, I think you need to be there by yourself, showing who is in charge and a new day has just arrived. If you need to dismiss anyone, doing it quickly will be the best way. All your training as Prime Minister will come in handy. You will be known as tough Amanda."

"My darling, I am sure glad I married you, not a dull minute between the two of us is there?"

Chapter 48

IT WAS EARLY IN THE morning and both Jeremy and Amanda were heading to the Doctor's. Once in the exam room, the Doctor checked him out and order a CT be done right away. He gave him a large amount of water because he needed to be hydrated for the test. They put him in the machine and started the scan. The test took them about twenty minutes, and he returned to the Doctors office and waited. It seemed so long but it was only thirty minutes when the doctor called him back to the exam room. The doctor came in and his face did not look so good.

"Jeremy the left kidney does not look very good. I think you do need a transplant but we still have time so we can search for a match. If it gets worse we can put you on dialysis while we are waiting. Let's hope that we don't have to. I will give you some medication to help with your symptoms and make you more comfortable. We need to take blood samples so we can use them for the search of a match. Tell all your friends to come in and get tested. Sometimes the supply of organs is very low, we wish that more people would agree to donate organs, it sure would make our life easier."

They left the office and headed to tell Samantha about the transplant. They made plans for Amanda to appear on TV to encourage people to agree to donate organs. After she dropped Jeremy home she went directly to the TV Station where Delores worked and made a tape with Delores so it could be shown many times, day, and night. Delores decided that they would do a show on transplants and have Jeremy be a guest.

Amanda then went to the Health Department to get them on this.

Being a retired Prime Minister did have privileges. As she was doing all of this, she thought of Rudolph, he needed to be told. She knew that Stan knew where he lived so she called him, "Stan, I need a favor, can you go see Rudolph and tell him that Jeremy needs a kidney transplant, and we need to find a match so it can work."

"I will contact him today and pass on the message. I think he will want to help."

Amanda felt relief, she knew that the days to come were going to be tough, she was glad she had Marv to lean on. She got home and when she saw Marv she broke down and just sobbed, she had to let it out.

Marv held on and said, "let it out darling, let go."

They embraced each other and she finally stopped, and Marv would not let go. He kissed her, held her tight, whispered, "I love you."

She sighed, "You are so good for me, thanks for being here. These coming days are going to be hard on Jeremy and Samantha so we need to help them as much as we can. That might mean watching Alli while they are at the hospital."

"Darling, everything will work out, stay positive. Right now you are trying to do too much. Scale back and relax a little. Let's go upstairs and we can settle in, read or other things."

"Marvin you are a devil. I can read that look in your eye. Well lover boy, follow me if you dare." The evening became romantic, and both enjoyed the other.

Chapter 49

MORNING ARRIVED QUICKLY; AMANDA DRESSED in a hurry because the appointment was for eight am. They were going to surprise all the workers, she asked Marvin if he wanted to go but he said, "No this is your show, I might be a distraction." She understood what he was saying, she kissed him and left.

She arrived at the plant and Stan and his crew were already there. As the workers came they looked and wondered who they were and what did they want.

Curious, the workers started talking among themselves and no one figured it out. Stan and Amanda walked inside and went to the intercom system. At that time the CEO came and greeted them. He saw Amanda and his nerves got rattled. "What brings you hear Ms. Watkins?"

"It's Mrs. Malloy now Mr. McGill. We are here to close the plant for the day, and this includes you and all others. I want this place empty in the next thirty minutes. Also tell everyone that they will be paid for the day.

"Why are you doing this it seems to me that you could have come to me for any answers you need. I advise you to stop."

"Before you say something that you will regret Mr. McGill, I do not have to notify you of anything. I and my grandson, own this company and we are here to look for anything that you might be doing wrong.

Go to your office and bring me all the keys for every door and safe in this building. No exceptions, do you understand?"

"Yes madam. Attention, the plant will be closed for the day, but you will be paid. Before you leave we need every key to every lock and safe in the building. Bring them to the intercom office now." He turned to Amanda, "Is that what you want?" She nodded yes, he shook his head, "What have I done wrong?"

He got no answer, so he went to his office along with a security person. He could feel something bad was going to happen. He became worried, he thought of the secret safe and hoped they would not find it. He was not going to give the combination, and tomorrow when they were gone he would remove all the papers of the illegal transactions. He felt sure they would not find it.

Stan spoke to Amanda and Jeremy, "something tells me Mr. McGill is hiding what we are looking for. What is your take?"

Jeremy spoke up, "I was watching him very close, and his body language gave him away, plus his hands were shaking. We need to concentrate on him first."

Amanda looked at both, "I trust both of your judgements and tomorrow he will no longer be with us. Now let's get to work."

They went back to check if everyone was gone. The security crew assured them that they were. Stan and one security person went to McGill's office and began searching. Stan pulled out a stud finder and started checking the walls.

Everything was fine until he came to the bathroom and discovered a space where there were no studs. He moved it around and found that the space was thirty-six inches wide. The security person went to get some tools from the maintenance room. When he came back he brought another man with him plus Amanda.

Stan took a long screwdriver and punched it through the drywall, then he pushed it slowly until he hit metal. He checked the wall looking for an opening or a door handle. Running his hand along the wall trying to feel a door.

Meanwhile Amanda was searching under the cabinets looking for a button or switch. She felt something and pushed it and a concealed door opened. It was camouflaged so well you could not see a door. They saw the safe's door and Stan called one other security person to the office. When she got there, he put her to work to open the safe. It only took her five minutes and she had it opened.

It had files dating back twenty-five years to now. They glanced through them and discovered evidence showing that Rudolph was indeed innocent.

Stan called Scotland yard, told them what they found and advised him to arrest Mr. McGill immediately before he could get out of the country. As they looked through they saw that illegal activities were still going on. Drugs, guns, girls, smuggling, and more. They found names of the persons who were still active. Amanda was amazed, she counted, six men and four women.

Stan called Scotland Yard back and gave them the information, names and addresses and suggested they move quickly and round them up. He sorted things out so Scotland Yard could make an airtight case.

He then searched and found out how Charles put together the evidence to frame Rudolph and Keith was heavily involved. He showed it all to Amanda and she had to sit down. All this time she had no idea Charles could be this bad. She remembered when she asked questions he would tell her she didn't need worry about it because he had everything under control. Jeremy had to sit down thinking his father Keith was a crook. He turned to Amanda, "grandma, how do I get through all this? I never would have believed it."

Of the men who were involved, three were executives and the other were in management. All the women were in management. Tomorrow was going to be a big shake up day.

She called the Vice president who was not involved to come back immediately. When he asked why, she said, "just get here." She turned around to Stan and Jeremy, "New management takes over today. The shakeup will be heard by all, and they will all know that this type of behavior is over."

Stan received a call from Scotland Yard that they did indeed arrest all the people involved and some were telling all the details of who, where, when, and how. They said, this case is going to be big. Stan decided to go and see Rudolph and let him know what is taking place.

Chapter 50

RUDOLPH WAS THINKING ABOUT DELORES and meeting with her tonight when there was a knock on the door. He looked through the peep hole and saw Stan there. He opened the door, "Hello Stan, what brings you here?"

"Well, I have good news. Today we raided Watkins and we found proof that you were indeed innocent of all wrongdoing you were charged with. Also we have proof that they are still doing illegal activities and ten people have been arrested and some of them are singing out loud."

"I can't believe it, after all these years, how long do you think it will take to clear my name?"

"Well Rudy, they tell me at least two weeks. They must go over the evidence before they present it to the court. Now for the reason I am here. Your son Jeremy needs a kidney transplant. He lost the right one about eight years ago and now the left one is bad. If he doesn't get a transplant he will have to have dialysis for the rest of his life. Amanda asked me to tell you."

"Have they found a donor yet?"

"No, they are asking people to be tested. We can function fine with just one kidney. If you choose to get tested just, go to the hospital and they will test you."

"I will do that. I know Maureen would want me to. Thanks Stan for believing in me, it means so much. I do not have bad feelings toward you because you caught William, we all must pay for what we do, and I talked to William and told him to plead guilty and to pay back the money he blackmailed from them.

I will go back and try to convince him to follow through. I also must tell him that I am not his real father. I adopted him when he was three years old, and he does not have any memory before that age. I found him in the same home that I came from. No one should have to be treated like they treated me when I was there. I ran away when I was thirteen. It was difficult but I worked at what I could find and managed to go to school. Now with this new development, I can become the man that Maureen loved."

After Stan left, Rudy got ready for his date with Delores, they were having dinner and then they would do whatever moved them to do. After the other evening, he already felt a closeness to her. She reminded him of Maureen. They were perfect together and now with Delores, he hoped that they would create a good connection. He looked at his watch, 5:20, so he called her. "Are you ready for our evening my lady?"

Delores laughed, "You better get here soon before I change my mind."

"I am out the door as we speak." He got in the cab and was off to see a beautiful lady. Twenty minutes later he was knocking on her door. She opened it, "What took you so long?"

He entered, gave her a passionate kiss, "My darling I would have run all the way here if I could not have gotten a cab, that's how I feel about you."

"You know, I think I should make our dinner and we should stay here and talk and get to know each other better. You make me feel like we are meant to be close. I have never in my life felt this way before, I want to pursue this."

"I also feel what you feel, and I have much to tell you about me. I will be honest, some good and some bad."

She prepared a cold dinner and they sat together, and he opened up with her about everything. As she listened to it all, she realized that she knew some of what he told her. She knew about William but not about Jeremy. She knew about Amanda's story but not about how Charles framed him. She knew about Stan and the investigation but not the results.

She opened to him about what she knew, and he was surprised. He then looked into her eyes, "Delores, I believe that perhaps we are meant to be together."

She leaned over to him, embraced him, said, "My feelings for you are very strong. I do not know where this will lead but I sure want to find out."

Chapter 51

E DWARD AND JENNIFER'S WEDDING WAS going to be tomorrow, and they were trying to think if everything was covered. License, flowers, rings, party, honeymoon.

Marvin was giving them the party at Editors, Amanda was taking care of the flowers, they had the license and the rings. They were very thankful Delores took care of the rings; she was fun to work with. Everything was all set.

They called Jeremy to find out how he was doing. He invited them over to his and Sammie's house for dinner. They drove over and were surprised to see that Marvin and Amanda were there.

Jennifer spoke, "You know Amanda feels like a mother to me. She has been so good to me. I know, tonight lets you and I write a thank you letter to them for all that they have done for us."

"What a wonderful idea. Marvin has treated me like a son. Without him I never would have advanced to where I am now. Let's do it."

They got out of the car and went inside the house. Alli went running to them and Edward scoped her up. Alli was a special girl, so happy and so smart. Jeremy was cooking. He showed them their new grill, I learned to do this when we were in Texas. He was grilling steaks and corn.

Jeremy spoke, "We have some news to tell you. After I get my transplant, we are going to move to Texas to live near Samantha's family. We fell in love with the place. Now I turn it over to Sammie."

"Well, Jeremy and I pray that a match is found quickly. The big news is that I am pregnant. I am ten weeks along."

Amanda and Jennifer both hugged her and the guy's shook Jeremy's hand. Alli shouted, "I am going to be a sister." It was a happy group. The food was ready, Marvin offered a prayer and they all sat down to enjoy the Texas meal.

Marvin remarked, "Just like home. All of you will have to get used to new things when you all move to the states."

Amanda turned to Alli, "Are you excited to be going back to Texas?" "Yes, I get to ride my horse. Grandpa gave me one."

"Oh that was a nice thing to do. So tell me, was it nice at your grandpa's and grandma's?"

"I had so much fun helping grandpa and then grandma showed me how to make cookies. Did you ever make cookies?"

"Yes I have made many, just ask you Dad about he and I making cookies. You know my grandmother taught me how to make cookies. Before you leave for Texas you should come over to my house and we will make some together. I will teach you how to make my special English cookies and then you can make for your Texas family."

"That sounds like fun. Mama, grandma wants us to come over to her house to make English cookies. Can we go mama?"

"Yes, we can do that, just ask when."

"When grandma, when?" 'How about next week Tuesday?" Samantha wrote down the date and time.

Jeremy got a phone call from the hospital saying that they found someone who was an 80% match which they could use if needed.

Amanda thought about Rudolph and wondered if Stan had spoken to him yet. Everybody was encouraged by the news, knowing people were getting tested. Amanda declared I have an announcement. I am writing a book. It is a romance novel based loosely on Marvin's and my story. Right now the title is The Widower, but I think I will change it. I have seven chapters written so far.

Marvin told Edward and Jennifer, "I have contacted New York about you two staying in my apartment for your honeymoon. Also they are searching for an apartment for you when you make the move. They are also going to furnish it completely, so you won't have to worry any."

Jeremy spoke up, "I thought we were going to work together." Marvin turned to Jeremy, "Edward will be directing the New York office, but he can still work with you doing what you need done. After a year I am bringing him back to be the director of the new London office."

Jeremy was impressed, "You two have hit the jackpot. Do you realize how much our lives have changed since Marvin wrote Grandmother a letter? None of this would be happening if that letter had gotten lost. I almost threw it in the garbage pile. Good thing I didn't pay attention to where I put it."

"Tomorrow is the big day; Jennifer and I better get home and rest if we can."

Everybody said good night and hugged one another, looked toward the sky and saw a full moon. "Now that is a good sign."

On the way home Amanda told Marvin that she had Stan notify Rudolph about Jeremy's condition. She decided to call him when she got home.

Little did she know, Delores talked to Rudy about being a donor and he agreed saying, "It is the least thing I could do for my son, but please don't tell Amanda that I am going to be tested. I want to stay anonymous if I happen to be a match. I made the decision to stay in the background about Jeremy."

Delores disagreed with him and told him so, "Your son needs to know that his father loves him, you are making a big mistake, but I promise not to tell your secrets. You must do that on your own."

Chapter 52

WEDDING DAY BEGAN WITH JENNIFER in a big panic. "I cannot find my earrings anywhere. I have looked high and low for them.

"Did you look in your ears dear?" She looked in the mirror and felt foolish, there they were. "I hope the rest of the day does not go like that."

Yes the bride was nervous, and the day was just beginning. Edward was calm he thought. When he looked down he saw that he had on two different colors of socks. He hoped Jennifer didn't see but she did.

"My my, the beautiful husband to be is so calm, not a bit nervous, Mr. Strong man. One brown sock and one blue sock, how nice, setting a new trend are we?"

That eased the tension, both finished dressing and gathered the things they wanted to hold on to during the ceremony. She had her mother's pearl stick pin, and he had his father's tie clip. Both of their parents were gone so they were going to place pictures of them on the altar so they could see them. They were gone but still loved.

The ceremony was at 11:00 AM in the Church of the Redeemer. They left to go to the Church but stopped and faced each other. Jennifer said, "Edward, when you came into my life I knew instantly that you were my person."

"Jennifer, the first time I saw you in Amanda's office, my heart fluttered, and I knew that you were special. The more I got to know you, the more I wanted to spend my life with you, I love you." They got in the cab and off they went to begin a new life.

The ceremony was beautiful, happiness filled the sanctuary, Alli giggled as she placed the flower pedals down the aisle, and everyone smiled when it was announced that Marvin was going to be the ring bearer.

The Minister spoke directly to Jennifer and Edward, "You are entering into a new beginning and go with love in your hearts. As you go, God wants you to share that love with others, Be the best you can be together, share the happiness, with all you meet."

When Amanda heard the words, "Share the happiness," she thought she had heard it somewhere before but could not remember where.

The Minister smiled and said, "I now pronounce you, Husband, and Wife. You may kiss the bride." He did just that, he gave her a passionate kiss and the guests started applauding.

The Bride and Groom came outside, and everyone smiled and clapped as they got into Marvin's car to go to Editors for a wedding lunch. They entered and were escorted to banquet room.

Delores looked around and in the far corner she saw Rudolph. He was hidden, so she knew the others could not see him. She was glad he was there, he needed to see for himself how Jeremy was doing. She wished she could convince him to let Jeremy know that he was his father. She knew that Amanda knew, maybe she could convince her to talk to Rudy.

As everybody sat down, they started to clink their glasses letting the newlyweds to kiss. Everyone was in a good mood. Happiness filled the hall. The door to the hall was opened and Rudy could see in.

Amanda glanced his way; she stopped and saw him. He knew she saw him, so he nodded his head, got up and left. Amanda saw him go and knew then that Stan had indeed told him about Jeremy, and she felt at ease. She also knew that the evidence they uncovered would clear him and she wondered if he would tell Jeremy that he was his father.

Delores was watching her closely. She got up, went over to Amanda, sat down next to her, and whispered, "You saw him, didn't you?"

Amanda was shocked, how did Delores know about Rudolph. So she asked her.

Delores replied, "Remember that lover I told you about, that is Rudy and last night he told me his whole story, which is how I know."

"I am glad you know, holding it all in has been hard for me."

Marvin asked, "What are you ladies whispering about?"

"Well if you must know, we just saw Rudolph in the main room and Delores knows all about Rudolph and Jeremy. I will tell you how when we get home."

They started to clink glasses again, so they kissed again. The party was very good and after three hours it thinned out until only Jeremy, Samantha and Alli were still there with Ed and Jen. They loaded up all the gifts and headed for Ed's apartment. After putting the gifts away, they said their goodbye's and left.

In the morning the newlyweds were leaving for New York. Jennifer said, "maybe we should go right to sleep so we will be rested for the trip."

Ed gave her a look, "you have to be kidding."

She smiled, "Yes I am."

Chapter 53

"R EMEMBER WHEN I TOLD YOU about Delores meeting a new lover? Well, Rudy is that new lover and he has told her all the details of his life. She knows that Jeremy is his son, and she knows that Charles framed him. She knows it all."

"How do you feel about all this?"

"I am glad someone else knows, carrying this by myself has been difficult, I need support. I must go to the hospital to check on how they are doing with finding a match for Jeremy. What are you going to do?"

"I am going to the studio first and do you want me to see Delores?"

"I don't think that is necessary, she will contact me if she needs too."

"Ok darling, I will see you tonight. Relax and enjoy the day."

Marvin left and Amanda left also and headed to the hospital. She got there and walked down the hall when she saw Rudolph in one of the examining rooms.

She looked in, "Hello Rudy!" Startled, he looked up and saw Amanda, "What are you doing here?"

"I am checking how the search is going for a kidney match for Jeremy. Are you getting tested?

"Yes I am, and I want to keep it quiet, I do not want Jeremy to know."

"Don't you think you should let Jeremy know the truth, after all you were in love with my daughter. It is time Rudolph, to face the truth, own up to all. We found the truth of what Charles and Keith did to you and I feel the company owes you for the eight years you spent in prison. I believe that if you hadn't been sent to prison, you and Maureen would be together today enjoying being grandparents. I am on your side Rudy, deal with it. Stop hiding."

She walked away and she could tell Rudy was shaken. He has never had to face the truth, but now was the time. She saw the Nurse that was conducting the search, and was told no match yet, but there has been a big response to her pleadings on TV.

She called Molly and Delores to see if they wanted to go to lunch. They did and she told them to meet her at Editors at noon. She came back through, and Rudy was gone. Her thoughts went to Rudy and Delores, she hoped that it would work out.

When Rudy left the hospital he went to the Scotland Yard office to find out how long it would take for the paperwork to be completed. The sent him to Mr. Livingston who was doing the work on this case. "Well hello Mr. Abercrombie, I thought you would be coming here. Sit down I need to ask you some questions.

This case is going to be very big. You can help us with whatever information you might remember. Your papers will be done tomorrow, why don't you come in and I will show you the files and just maybe you will see something we can use."

"I will do that. I am so happy that this is going to clear my name. I can start my new life. See you tomorrow."

Chapter 54

THE GIRLS MET FOR LUNCH. You would think they were teenagers, telling each other details of their love lives with all the juicy details. They were giggling the other patrons were staring.

Molly noticed, "We better quiet down everybody is looking at us." This made them laugh harder. Amanda told them, "You know, since I retired I have never felt so loved, and now that my breast cancer is gone, I feel free to be and do whatever I want to. I am having so much fun writing the book, one chapter just leads me to the next. I cannot believe how fast it is coming."

Molly turns to Delores, "Now tell me everything about this new man in your life. Who is he and what does he do and are you going to try and become him and her?"

Delores smiled, "Amanda already knows who, so I guess I can tell you if you promise not to spread it around for now."

"I promise."

"His name is Rudolph Abercrombie and,"

"Wait a minute, isn't he the one that Stan has been investigating?"

"Well yes he is, but Stan, Amanda, and Jeremy found the evidence to clear him of all charges. He told me the whole story the night before last, and you have never seen such a happy man. I will tell you this, but please keep it quiet for now, we both feel that we have something special, so we are going to explore it."

Amanda smiled, "ladies in the very recent past, our lives changed drastically. Think back, mine because of a letter a man wrote me, Molly, you because I had Stan investigate, and Delores, you had this great makeover and then you ask a man to join you for dinner. I am beginning to think that we are the luckiest three ladies in London."

As Amanda was talking her phone rang, she saw that Samantha was calling, "Hello Sammie, what do you need? I see, I will be right there. Jeremy was rushed to the hospital; his kidney is failing. I must go."

"We will go with you." They rushed out of there and headed for the hospital. Amanda said a prayer and hoped for the best.

Once at the hospital they found out that his left kidney had shut down and he would have to be put on dialysis. Samantha told them that he would have to stay overnight so they could coordinate everything. He would have to stay on the machine unless the left kidney started working again. Amanda said to no one in particular, "Please God, find us a kidney." She whispered to Delores, "call Rudy and let him know."

Chapter 55

JEREMY HAS BEEN IN THE hospital for two days now and the family was anxious for him to come home. He was complaining that he needed to get back to his studio because he has been working on a painting in secret and he would like to finish it. Samantha didn't even know what it was. Marvin and Edward knew but promised not to tell anyone. Amanda grabbed Marvin's arm, "come on, you can tell me."

"No, I have been sworn to secrecy, my lips are closed."

Jeremy was being wheeled down the hall, "let's go home." He was a little anxious on getting home. He knew his life was going to be much different, but he also knew that he would adjust. For the sake of his family he had too. The nurse who oversaw finding a match for Jeremy came into the waiting room. "Before you go, I have wonderful news, we have found a donor that is a 100% match. He wants his name to remain secret, but he has agreed to the procedure. Tomorrow we will let you know when we will do the procedure and all the details that go with it.

The family was so happy and there were hugs all around. They left a happy family.

Amanda decided to tell Jeremy everything about his mother and his father. She knew she was going against Rudolph, but the time was now, and he needed to know the truth. It was going to be a difficult conversation, but it had to done. Also she needed to discuss the CEO position at Watkins. She wanted to offer it to Rudolph. He worked there for four years, and the company owed him for the prison time, besides he was qualified.

As they left, she asked him if she could stop by tomorrow because she needed to talk about the plant and other topics. He agreed and set the time over lunch.

When she returned to the farm, she told Marvin what she was going to do, and he approved. She went to her studio and made notes for the book so she would not forget the details. She opened her computer and began writing. When she stopped, she had written four more chapters. The book had a life of its own and she loved writing it all down.

The publishers were hounding her to write a book about her time as the Prime Minister, but she was happy writing fiction. Marvin walked in with a tray of food for supper. He set it up and they ate in the studio.

She told him it was romantic and then she saw the look in his eyes, and she knew what he was thinking. She thought that a little teasing would liven things up. She came up behind him, kissed him on the ear, he shivered and pulled her down in his lap. He heard her say, "shall we retire to the bedroom?"

"No, here is just fine." He pulled her into his lap and the dance began. No more chapters tonight.

Chapter 56

A NEW DAY ARRIVED, AND IT was sunny and warm with a slight breeze. The clouds white and puffy. A good day to just be lazy. Jeremy felt lazy, he turned to Sammie, "Let's have a picnic today after grandma leaves. We can go to grandma's lake."

"That would be a wonderful idea. I will fix the food and Alli will love it. Then we can see Amanda's horses. You know how much Alli loves horses. What time is Amanda coming over?"

"I will call her and ask."

Amanda talked to Jeremy; told them she would be there before 10:00 am.

Marvin came into the kitchen, "darling I found out what Jeremy's big surprise is. He is doing a life-sized painting of Maureen and he wants to place it in the company offices."

"Wow, that's wonderful, now we can remove the one of Charles and burn it. That young man is going to go a long way. He and Sammie are going to picnic at the lake. I told him I would be there by ten, so I had better get going. Love you!"

She got there in record time, now she had to let Jeremy know things that have been hidden for so long.

They sat around the kitchen table and looked out the window. Amanda smiled, "sitting here I just thought of something I could add to my book. The meaning of looking out the kitchen window.

A writer I follow at times wrote about looking out the kitchen window and it was very profound. I keep all his postings; I will use it and make sure he gets the credit.

Now Jeremy, we need to find a CEO, someone who has experience and understands our company. The man I have in mind is one who was with the company for four years until your grandfather had him sent to prison for eight years. His name is Rudolph Abercrombie. I have not spoken to him yet because we need to agree with the person we ask."

"I know we found proof that Mr. Abercrombie was framed, but why do you think he can do the job?"

"First I know he is qualified. He has great credentials, and his mind is geared for business and the company owes him a large amount of money for his incarceration."

"I agree we owe him a large amount of money, but I still do not understand why we should offer him this job. I am missing something, what is it?"

"Ok Jeremy, I am going to tell you the story. I did not find out about this until just before I retired from the Prime Minister's job, and it rattled me."

Amandas hands were shaking and noticed by Sammie. She reached over and placed her hand on Amanda's, and she calmed down.

"A short time ago I was notified by the bank that there was a safety box, and they were instructed by your mother that they could notify me five years after her death. What was in the box were letters, one from her, and the others were love letters from her lover." Jeremy looked puzzled and shocked.

"Her letter contained information about her marriage and how her husband Keith abused her throughout their marriage, both verbally and physically. She explained she fell in love with someone else and they had an affair that lasted for four years. She was afraid of her husband and her father and what they would do if they had found out. She had so many happy times with this man, but she got pregnant with him. She told him but because she lived with fear she would not divorce Keith. He was devastated and when your grandfather found out he set a trap for him, and he was sent to prison. Yes, your real father is Rudolph Abercrombie and not Keith O'Dell.

I had Stan investigate and we found that Keith and grandpa forged a birth certificate, and we found the real one which I will have Stan give it to you. All these years you have become the family secret."

She pulled out a copy of the certificate and showed it to him. "One other thing, Rudy does not want you to know he is your father and William is his adopted son. I think he is wrong, but it is his call, and he is the one that is a perfect match for your transplant.

Jeremy just sat there in wonder. This information filled in some gaps he had but never knew why. His mother use to step in between him and his so-called father. When she did, Keith would just walk away. Now he knew why. "So, you want me to keep this between you and me?

"Just for the time being, I am trying hard to convince him to come forward and tell you the truth."

"Well if you think this man is qualified for the job, let's do it because if it doesn't work out we can let him go. We need to write his contract with that clause in it."

Amanda smiled at him, "My you are quite a businessman. Let's do it." She had gotten Rudy's number from Delores and called him. "Rudy can you come out to my house this afternoon for lunch, I have some business to discuss with you. So you will know, Jeremys family will be out here at the lake, but they won't see you, I will make sure of that. I will send my car for you."

"As long as they will not see me, I will come, thank you. How about 1:00, is that ok?"

"I will have the car pick you up at 12:40. See you when you arrive."

She called transportation to pick him up and they told her it would be done. She thanked them and turned to Sammie, you take care this man, we need him. She gave hugs all around, went out the door saying, enjoy the lake. From the car she called her cook and told her there would be two for lunch. She then called Delores and told her what she had done so she could help Rudy if he needed any.

Marvin called and asked, "how did it go?" She told him the facts and how she felt. She told him that Rudy was coming for lunch, and she was going to offer the job to him. He wished her luck then told her "Last night was special and you make me feel blessed." With that statement he ended the call.

She was feeling so loved, she thanked God once again for bring Marv into her life. She wrote down on her note pad what he said because she would use it in the book. She went to the study and started to write. She got lost in her work until Rudy arrived. She looked out the window toward the lake and she could see them having their picnic. She then went to the door and welcomed Rudy into her home, saying as they went to the breakfast nook, "I bet that you never would have guessed you would be invited to the Watkins home?"

"No, not in a million years. I used to dream in prison, coming here and beating Charles for what he did. Now thanks to you, my life is changing so, Mrs. Malloy, I am ever in your debt."

"Sit down Rudy I have a very important offer for you, and I hope you will accept." They sat down and while they ate their lunch Amanda told him just what she had to offer. "Rudy, I want to offer you the CEO's job at Watkins. I know you would be good there, with your experience and we sure do owe you a lot but even if we didn't, I still would make this offer. We need you there. Now tell me what you are thinking."

"Well now this is a big surprise. First I ask why do you think I am qualified? Second, if I accept will I have full control or would I have to do only what you say. Third, what did Jeremy say about this, and did he object?"

First, I did my research and I checked back when you were first here, and I concluded that you would have been my first pick even without our past. Rudy, we as a company owe you much, but this is not a payment for what we owe you. This is for keeping this company as a leader in industry and with the illegal activities that have taken place we are going to be placed in trouble if we do not have leadership to pull us through. You will be under watchful eyes, but you can do it Rudy. Second, you will most certainly have full control and you will be allowed to make changes that are needed. The board which I am chairperson, will overlook financial records and give you a free hand. Third, Jeremy asked why I would ask you and I explained everything to him. He did not object, he only asked what my reasoning was, and when told my thoughts he agreed to say yes if your contract contained a clause that you could be removed if your job performance is below standards."

"It sounds like you and Jeremy have been done your homework. Can I have 24 hours to consider this proposal? Also if I say yes, when would I start."

"Yes I will allow you the privilege of 24 hours, shall we say we need an answer by 2PM tomorrow? We would expect you to start after you recover from the kidney surgery. Does this meet your requirements?"

"How did you know I was going to donate my kidney?"

"I just put two and two together, but Jeremy does not know yet. I say yet because you should be the one to tell him."

"It may surprise you, but I have thought of telling him."

"When you deliver your answer, I hope you tell me, you will tell him when you are ready."

"I decided to accept but, let me think about Jeremy."

"We have a deal Rudy. Meet me there tomorrow and I will introduce you to the Vice President and the two of you can start planning your direction. I will meet you there at 10:00. We will make the formal announcement after you recover."

"Thank you Amanda, I will make you proud, I promise."

Chapter 57

RUDY CALLED DELORES AS SOON as he was outside of Amanda's house, "Are you busy tonight? I have some news I need to tell you. I can be there in about thirty minutes. Ok I am on my way."

"Hello, I am Alli, who are you?"

Surprised Rudy didn't know if he should talk to her or not. As he looked at her he could see that she looked like Maureen. "My name is Rudy; do you know Ms. Amanda?"

"Yes, she is my great grandma. Do you know her?"

"Yes, she is a friend." Just then Jeremy and Sammie came around the corner and Rudy almost panicked, but he controlled himself and calmed down. "Hello, my name is Rudolph, and you are?"

"MY name is Jeremy O'Dell, and this is my wife Samantha. Are you here to accept the job as CEO?"

"Yes, I accepted it. I look forward to your intel. Just call me anytime, Goodbye now, I must run." Rudy left in Amanda's car and headed for Delores's place. When I tell her I talked with Jeremy she is going to say, "Did you tell him?"

Jeremy stuck his head in the door and hollered, "We are going to look at the horses." He heard an ok, from Amanda, so they went off to the barn. While he was in the barn, the hospital called and said the surgery was going to be Friday, only three days away. Both Rudy and Amanda got the same notice. Amanda sat, looked, and thought three days and Jeremy's life will be changed. I pray all goes well.

Chapter 58

RUDY ARRIVED AT DELORES HOUSE in record time. He did not get a chance to ring the bell, she was waiting for him, and she opened the door and let him in. He kissed her and she asked, "Well what happened?"

"I met with Amanda, and she offered me the CEO position at Watkins. After some thought I told her that I did not want Jeremy to find out I am his father. She accepted that but she told me I need to tell him."

"Well I agree with Amanda, and I believe that by not telling him, you will live to regret it. Rudy, put yourself in his shoes, what if he finds out from someone else?"

"Do you really think he would be upset? Do you think he would hate me because I haven't told him?"

"I think he might be so upset that he would not have anything to do with you. I also believe he needs you in his life, you both have a lot of catching up to do. You could tell him how much you loved his mother and how the two of you got together. Yes you need to tell him, and I think it should before the transplant but if not then do it right after."

"I am leaning towards telling him, but I need to think on it some more."

"Let's go to dinner later and we can discuss it more if you want to. For now let's take a walk and relax and think about us." So they left the house and walked and held hands looking like love birds. The more they walked the more relaxed Rudy became and Delores told him she was on his side.

"Ms. Delores, I think I am falling in love with you, I feel more at ease around you."

"Well Mr. Rudy, I am feeling the same."

They looked up and they were standing in front of the pub, so they entered, and the regulars hollered, hey Delores, who is the fellow?"

She laughed and told them, "Just someone I picked up around the corner." Even Rudy was laughing at that, they sat down and ordered a pint. When it came, the two of them looked into each other's eyes, smiled and Rudy mouthed the words, I love you and a tear rolled down his cheek and Delores wiped it away and said, "It will all work out."

He took her hand and placed a kiss on the back of her hand, said thank you. It was at that moment that Rudy decided to tell Jeremy is his son. It was also the moment he decided to tell William that he was adopted.

Delores could tell that he had made some decisions. She asked, "What are you going to do?"

All he said was, "You are right, I need to tell both of my boy's the truth, and I will do it after the surgery."

Chapter 59

A MANDA WAS TRYING TO THINK how to write the next chapter and which characters to write about. She was finding that at times things did not go well but you had to keep writing because you could always delete it if you had to.

She remembered the picnic they were on and how nice it was so; she began to write about it. She embellished it some, but it would make the reader want to have a picnic of their own. While writing, thinking about the reader helped her immensely. Marvin was going to love this book. It was their story.

Friday came into her mind; a kidney transplant was a serious thing for both parties. I just hope that Rudy tells Jeremy. Even though Jeremy knows the truth, coming from Rudy would go a long way.

Then she thought of Maureen and how she managed to keep secret her problems. She knew that she truly loved Rudy but did not know why she stayed with Keith. Every family has its secrets, this one is ours.

As she was writing she managed to get Maureen's story in the book. It was time to take a break from writing, she was thinking about the surgery and the preparations they were going to go through. No food tomorrow, just clear liquids. The surgery was scheduled for 8:00 AM and they had to be there by 6:00 AM. It's going to be a long day. I should call Samantha and see how she is doing. Going to miss them when they move to Texas. Oh well that gives us one more place to visit.

Marvin was at his studio working on the new painting and he was about half done. He cleaned his brushes and decided to go home early and surprise Amanda. He knew she was concerned about the surgery, so he was going to picnic by the lake.

He called ahead so the cook would have it all ready. Marv arrived home, came through the door and hollered for Amanda.

She came out of her study and Marv said, "Come on, we are going down by the lake and have a picnic."

She smiled at him, "How did you know that I needed time with you. Are you a physic?"

"No, I just knew you needed relaxing time. Darling, everything is going to turn out alright. I called and had a basket prepared for us, so let's do it."

"Marvin, you keep surprising me, please don't stop, I love it." She gathered her sweater and book, took his arm, "My love, I am yours, let's go."

They got the basket and wine and headed for the lake. When they got there they went to the picnic table, but Marvin said, "It's not a real picnic unless we spread a blanket and eat down on the ground."

Amanda laughed, removed all from the basket and had Marvin open the wine. He poured and offered a toast. "This is for Amanda who is my special person. I love her so much and God I thank you for sending me to her. Amen.

Amanda hugged him, sat down together, and began the feast. Marv quipped all we need is candlelight. He raised his glass and offered a toast. "My darling Amanda when you came into my world it changed completely. I was just going through the motions, and you re-energized me. I love you with all my heart."

Amanda spoke, "Marv, you have been such a joy to me, you make me feel young again, I love you."

They both had a drink and then went after the food. It was a perfect ending to their day. When the sunset they admired it and walked back to the house. Friday was going to be long and tiring.

Chapter 60

ALLI GOT OUT OF BED and ran into Jeremy's and Samantha's bedroom and jumped into their bed. "Come on, time to get up. Time to feed the horses." She told them that she was practicing for Texas.

This is the day that Jeremy could not eat, just clear liquids. They got up and Sammie went to start breakfast. While it was cooking she got a phone call from the manager of the local club. He asked if she would sing with the local band tomorrow night.

She said NO because her husband was having surgery tomorrow. Jeremy heard and told her to do it because he would be in the hospital.

So she told him she would. The thought of singing excited her. Jeremy said, "This could be the beginning of your singing career."

Amanda decided to call Jeremy and ask him to come to the plant and be there when Rudy came so he could learn where Rudy wanted to take the company. He turned to Sammie, "Why don't you and Alli come with me to the plant, and you will be able to see just what they do and how it's done. I think you would enjoy it."

"That sounds like it might be fun, let's do it. So they put things away and headed for the plant. When they got there, Sammie was impressed, everything was organized like it should be.

Jeremy escorted them to the offices, and they met the Vice President Mr. Cassidy. He took them in and introduced them to Rudolph. Of course Jeremy already knew him, but he was meeting Samantha and Alli for the first time, "How do you do Mrs. O'Dell and who is this beautiful young lady?"

"This young lady is our daughter, Allison but we call her Alli."

You could see Jeremy tighten up a little because knowing that Rudy was his father felt strange to him. Also knowing he was going to receive his kidney tomorrow, he wanted to say thank you dad, but knew he couldn't. He would wait for his dad to tell him.

Amanda walked in and they began the meeting. Sammie tried to excuse herself, but Amanda would not allow it. "You are now part of this family, and you need to know what goes on in the family business.

So the meeting began with Rudy already presenting a plan. They asked questions and presented further ideas and soon they agreed on a plan.

Amanda shook Rudy's hand said, "Good job, I am impressed." Samantha told Jeremy, "This new President seems to know his business."

Jeremy said, "Yes he does, I think grandma made a good choice. Let me show you around the plant. So they took the tour. As they went around many of the workers greeted Jeremy by name and some of them even complimented him on his show. He felt so good, and Sammie said she was so proud of him and Alli was having a good time seeing all the people that worked there. Jeremy said, "We should go before I get too tired."

Chapter 61

THE BIG TRANSPLANT DAY WAS here. Both were being prepped but not in the same room. They would never see each other according to plan. The hospital respected Rudy's wishes to stay anonymous. There were placed in two separated surgeries and the operation started.

Jeremy was being prepped; Rudy was having his right kidney removed. They rushed the kidney into Jeremy's room and proceeded to put into place, they checked for function and closed him up. Rudy was already being taken to recovery, and soon Jeremy was there too. Now the wait.

Of course everybody was in the waiting room, anxious for news. The doctor came in and told them that the surgery went just fine and both parties were in recovery and expected to be fine. We will know more after they wake up. That was good news, so now more waiting.

Marv went after coffee and soft drinks for Sammie and Alli. Amanda did not want anything just yet. When he got back the Doctor was there telling them that they were doing just fine, and they expect a complete recovery. The patients were back in their rooms, and they could see them although they were still groggy.

Amanda was going to go see Rudy and Sammie and Alli were on their way to see Jeremy.

Amanda walked into Rudy's room, thanked him helping Jeremy. He tried to smile but he hurt. He did manage to say, "That's what fathers are supposed to do." "Does that mean you are going to tell Jeremy you are his father?"

"Yes, but I will wait until we both have recovered from surgery. You and Delores convinced me I should, and I hope that he won't be to upset with me."

"After you explain how you and Maureen got together, and how much you loved each other, I think he will accept you as his father. If you need anything call me."

"I also need to see William and tell him the truth. I know you are upset with him so I will not talk to him about you. Right now he's only sorry he got caught. As Amanda was leaving she saw Stan coming down the hall. She asked, "What are you doing here?"

"I am here to bring Rudolph his papers that show that he was falsely accused and his records and been straighten out. He's going to very happy about it."

"You do know that Jeremy and I have hired him to be CEO of Watkins. The company owes him a great deal, but we hired him because he's qualified."

"My goodness, he's come a long way since prison. I knew deep down he is a good man and now he can show it. Did you know about him and Delores?"

"Oh yes, Delores has told me all that's going on. She should be here shortly. As she said this, Delores was coming down the hall, checking room numbers until she found the right one. She waved at Stan and Amanda, entered his room, and closed the door.

"Rudolph, you have done a great thing, I am so proud of you. Your son is a good man, and he has a wonderful family, who is now your family. When you get to know them, you will cherish them, and you will learn what you have been missing all these years."

With that she leaned over and gave him a big passionate kiss, "Now, get better, because you are coming to my house to finish your recovery and don't you bother to resist, because it won't do you any good." He smiled up at her and all he could say is, "Yes dear."

Chapter 62

AMANDA HEADED DOWN TO JEREMY's room, saw Sammie and Alli along with Marvin and Edward. She thought to herself, the gangs all here. She could feel that all was going to be ok. She decided to put this in her book. She was nearing the conclusion of it but by adding this, it would help bring it all together.

The happiness in this room was exciting to see, she took hold of Marvin's arm and began crying and she could not stop, she was so happy.

Marvin held her and then Alli hugged her saying, "Don't cry grandma, we love you." All eyes were on her, and she smiled and picked up Alli and said, "I love you child." She went over to Jeremy and kissed him telling him, "Get well, Texas is waiting for you."

Jeremy smiled at her, "As soon as I am recovered we will be gone, but we will miss you very much, they told me it would take me at least 6 months to recover."

"Oh Marvin and I will visit you often, we are going to become world travelers, so when my book is done, we will be off. We must be in New York in June and then it's off to Montana. Didn't you say they are coming here for Christmas?"

"Yes and it should be fun. I think they will be overwhelmed with London, although they do spend time in Dallas. We will see what happens."

Everyone is in a good mood and suddenly Rudolph was being rolled into the room and asked, if he could have a minute with Jeremy. Everyone in the room knew what was coming so they walked out to give them some privacy.